"You promised," she said. "About my baby?"

Greg felt a spurt of admiration. She stood there in a corner of the interrogation room, a skinny figure in old clothes, but a figure possessing a singular dignity. "Absolutely," he replied. "You have my word."

She moved toward him and held out her hand. "We have a deal then, Mr. Tyrrell."

He stared at her for a moment, caught off guard. Finally he reached out and enclosed her hand in his own. How small and cool her fingers felt in his. How trusting.

"Deal, Miss Bryson," he said solemnly. This woman might have made some mistakes, but she had courage. Here she was, all by herself, a thousand miles from home—and four months pregnant.

Yes, she had courage.

Dear Reader,

The Baby Contract is our first book set in Tucson, one of our favorite cities, and it's also our first book with a pregnant heroine. Between the two of us, we've had every symptom of pregnancy there is, and we were glad to be able, finally, to put our expertise in this area to work!

There is a very real problem with illegal adoptions in this country—and there are some very unethical people who take advantage of childless couples' desperation. Our hearts go out to all these couples.

We hope you'll find the story's premise interesting; we also hope you enjoy our depiction of the setting. There's a story we like that's told about Tucson. A busload of tourists climbed down from their tour bus and looked around, saw the infinite varieties of cactus and creosote bush and mesquite trees and all the other desert growth, and they looked at one another and said, "So where's the desert?"

And please bear in mind that the saguaro (sa-wharo) cactus, the huge sentinels with their crooked arms, grow only in the Sonoran Desert around Tucson and down into Mexico and nowhere else in the world, despite their being pictured everywhere in the West.

We hope you enjoy *The Baby Contract*.

Sincerely yours,

Carla Peltonen
Molly Swanton

Lynn Erickson

THE BABY CONTRACT

Harlequin Books

TORONTO • NEW YORK • LONDON
AMSTERDAM • PARIS • SYDNEY • HAMBURG
STOCKHOLM • ATHENS • TOKYO • MILAN
MADRID • WARSAW • BUDAPEST • AUCKLAND

ISBN 0-373-70690-1

THE BABY CONTRACT

Copyright © 1996 by Carla Peltonen and Molly Swanton.

ABOUT THE AUTHOR

Lynn Erickson is the pseudonym for the writing team of Carla Peltonen and Molly Swanton. They are known for their suspenseful, adventurous and fast-paced stories.

Carla and Molly and their families live in Aspen, Colorado. The town of Aspen was the inspiration for their first single-title release, *Aspen*, published by MIRA Books in 1995. Watch for their upcoming MIRA title, *Night Whispers*, appearing in January 1997—it's also set in Colorado, but in Denver this time. Their next Superromance will appear in December 1997.

Books by Lynn Erickson

HARLEQUIN SUPERROMANCE

CHAPTER ONE

BETTIE GAY BRYSON propped her knees against the dashboard and shivered. "I'm freezing, Jay. Turn up the heat, will you?"

"I'm hot, I'm cold, turn up the heat, turn it down," Jay mimicked, reaching for the sliding control on the dashboard of the old Cadillac. "I swear, B.G., you sure are a pain in the butt lately."

"Sorry," she muttered, "but I thought the desert was supposed to be hot." Boy, was he in a bad mood.

"It's March and it's four o'clock in the morning," Jay said matter-of-factly.

Bettie Gay opened her mouth to say something clever in return, but nothing came. She was too cold, too tired and, she realized, too worried. Here they were in the middle of nowhere, on a desert road somewhere outside of Tucson, Arizona, at four in the morning. They were practically out of gas, hadn't eaten since yesterday in Los Angeles, and between them all they had was eight or nine dollars.

Jay had a great gig waiting for him in Phoenix, but then, he'd had a great gig waiting in L.A., and it hadn't worked out. Oh, Jay had been full of enthusiasm back in Florida when she'd met him. This L.A. gig was his big break, a chance to audition for a really popular country-and-western band that needed a replacement guitar player.

She'd been so in love, so blind all those months ago, leaving Mayport to drive cross-country with Jay. It had sounded good, so exciting, so hopeful.

But bad times had hit. The audition had gone badly, Bettie Gay's one credit card had reached its limit, and now they were just trying to get to Phoenix in the old yellow Caddy. At least it hadn't broken down. Yet.

"Couple hours," Jay Pearson was saying as he tuned the radio. "Couple more hours and we'll be in Phoenix. We'll pull over there and catch some sleep in the car. This gig's got promise written all over it, B.G. 'Bout time I got a break."

Bettie Gay switched her glance to the gas gauge. About an eighth of a tank. "We've got to get gas, Jay, and I've got to find a washroom."

He shook his blond-streaked mane. "Man-oh-man," he said. "It's like you gotta go every two minutes, baby."

"You know why," she said defensively.

"I didn't think there'd be so many weird things about it, though," he answered. "You're, like, different."

"Yes, I am," she said.

"Hey, don't sweat it. You know I told you I'd take care of everything, and I will. I'll be making fifty, seventy bucks a night. I got a three-week run at Maverick's. We'll handle it."

"Mmm," B.G. said. "What about gas? I don't think the old guzzler's going to make it on eight dollars, Jay. What're we—"

"Just relax," he said, and she knew he was trying hard to sound unconcerned. "I've got everything under control. You don't trust me enough, B.G."

"I'm worried, that's all. I don't want to get stuck out here in the middle of the desert."

But all Jay did was roll down the window, prop his arm on the sill and whistle to the music that blared from the radio.

B.G. reached in back and found a windbreaker and huddled under it, sliding down in the seat, sticking her feet up against the floor heater. She was very close to tears, but she'd be darned if she was going to let him see her cry. No guy was ever going to see her cry.

She gave her boyfriend a quick sidelong glance in the dark interior. The dash lights cast a soft orange glow on his profile and, as she'd thought a thousand times before, he was a great-looking guy. Lean, golden-skinned, with that shoulder-length blond hair and the cutest sexiest face she'd ever seen on a man. He was her age, twenty-six, but he could have been sixteen or sixty—it didn't matter. Jay Pearson, aspiring country-and-western guitarist and singer, was always going to be drop-dead adorable.

But then there was his character.

Jay, she'd discovered, was a user. One of those people who'd been raised to believe the world owed him a living. He was special, gifted, or so he thought, and that made it okay to borrow from friends and never pay them back, or to snitch food in a grocery or cassette tapes from a music store. He acted more like a teenager than a twenty-six-year-old. A teen could snitch things and you chalked it up to youth. But at

Jay's age, it was downright criminal. And whenever B.G. said anything to him about it, he'd grow mean and defensive and threaten to leave her high and dry.

She'd put up with it so far, though, because she'd loved him once and sometimes she still did. They were in a real bad position right now, and she couldn't leave him for so many reasons—no money, no place to go, no friends, and then there was the biggest reason of all...

Her grandmother once told her that she, B.G., had trouble keeping men interested because she thought so little of herself. At the time Bettie Gay had thought that was mean, but now, thinking about how Jay treated her, she was beginning to believe Grandma was right. The way things were, though, she didn't see what she could do about it.

It must have been ten minutes after B.G. said they needed gas—and she really could use a washroom—that Jay bit his full lower lip and muttered, "We gotta get gas."

"Well, all I see around here is cactus and rattlesnakes," she said, sitting up straighter, her bladder beginning to ache.

"Rattlesnakes," he snorted. "They only come out in the sun."

"They're cold-blooded, Jay. I know that. I just meant—"

"Let's drop it," he said, "and find a gas station. There better be one in the next few miles or we're flat outta luck." B.G. stared at the black ribbon of road ahead. Other than the stars glittering in the sky and a horizon of cactus-dotted low mountains, she couldn't make out a thing—at least no city lights from Tucson. But there had to be something. A truck stop, a strip of motels where the interstates outside Phoenix and Tucson intersected, something. They just couldn't get stuck alone out here. Lately she'd been through enough.

A few minutes later she said, "I really have to go, Jay. Maybe we better just—"

"You'll have to hold it. If I stop now and start up again, it eats twice the gas. Okay?"

"Sure."

And then the gas gauge read empty. Jay swore and shifted his lean frame angrily in the seat. B.G. stayed quiet, trying not to say anything about how she'd told him a hundred miles ago when they'd passed that exit with the all-night gas station that they'd better stop. Water under the bridge.

At last, finally, they spotted a green-and-white exit sign—two miles. "We'll make it," Jay said triumphantly.

"I hope so."

"We'll make it."

"But do we have enough money? I mean, eight dollars—"

"Hey, let me do the thinking. I'll figure it out."

"Okay," she said, "okay." But then she wondered if there was even an all-night station at the exit.

There was. In a minute they both spotted the well-lit sign perched on a pole fifty feet high: Food, Gas, Indian Trading Post, 24 Hours.

"Thank God," B.G. muttered.

They pulled off onto the ramp, turning into a brightly lit gas station made to look like a log stockade. Jay maneuvered the Caddy up next to the pumps while B.G. scrambled out of the car. She was aware of little except the terrible pressure. And then she was past the neatly planted cactus garden out front and inside, ignoring the rows and rows of factory-made Indian pots, the aisles of food and curios—barely giving the clerk on duty a glance—and into the ladies' room.

She was in there a long time. And when she was done in the stall, she washed her hands and her face and combed her long brown hair. She straightened her T-shirt under the big plaid shirt of Jay's and retucked it into her jeans, aware of how baggy they were, how desperately hungry she was. If only... But the money had to go for gas, she knew, and even so she wondered if they'd make Phoenix.

"Oh, well," she said to herself, trying to put on a good face. Jay did have this gig starting tomorrow night. Well, tonight now. And Maverick's had a pretty good reputation. Maybe this would be the break. Maybe in a few months they might even be settled in and they could think again about getting married. She had a lot of misgivings about Jay, but there was so much to hold them together. They should get married, they really should. It was worth a try—she had to believe that. She had to believe he cared enough for her to marry her. She and Jay and... But she wasn't going to hash that over right now. Especially with Jay. For now, it was one day at a time. Things had been rough out in L.A. They had to get better. They had to.

Life couldn't just keep kicking you in the rear without taking a breather once in a while.

She pushed open the washroom door, took a breath—hunger was making her a little dizzy—and glanced around the store while Jay finished pumping the gas and crunched across the gravel drive toward the entrance.

She touched a little Indian drum with red and orange feathers pasted on its sides—tacky, she thought. She tilted her head and looked at some silver earrings on squares of cardboard—probably not silver and for sure not real Indian stuff. Same with the rows of painted earthenware pots. All factory junk. If her grandmother had taught her one thing, it was that you had to pay for the genuine article; nothing worthwhile in life came cheap.

Her eyes settled on the food aisle facing her. Doritos, nuts, chips and popcorn in bags. Candy bars.

Her stomach knotted and the dizziness returned. She was already thin, and now, especially now, she couldn't afford to be dropping weight.

Boy, she was hungry, she was thinking when she heard Jay's voice over by the checkout stand. He sounded . . . angry.

She turned away from the chocolate-covered doughnuts and looked in his direction, heard a few words. ". . . money in a bag and don't try anything stupid."

What? An alarm clanged in her head, and that was when she saw it. A gun. Jay had a gun!

Everything seemed to grind to a halt in her vision. Her brain, her hands, her feet were suddenly encased in cement. Things became extraordinarily clear and bright: the overhead lighting in mock wagon wheels, the blinking red-and-white Coca Cola sign on the wall, the blue-and-white ice sign on the freezer. The gun in Jay's hand and the frozen look of fear in the young clerk's eyes.

Slowly, slowly, the boy put up his hands. "Whoa, mister," he said, his voice quaking. "Money's yours. Don't hurt me."

And Jay. "I said put the money in that bag. Hurry!"

B.G. stared in horrified disbelief. She thought she heard herself cry, "No! Jay, no!" But maybe the scream was only in her head.

The boy did as he was told, and then Jay turned around, the gun still on the kid, and looked around, and the thought flashed through her mind that he was looking for her, but his eyes were so wild. He didn't even see her. It was as if he'd forgotten her completely.

She couldn't move. The cement holding her feet thickened.

"Jay," she mouthed, but he was turning back to the kid, sticking the gun at him again, threatening, and then he went careering out the store, smashing the door against the wall of the building, breathing heavily, swearing.

She watched in mute horror as he leapt into the car, looked back one last time, and the next second all she could hear was the gravel shooting from under the Caddy's tires and he was gone, swallowed up by the black desert night.

A moment slid by, two. And then everything came back to life inside the store. The clerk was grabbing the phone, dialing 911, yelling into the receiver. B.G. stood there gaping, her brain trying to function again. Jay. Jay had just robbed the store. Armed robbery. Where had he gotten that gun? And here she was, suddenly alone, abandoned, *dumped,* somewhere between Tucson and Phoenix with this terrified kid.

She moved her feet, felt dizzier than ever. Toward the door. Yes. She better get out of here.

Jay would come back. In a moment or two he'd come speeding into the lot again and she'd hop in and they'd be free . . .

She caught the kid's terrified glance. She stopped. She wasn't going anywhere. Jay would realize the crazy thing he'd just done, and he'd come back, tell the kid it was all a mistake. Sure. Sure. *Oh, Jay! What have you done?*

She had no idea how much time had passed. She was still looking at the kid frozen behind his register. And he was staring back at her for what seemed like forever. Finally she sat down on a stack of newspapers and put her face in her hands. "I'm sorry," she mumbled through her fingers.

"Jeez, lady" was all the kid said.

And then in the distance, a siren wailed, coming closer by the second.

The cops. Her brain spun. If Jay came back now they'd arrest him!

The door swung open abruptly, and in a flash two uniformed deputies rushed in, crouched, guns sweeping left to right, back again. B.G. could only stare in shock, the lump in her chest a desperate knot of fear.

"Let's see those hands, lady," one of the deputies said harshly.

Oh, my God. Here she was in the middle of the desert a thousand miles from home, everything she owned in the world careering down the highway with Jay, abandoned, four months pregnant.

And two sheriff's deputies holding guns on her.

CHAPTER TWO

IT WAS A NIGHTMARE but she was awake. Questions, hard eyes on her, the eyes of men who saw her as a menace, a criminal. No one had ever looked at her like that before.

"I didn't do anything," she kept saying. "I was in the bathroom. I didn't know he was going to do that. I didn't know he had a gun, I swear."

She wouldn't tell them his name: she owed Jay that much. He wouldn't have given *her* away, but then, she never would have done anything like he'd pulled, would she?

And she was innocent. Didn't that count for anything? This was America, and she was presumed innocent, and they had no right to force her to give them information.

She'd told them that, trying to be tough, but her voice had quavered, and they'd smiled condescendingly at her.

"You're an accessory to a felony," they told her there in the bilious green light of the trading post, "but maybe if you cooperate, give us his name and where he's headed, we'll go easy on you." They even tried the good cop/bad cop routine on her, one threatening her, the other cajoling. All the clerk had seen was a big old yellow car, no license-plate number, but he could describe Jay pretty well.

"Okay, lady," the older deputy finally said, "let's go."

"Where?" B.G. asked fearfully.

"Tucson. To jail," the younger one said tersely.

"Jail," B.G. breathed, feeling the bile rise in her throat.

"Unless you feel like giving us your boyfriend's name."

"I can't," she whispered. "I won't. I don't have to."

"Too bad, then. Come on, we're almost done with our shift. We'll really get ticked off if we have to put in overtime booking you, lady." And the older deputy took her elbow and steered her through the door out into the night, pushing her head down as his partner held the back door of the squad car open for her.

She sat there in the back seat, her hands in her lap and clutching her shoulder bag, a heavy wire-mesh screen between her and the deputies. She listened to the rasp and chatter of the police-band radio. Her mind refused to work, denying the situation she was in. This couldn't be happening. She hadn't done anything. She was innocent. Completely innocent.

Oh, Lord, what would her grandmother say? The tough lined old face came to her like an apparition, and B.G. could hear Grandma's words: "We don't lie and we don't steal. We've got our pride, us Brysons. We may be common folk, but we don't take handouts, and we don't break the law."

Grandma, B.G. cried silently, *I didn't break the law. I'm innocent.*

IT SEEMED as if they drove for a long time, southeast, into the pale predawn of a desert morning. Then they were in Tucson, a dark quiet city, its long straight thoroughfares empty and palm-lined and studded at intervals with the colored blinking eyes of traffic lights.

Off in the distance she could see the lights of downtown, where the buildings were taller and closer together, but the deputies turned away from there, crossing under the interstate to a neighborhood that wasn't built up at all, and swung into a parking lot. They got B.G. out of the car, marched her into the two-story concrete building, one on either side of her, like bodyguards.

It took a long time after that. Questions and more questions, papers filled out by the deputies, her handbag searched and tagged. She moved through the procedure in a daze, exhausted, nauseous, weak with hunger, alone. But she wouldn't give Jay's name to them. "You don't rat on your friends," Grandma used to say. Maybe, she thought, Jay would turn himself in, and then she wouldn't have to say anything.

She kept telling them she hadn't done anything, but she could see they weren't impressed.

"Are you arresting me?" she asked with false bravado. "I want a lawyer. I have a right to a lawyer."

"We're not arresting you—yet," one officer said. "Calm down. You're being held as a material witness for now."

"You can't hold me. I didn't do anything."

"We can detain you for twenty-four hours. Of course, if you tell us about your boyfriend, we might let you go sooner. And then again, if you don't, we may have to arrest you.''

One of the female officers at a nearby desk gave B.G. a perusal and said, "You don't look so good, honey. You sick?''

B.G. felt tears come to her eyes at this, the first kind word she'd heard in days. She blinked them back, then stared down at her lap. "I'm really hungry," she said.

The woman gave an impatient snort. "All we have are doughnuts, but you'll get breakfast later. Want a doughnut now?''

"That'd be wonderful," B.G. said. "If you don't mind.''

It was a fat greasy cruller, but it tasted like ambrosia. So did the cup of hot sugary coffee with globs of undissolved powdered creamer in it. She sipped and chewed, and for a minute it didn't matter that she was dirty and tired and all alone in Tucson, Arizona, and being interrogated by the police.

"Better?" the female officer asked her.

"Yes, thanks," B.G. replied.

A dark-complected man with a Pancho Villa mustache came into the room. He wore a suit with his ID clipped to his pocket. He was holding the papers they'd filled out about her. "I'm Detective Manzanares," he said.

B.G. looked up at him silently.

"Your boyfriend left you, Miss Bryson. Why are you protecting him?''

She shrugged, beyond argument.

"You're pregnant, I see here.''

She flushed.

"He wasn't going to marry you," Detective Manzanares said. "Quit fooling yourself. He left you, dumped you like an unwanted kitten. He doesn't deserve your loyalty."

B.G. looked down and shook her head.

The detective sighed. "Okay, Miss Bryson, I'll have to hold you until tomorrow. We'll want to do some checking on you."

"I want a lawyer," B.G. said stubbornly.

"We can see about that tomorrow. No rush. No charges are being brought against you. Yet."

That threat again. "You can't hold me," she repeated, her voice trembling.

"Oh, yes, we can. Detective Lewis, take her away, will you please?"

Detective Lewis, a tall stern-faced woman, took her by the elbow and led her out of the room, through a bewildering network of corridors, through a steel door, down a dim hallway between barred cells. She opened a door and pushed B.G. inside. "Sweet dreams," she said, then slid the door shut and left.

There were three other women in the cell. Two were asleep, dark humps on double-tiered bunks. The third, a gargoyle with too much makeup, a short tight skirt and patent leather boots up to her thighs, sat on her bunk and grinned at B.G.

"What's your name, toots?" she asked.

"Bettie Gay Bryson," B.G. whispered, hugging herself.

"Well, Bettie Gay, what they put you in here for? Drugs or johns?"

"Johns?"

"Drugs, then. You don't look like a working girl." The woman snickered.

B.G. stared at her, fascinated and horrified. The woman was a prostitute, she realized.

"You can have the top bunk," the woman said, "if you wanna sleep."

B.G. sidled around the edge of the cell, keeping as far from the woman as she could. She pulled herself up to the top bunk and lay there shivering, the greasy doughnut heavy in her stomach, her head on a pillow smelling of mildew. She'd hit bottom this time. This was as low as you could go. In jail. Pregnant, abandoned and in jail. She huddled there on the hard bunk, dry-eyed, desolate. She'd taken the wrong turn this time, and this was the end.

She closed her eyes, then jerked them open as an eerie cry came from another cell. Then curses and a new silence. B.G. smelled harsh disinfectant and the prostitute's sickeningly strong perfume and the sour reek of vomit, the sharpness of urine. Oh, God, jail. They had to believe her and let her out tomorrow. They had to.

But then what would she do?

B.G. HAD NO IDEA how long she'd been lying in stomach-churning sleeplessness when a woman came to the barred door. "Bettie Gay Bryson," she called out.

B.G. sat up quickly. "Yes?"

"Come with me."

Awkwardly B.G. climbed down from the bunk. She felt awful. Shaky and sick. She knew she must smell.

Nervous sweat, no shower, no toothbrush. Where was this woman taking her? Was she going to be released?

"What time is it?" she finally asked.

"Nine a.m."

"Uh, where are you taking me?"

"Interrogation." B.G.'s heart sank.

The interrogation room had institutional gray walls, windows covered with stout wire, a long table, four straight-backed metal chairs, a full ashtray that stank. She was shown in, then the woman turned to go.

"Wait," B.G. said. "What's going to happen?"

"Someone'll be in to interrogate you. Just sit down and hang on till it's your turn."

"But—"

"Sit down and wait," the officer said, then left, closing the door behind her.

B.G. sat in one of the chairs and looked around. *I've seen this movie,* she thought. *I've seen it a million times, but not with me in it!*

She crossed her legs and fidgeted, then ran her fingers through her tangled hair. She bet she looked a wreck. She didn't even have a comb anymore or a change of underwear. Nothing. Her purse was being held and everything else was in Jay's car.

She was so tired. All she wanted to do was put her head down and sleep. No, she wanted to eat first, a big plate of ham and eggs and biscuits, a glass of fresh-squeezed orange juice. Then a clean bed and a soft pillow and oblivion.

They had to let her go. And Jay—where was he? Had he reached Phoenix? Had they caught him? He'd turn himself in soon. She was sure of it.

She sat there, rested an elbow on the table, her head leaning on her hand as if it was too heavy. How had she gotten herself into this predicament? How could she have been so stupid, so naive? A desperate hopelessness gripped her, and suddenly she felt deathly ill, cold and trembling. Her baby couldn't be born in prison. It just couldn't be!

GREG TYRRELL, chief investigator for the Pima County Attorney's office, stared through the one-way glass at Bettie Gay Bryson.

"God, she looks young," he said to Stan Manzanares.

"Twenty-six," Stan said.

She looked like a skinny kid, Greg thought. Worn jeans, a man's creased flannel shirt, tangled long brown hair, a pretty face from what he could see. She was very pale and she was slumped, sideways to him, her head on her hand as if she was totally done in. Well, she probably hadn't slept all night, but that was okay—it'd make her easier to manipulate.

"She doesn't look pregnant," he remarked.

"Only four months. Sometimes it doesn't show much by then," Stan replied. "At least with the first one."

"Oh," Greg said. Stan had three children, he thought. He must know about things like that.

"Okay, I guess you can go in," Greg said. "I'd like to hear what she has to say. But if she's too dumb, it's just not going to work."

"She's pretty much out of it," Stan said. "No sleep. But I don't think she's too dumb. Maybe naive." He shrugged. "You know, after all these years, I've got real good instincts. You just get a feeling about some of the people that're brought in here. And this girl—" he gestured toward the one-way window "—well, I'd bet my last dime she wasn't in on the robbery."

"So you can't hold her?"

"Not for long. Not without charging her. Twenty-four hours."

"That'll have to be long enough," Greg said.

He studied the girl as Stan entered the interrogation room. She lifted her head when she heard the door open, her eyes wide. Pretty eyes, big and a light color. Not blue. Hazel. He could see the effort she made to straighten her back. Her neck was very slim and white, her profile nice. He felt a moment of pity for her, followed by a moment of contempt, then he put his feelings out of his mind and listened closely as Stan began to question her.

Coming through the intercom, the voices had a tinny quality. Hers was so faint he had to strain to hear. Stan went over all the routine questions again: name, age, permanent residence, job. She had no real home, only gave Stan a town in Florida—Mayport— where her grandparents had raised her.

"Don't I have the right to a lawyer?" Bettie Gay asked then.

Stan was ready for the question. "Has anyone charged you?"

"I'm in jail," she protested.

"Right now you're only being detained, Miss Bryson. What happens next is up to you." He'd side-stepped the lawyer issue neatly, buying time. But if she pressed him, he'd either have to back off or book her as an accessory, allow her to talk to a court-appointed lawyer. She did have rights, and apparently, she had some awareness of them, but she sure was unsophisticated, thinking that just because she hadn't done the robbery herself they'd let her go. Didn't she know how the law worked?

Greg looked at her sitting there, her big eyes guileless, her hands clasped tightly together. There was a simplicity about her that made him believe every word she said. And yet there was also stubbornness. She was green all right, but she was no pushover.

Stan went over the crime again step by step. She kept saying she was innocent, hadn't known her boyfriend was going to hold up the store. She'd been in the washroom.

"What's his name, Miss Bryson?" Stan asked.

"I can't tell you," she said in a broken voice. "But I didn't do anything. Really, I didn't."

Greg believed her. For that matter, so did Stan. But they needed leverage against Miss Bryson. They needed her cooperation.

"This boyfriend of yours. Where were you two headed?"

She hesitated. "Just driving. I don't know."

"You don't know," Stan said. "I find that hard to believe."

She said nothing, holding herself rigid. Greg could see that her hands were shaking.

"How are you going to contact him?"

"I can't. I don't know where he is. I don't know where he was going."

"You're lying, Miss Bryson."

"No," she said.

Greg knew she was lying now. She was a lousy liar. She wasn't an accessory to the robbery, not really, but she wasn't ratting on her boyfriend, either. He found himself admiring her for that.

Stan stood up and leaned over her, deliberately invading her space. Greg could see her flinch.

"This guy, this bum, left you holding the bag. He took off with sixty-five lousy bucks and left you to face the law and maybe jail time. He abandoned you, Miss Bryson, you and your baby. He deserves to be apprehended and to pay for his crime. Then maybe you'd get some child support from the guy."

Bettie Gay Bryson turned her face up to Stan, scared, shaken, cornered. On the verge of tears, her lips quivering. "I don't know where he is," she whispered. "I don't."

"You planned that robbery with him, didn't you?" Stan asked.

"No, no." She shook her head and shifted in the chair, trying to move away from her tormentor.

Greg was studying her the whole time, her poise, her profile, thinking about how she'd look if she were cleaned up, her clothes nicer, a girl you might see in the street, when he realized with a start that Stan had asked another question, which he hadn't heard. He pulled his gaze away from the girl's face and listened to her answer, trying to judge her. He wasn't there to stare, to wonder, to hold any opinion of her looks whatsoever; he was there because Detective Stan Manzanares had notified the county attorney that the Pima County Sheriff's Department had in their hands a young unmarried pregnant woman. Finally.

"Los Angeles," the girl was saying. "We came from Los Angeles. We were almost out of gas. I don't know, I guess . . . he got desperate. But I didn't know he was going to rob the store. You have to believe me."

It was looking good. This girl wasn't just pregnant but completely alone, not a penny to her name, and she wasn't a local girl with family or friends to complicate matters. She had very little choice really, except to go on welfare, and Greg could offer her better than that.

He'd watched girls before through this one-way window. The sheriff's department called his boss every time they arrested a pregnant woman, but until Miss Bettie Gay Bryson, none had been right for the job— or they'd refused to do it. He'd been waiting months for the right girl to come along, and now he just might have hit the jackpot.

"Come on, Bettie Gay," Stan was saying, Mr. Nice Guy now. "Give us his name and things'll change. We'll go easy on you."

She shook her head, then she put her hand to her forehead as if she was dizzy.

"You okay?" Stan asked.

"I'm awful hungry," she said. "I didn't eat last night."

"You'll get breakfast soon enough. Sooner if you tell me what I want to know. What's your boyfriend's name?"

Greg studied the girl more closely. Broke, pregnant, alone and hungry. My God, he'd never been hungry in his life, not really. Only the healthy hunger before a meal, a few hours' worth at most. But this poor girl was really hungry. He wondered how it felt and disliked himself suddenly for what he was going to do to her.

His boss, County Attorney Dick Mayer, had sent him to see if she would strike a deal with his office. All her sins would be forgiven if she'd do a particular job for him, and Greg had been well prepped on what he could offer her. All in all, it would be a very good deal for both the county attorney and Miss Bryson. If she accepted it.

"I won't tell you," she was saying plaintively, "I just won't. I'm so tired. Please leave me alone now. Please."

Stan threw up his hands and shrugged. "Okay, fine, have it your way."

She looked at him, her hair a tangled frame for her wan face. She was near tears, Greg could tell. He watched as Stan stalked from the interrogation room, slamming the heavy metal door behind him. Bettie Gay put her face in her hands as the door closed, her shoulders shaking.

Behind him Stan said, "I got her all softened up for you, Tyrrell. Go for it."

A wave of guilt swept through Greg, but he ignored it. The means justified the ends in this case. He nodded to Stan. "Thanks," he said.

"Good luck."

"Yeah." Greg looked into the room again, saw the girl raise her head and rub tears from her eyes angrily. Her narrow back straightened. Admiration vied with pity in Greg's mind. She had guts. He moved away from the one-way window, took a deep breath and squared his shoulders. Then he opened the door of the interrogation room and went in.

CHAPTER THREE

WHEN SHE HEARD the door open, it was all B.G. could do to square her shoulders for this next onslaught from Manzanares. It was too crazy, too awful. And she was so awfully tired. She'd ask for a lawyer again, that's what she'd do.

She'd tell him that right now. And she'd also tell him that they had to feed her. My God, B.G. thought as the door was opening, this was worse than a Turkish prison! Or, at least, how she imagined a Turkish prison!

"Look..." she began, her chin tipped up defiantly. But it wasn't Manzanares.

"Hi," this new man said, closing the door behind him. "My name's Greg Tyrrell. I'm with the Pima County Attorney's office. Mind if I sit and talk for a minute?"

"I...ah..." Words failed her. She hadn't expected this other person, this change in tactics. She stared at him as he strode to the table, pulled out the chair across from her and lowered himself casually into it. He folded his hands on the tabletop and smiled.

"Are you a lawyer or something?" B.G. said finally.

"Almost. Soon to be one," he replied, and she was struck by the deep even timbre of his voice and his boyishly handsome face.

"Oh," she said, bewildered.

"I'll explain." And again he smiled. "Right now, I'm the chief investigator for the county attorney here in Tucson."

"You're a...a private eye?" What was going on here? Surely she wasn't this important!

But he was shaking his head. "No, Bettie Gay," he said. Then, "May I call you that?"

"Uh, B.G. I go by B.G."

"Okay, B.G. it is. No, I'm not a private eye. I'm more of a detective, but with the county attorney. I'm not a policeman."

"Oh. And why do I need detecting, Mr.... Mr. Tyrrell?"

"We'll get to that in a minute," he said. "Say, would you like your breakfast in here? You could eat while we chat."

Oh, brother, she thought, *guess this is the good cop/bad cop routine again.* Still, she was famished, and maybe with a little food in her stomach she could collect her wits.

She fought off her weariness. "Yes, I want breakfast. And then I want a lawyer. I'm entitled to a lawyer for free, aren't I?"

"Of course you are, B.G. And I'll get you one if you insist. But we're kind of jumping ahead of things here. Let's get you some food and we'll talk, and then you can decide if you still want a lawyer. Is that okay with you?"

"I suppose," she said suspiciously.

He rose then, unfolding his body with a masculine grace she didn't fail to notice. He was tall. Over six feet, anyway, midthirties, and lean and fit beneath the dark gray lightweight wool suit.

He went to the door, opened it and quietly asked someone she couldn't see if he could get Miss Bryson a breakfast tray. And then he closed the door and turned back to her. The whole time B.G. had not been able to take her eyes off him. His light brown hair was perfectly razor cut; his white shirt was immaculate and starched, his tie a gray-and-burgundy-striped silk, a beautiful tie, very conservative.

But it was his face that held her, making her tongue feel cottony and her brain mushy. Smooth, with long-lashed blue eyes, short narrow nose, generous mouth. Investigator—almost lawyer—Greg Tyrrell belonged in the movies or at least in a TV ad, the sort where an incredibly handsome man with a heartbreakingly boyish smile is sailing a boat or plugging a beer with some of his other knockout buddies. He was absolutely the most all-American great-looking guy she'd ever seen.

And that, B.G. realized suddenly, was not good. He was making it impossible for her to think straight. Oh, God, this was worse than Manzanares's grilling. They'd sent in Mr. Perfect!

He sat back down and rested his clear blue gaze on her, and automatically B.G. ducked her head, self-conscious in her unwashed state and ratty clothes, in her humiliating position.

She thought about Jay then, saw his face as clearly as if he was in the room with her. Yesterday, when they'd left L.A., she'd thought everything was going to work out—the new gig at Maverick's, their relationship. She'd felt the growing bulge in her belly and honestly believed it was all going to be okay. Jay had even kissed her long and lovingly and said how much he loved her and how glad he was about the baby. "Really," he'd said.

But yesterday was a million years ago.

"I'm sure it won't be long," Greg Tyrrell was saying.

"What?" She looked up.

"Breakfast."

"Oh."

"Maybe while we wait," he said casually, "you could tell me a little about what happened out at that place on the interstate this morning."

"I've been over and over that, and I can't—"

He held up a hand. "Okay. I get it, B.G. But I really would like to hear how you feel about it."

"About what?" This was a new approach, she thought, wary.

"About your friend driving off that way. Leaving you holding the bag, so to speak. How does that make you feel?" He leaned forward a little. His expression was kind.

B.G. squirmed. "I won't tell you his name. I won't."

"I know that," the almost lawyer said. "And some people might even say that's very commendable of you, B.G. I'm only asking how you feel."

"Lousy." She met his eyes with a flash of sudden anger. "I feel lousy. I'm scared, I'm humiliated... Do you know I'm pregnant?" *Don't cry now,* she commanded herself. If ever she needed to be strong, this was the moment.

He sighed, sat back, folded his arms across his chest and held her gaze. "I know you are, B.G. Is your friend the father?"

Slowly she nodded.

"And that's got to hurt."

"Yes... it does," she said, and her voice began to crack, but mercifully a knock came at the door just then, and the tray of food was brought in.

With Greg Tyrrell looking on, B.G. ate with as much finesse as she could, considering how hungry she was. Eggs, bacon, whole-wheat toast and strawberry jam. Coffee. Juice. Never had anything tasted so good. The whole time she ate, he merely sipped on coffee from a paper cup, his gaze on her, weighing, concerned, but always assessing. She wondered if he was doing that on purpose, throwing her off guard. And why was she so darned important to the Pima County attorney's office, anyway? A sixty-five-dollar robbery couldn't possibly merit all this attention.

She ate and she thought again about Jay. She took on a far-off stare for a minute, fork poised over the eggs, and wondered where he was and just how he was feeling about leaving her like that.

The rat.

She frowned and collected herself, her eyes shifting back to Tyrrell. She pushed the tray aside and straightened her shoulders.

"Better?" he asked.

"I guess so. Sure."

"Good."

"So what now? This is all real nice, Mr. Tyrrell, but I don't buy my deserving all this attention over a convenience-store robbery I didn't commit. What's the catch?"

"You *are* feeling better," he said, and he gave her what seemed to be a smile of approval. "I've got a proposition," he said then, "but I'd really like to know a little more about you, B.G., before we get into that."

"This is pretty strange," she said, suspicious.

"I'm sure it must seem that way. But in a little while I'm certain it'll all make sense."

"You're not trying to put something over on me, are you?"

He raised a sandy brow.

"Trying to get me to relax and tell you my friend's name?"

"Not at all. I promise. Scout's honor," he said, and made a sign over his heart.

"I knew you were a Boy Scout," B.G. couldn't help saying.

"You got me there, B.G. Were you ever a Girl Scout?"

She shook her head. "I was always too busy. I used to help my grandmother in her restaurant."

"Was that in Florida?"

"Yes. Mayport. You know, a real good fish place. Shrimp, grouper, all kinds of fish in season."

"Sounds great. Does she still run it?"

B.G. shook her head. "No. It finally went belly-up. The health inspector was driving Grandma nuts—you know, you've got to put in new refrigeration, new washrooms, all that stuff. Grandma just barely made ends meet as it was."

"Tough business, restaurants."

She nodded. "It was the pits. So much work."

"But I'll bet you learned how to work."

"I guess."

"So why'd you leave Florida?"

She gave a tired laugh. "I wanted more. I didn't want to be your average Southern cracker—you know, married with four kids before you turn twenty-five."

"So you left...uh, Mayport."

"I met this guy and he had an audition in L.A. It was a great chance, and he wanted me to go along."

"So how was it out there?"

"Out where?"

"In the big wide world."

"Okay."

"And?" he prompted.

"And what? What's it to you, anyway?"

"I'm just curious," he said evenly. "You seem like a girl...excuse me, a woman with a level head. I'm only wondering how you ended up in this mess."

B.G. sat back and, avoiding his gaze, said, "Don't I wish I knew."

An uncomfortable silence filled the room, and then he said, "So you ended up here, alone and broke."

"I guess I did. So what?"

"So, if you get out of this situation here at the county jail, what are you going to do?"

"That's none of your business. And why should *you* care?" she said, defiant, anxious.

"Well," he said in a deep, strangely soft voice, "maybe I can help."

B.G. looked up. "Help? What are you saying?"

"Let me tell you how I see things. If I'm off base, let me know. But the way I see it, you're broke, totally alone in a strange city and haven't got a friend in sight. You're also pregnant. Am I right so far?"

She couldn't help it; she couldn't stop the tears burning behind her eyes. Damn. She said nothing.

"Okay," he said, still softly, carefully. "And I think...I hope, anyway, you won't try to link up with this guy of yours again when...if you get out of here." He waited, but still she said nothing. "I think you know better. He committed armed robbery, B.G., and he left you flat. You don't want to live with a guy like that. I have a feeling your family instilled better morals in you." He paused for effect. "What I'd like to do here," he went on after a moment, "is propose a solution. You might be able to help out the county attorney, and in turn, he could make your life a whole lot easier."

"I don't get it," she said.

"Let me explain. There's a certain unscrupulous lawyer here in Tucson we'd very much like to put behind bars. The trouble is, we need some help."

"Help?"

He sat forward, clasped his hands and pinioned her with his gaze. "You see, B.G., this lawyer sells babies. Sells them just like they used to sell people at slave markets."

"So...how do I fit in? You can't mean that I'd actually sell my baby!"

"No, absolutely not. It's your baby, B.G. Any decisions you make about your baby are yours and yours alone."

"Oh," she said, relieved.

"It's like this. You go undercover for the C.A.'s office, try to get enough on this lawyer so we can put this person behind bars, and the C.A. will drop all charges against you, as well as pay all your living expenses."

B.G. sat back and shifted her eyes away from his. *Wow*, was all she could think. Nothing more. Just, *Wow*. She put a fist to her mouth and chewed on her knuckles.

"It's something to consider, anyway," he said.

"What would I have to do?" she asked.

"Well, I really can't go into details now, but it would be easy, nothing taxing. You'd just have to visit the lawyer and report back to me. That kind of thing," he replied.

"Nothing that would hurt my baby?"

"Absolutely not."

"And you'd pay me?"

"I'm authorized to offer you a house to live in, an allowance until you have your baby, and we'll cover all prenatal care and hospital bills."

"No strings attached? Like, I wouldn't have to pay you back if things didn't work out?"

"No strings, B.G."

She thought a minute, hoping her brain was working properly, tired as she was. "Have you tried this before, I mean, getting some girl to go to this lawyer?''

He shook his head. ''We haven't found anyone promising till now. Till you.''

''Um.'' She stared at him, then hooked a strand of hair behind her ear. ''Why am I promising?''

He looked at her, apparently mildly surprised at her question. His answer came very cautiously. ''You seem intelligent and honest. And you're...in a spot. We can offer you help.''

''What you mean is, I'm easy to take advantage of,'' she said bitterly.

''No, not at all. This is a mutual thing, B.G.''

''Sure it is.'' Then she fell silent, thinking hard. He was so smooth, so convincing, she almost believed him. Almost.

After a long minute, Greg said, ''Hey, look, I know this is a lot to digest. Why don't you get some rest today, think things over, and I'll stop back this evening. If you're at all interested, we can go over more details then. If not . . . well, we can cross that bridge when we get to it. Okay?''

''Huh?'' she said. Then, ''Sorry, I heard you. I'm just very tired.''

''I'll go now.'' He pushed himself back from the table and rose, buttoning his suit jacket with one hand. He smiled again at her. ''Give it good long thought, B.G. If we go through with this deal, you've got to be committed.''

''I understand,'' she said, knowing she really didn't. Not yet. There was an awful lot to consider.

He walked to the door. ''I'll stop back around six.''

"Oh," B.G. said. "I guess I'll still be here."

"Uh-huh," he said. "If things work out, you can be out of here tonight. We'll talk later, okay?"

"Sure, yes, later."

He lingered a moment longer. "You get some rest, hear?"

"Sure," she said, and as he left, disappearing into the labyrinth of the county jail, B.G. wondered if she'd heard real concern in his voice. But why should a guy like that give two figs about her?

Before B.G. was escorted back to her cell, she was allowed to take a shower. Of course, there was an officer there supervising her, but the woman was very kind, giving B.G. her privacy, even remarking that it was tough being pregnant and alone.

"How did you know that?" B.G. asked, a towel wrapped around her.

"Greg . . . Investigator Tyrrell asked me to look out for you today," the woman answered.

"Oh," B.G. said.

They let her stay in her own clothes—not that her jeans and shirt were any too clean—but at least she didn't have to wear one of those horrible orange shirts with the big PCJ, for Pima County Jail, on the back. And she noted, too, that this morning no one had spoken of actually booking her. It occurred to her that they'd been holding her specially for Greg Tyrrell, that he'd been notified of her existence. It had been unspoken but still there—what would happen to her if she didn't go along with this deal? Would they book her?

She sat cross-legged on the top bunk and thought. They couldn't hold her past twenty-four hours. They had to either charge her or let her go. If she turned Greg Tyrrell down and they tried to book her, well, she'd demand a lawyer then. Yes, she could do that.

After all, she was innocent. Even the clerk at the store had seen her go to the washroom. She hadn't been the one holding a gun on him, for Pete's sake.

The gun. B.G. couldn't get that out of her mind. How long had Jay had it? And why?

For the hundredth time that morning she wondered where he was now. Phoenix? And was he in a panic, knowing she had to have been arrested? Was he going to turn himself in? Was he worried about her?

Oh, God, she thought, head in her hands, she should have run out and jumped in the car with him. She should have! But then she'd have been an accessory to armed robbery.

Well, she was through with him. The cops were right—he'd abandoned her. He was a thief and a coward and she wasn't going to have anything more to do with him. Ever.

She stretched out on the mattress, one thin arm behind her head on the dirty pillow and wondered where her cellmates were. Maybe they'd had bond posted for them and were free now. Of course, they were local. She, on the other hand, was very far from home. No one was around to risk bail on her.

There was Greg Tyrrell's offer. He'd said she could be free tonight, taken care of. All she had to do was get the goods on some sleazy lawyer. A lawyer who sold babies. Like at a slave market.

Her other hand automatically rested on the small swell of her belly. Her baby. Recently she'd felt tiny twitches inside her and known the baby was moving. She'd seen that film on PBS years ago, the one that showed the growth of a fetus in a mother's womb. Her grandmother had called her into the living room in their four-room clapboard house.

"Would you look at this on TV," she'd said. "B.G., you've got to see."

And B.G. had ambled in, not really interested, but then she'd started to watch the miracle unfold.

It *was* a miracle.

And now, because she'd screwed up taking her birth-control pills, the miracle was happening to her.

She must have drifted off to sleep then, because the next thing she knew, the cell door clanked open and a woman who looked to be in her forties was ushered in.

"Got a friend for you, Bettie Gay," the female officer said. "Now you girls be nice to each other."

The woman was dressed in a loose housedress, and she was obviously drunk. She had bruises on her round arms and face, recent ones. She staggered a little, then half fell onto the lower bunk across from B.G.'s.

"That son of a bitch," she grumbled. "Cops hadn't'a come, I'd'a laid his ass out a whole lot flatter." Then, amazingly, she giggled. "Caught him upside the head with the frying pan, though, before that son-of-a-bitch cop could stop me."

"Who'd you hit?" B.G. had to ask.

"Why, that no-account crud I got for a husband, that's who. Las' time he'll ever smack me around."

"Uh-huh," B.G. said, not wanting to hear any more. She had enough troubles of her own.

In about five minutes the woman was on her back and snoring. The snoring was irritating, but B.G. had no intention of waking her to get her to roll over. And then the snoring reminded her of home. Her grandfather, before he'd died, had snored to beat the band, and in that tiny house you had no choice but to put up with it.

Of course, the house was gone now. Well, maybe it still stood, but her grandmother was in a state retirement home in Jacksonville. She was doing all right, but all those years of hard work and little reward had taken their toll. She and Grandma still talked on the phone every Sunday. Even if she hardly had a dime to her name, she always found a way to call her grandmother.

Sometimes she thought about Liddie, her mom. Mostly she didn't. After all, Liddie had left her with Grandma and Grandpa when she was six months old and had only come back a few times in all these years. As for her real dad, well, Grandma never said much about him, except that he was a shrimper and had moved to the Gulf Coast. Her mother and father had never been married.

Now here she was in a similar boat. Unmarried, pregnant. No way to support herself, much less her baby.

She rolled over and faced the painted cement-block wall of the cell. Up until the robbery this morning, she'd half believed she and Jay were going to get married and raise the baby. That was the pretty picture she'd had in her mind all along, the perfect family. Once it had actually seemed possible, back at the beginning. Jay had been so nice, so good to her, so loving. She'd had a dream, she guessed, and she'd hung on to it even after Jay turned out to be not so nice. And then she'd found out she was pregnant, and she'd hung on to the dream even more desperately.

Well, she guessed she'd been pretty simple-minded, because Jay obviously hadn't shared her dream. She just hadn't wanted to see it before; she'd been deliberately blind. But, she should have known. What was it she'd heard once in church? The sins of the fathers. That was it. The sins of the fathers visited upon her own baby. Bettie Gay Bryson had been dumped as an infant, and now her own innocent child was in for the same awful fate.

She set her chin. She wasn't going to let it happen. She was going to see that her baby had all the advantages.

Somehow B.G. managed to fall asleep. She awoke to noise again, and this time it was her cell-mate being taken away. Maybe a lawyer had gotten her out. Maybe she was being arraigned. B.G. didn't know and she didn't care. Her problem was that in a few hours Greg Tyrrell was going to return, and if she said she was interested, he'd go over some details about the county attorney's offer. She had to think about that. She had to think about what was best for the baby. There was no more putting it off. Jay was gone. And even if by some miracle they got back together, worked things out, she couldn't let a man who'd done such a rotten thing raise her child. The only reason she considered him at all was that she was pregnant, and remembered with lingering regret the good times, the way he'd been at first, his charm, his smile. She'd thought he loved her, but now she knew. Jay didn't love anything but his own image of himself.

So what were the alternatives? She knew that eventually she'd get out of jail. But she was penniless. She was a good worker, had experience managing a restaurant—well, a small café actually—but she could get a job. She'd lie about being pregnant.

No, it was hopeless. Even if she got a place to live, an impossible task without money, and even if she got a job immediately, she wouldn't get a paycheck for a week at the very least.

There was always welfare. She thought about the possibilities of staying in Tucson and living off the social services, but in less than a minute she dismissed the idea completely. No one in her family had ever resorted to welfare. She simply couldn't do it.

Her thoughts circled back to the county attorney's offer. She didn't know much about the details of how she would live or where, but Greg Tyrrell had sounded as if she'd be well looked after. She and the baby. He'd said, too, that what became of her child was up to her. And she couldn't help wondering if somehow they could find a good home for the baby. The hard cold reality was that she was utterly incapable of caring for her own child at this stage of her life. She had no husband, no money, no job, no prospects, and wouldn't she be showing her child more love by providing it with a good secure future?

She tossed and turned for the rest of the afternoon, ate something tasteless from a tray, weighing everything in her mind over and over.

The deal sounded good, a way out. But then, taking off with Jay Pearson had sounded good, too. In the end, it had been a wrong turn. Maybe this deal was, too. Maybe it wasn't. With the latest bad decision she'd made, how was she supposed to know?

CHAPTER FOUR

GREG'S LUNCH was a messy Reuben sandwich at his favorite deli. All the while he ate it, wiping coleslaw juice off his chin, he thought about Bettie Gay Bryson and how hungry she'd been. Jeez. In this day and age.

After lunch he walked back to his office building on North Stone Avenue in the Great American Bank Tower building. He took the elevator up to the floor where Dick Mayer had his office, two floors above his own.

"He's waiting," Rosemary told him. "Any luck?"

"Maybe." Rosemary knew everything. Sometimes Greg thought the entire office staff should quit and leave Tucson and Pima County to Rosemary. She'd probably run things just fine.

Their boss, Dick Mayer, could be a hard man. He'd been in the military, an army lawyer, then retired to Tucson and taken the job of county attorney when watering his cactus plants began to bore him. He was a tough taskmaster but he was fair, and Greg appreciated that. As a matter of fact, he aspired to be like Dick when he passed the bar, although he'd already decided he'd prefer private practice. More money in it.

Dick Mayer was drinking a Diet Pepsi. He gestured for Greg to sit and cradled the sweating can in his hands.

"So, you talked to her," he said without preamble.

"I did."

"Well?"

"She was a mess, no sleep, pretty upset. She listened, though. I told her I'd be back this evening."

"What did you think of her?"

Greg tried to sort out his impressions of Bettie Gay Bryson. Dick liked facts, not opinions, but this was a pretty subjective judgment. Greg tried to be as accurate as possible.

"Well, she's down on her luck, no doubt about it. Not a cent to her name, not even any clothes. The boyfriend took off with everything. Alone. Only a grandmother back in Florida. No ties, no job, no friends."

Dick Mayer nodded, his bristly gray crewcut catching the bright spring sunlight that flooded through the window behind him. Later, in the summer, the blinds would be tightly drawn to keep out the brutal desert heat. "Good, real good. What about her personality? Is she trustworthy? Will she stick to her word?"

Greg ran a hand through his hair. "That's a hard call at this point. My feeling is that she's naive, not dumb but naive, and that she's reliable, kind of old-fashioned almost. Believes in justice and loyalty and all that." He hesitated. "But she's tough, too. No, not tough. Spunky, I guess. Shrewd."

"Mmm."

"I'm not sure she'll go for it, Dick. She's in a pretty bad spot right now, but she could go on welfare. And the police can't keep her past twenty-four hours without charging her. I think she may suspect that. Like I said, she's not stupid."

"The boyfriend?"

"She won't give his name. But I believe her when she says she had nothing to do with the robbery. No record—we checked."

"You know what to tell her, Tyrrell..."

"Sure, I know. I'll be as persuasive as I can, but she may not go for it. And to tell the truth, I feel like we'd really be taking advantage of her." Greg rubbed his chin. "I intend to make the possible danger fully known to her, Dick. I won't lie."

"Don't exaggerate the danger, for God's sake. Chances are nothing will happen," Dick Mayer said.

"Yeah, I know but... Hell, this girl is in a real fix. I mean, I don't want to be unethical, bulldoze her. She does have other choices."

Dick Mayer leaned forward, set his Pepsi down on the desk and drew his brows together. "We need this girl, Tyrrell."

"I know."

"I want her signed, sealed and delivered tonight, and I want you to be her new best friend. I want her to be dependent on you for everything. I want you to be her mommy and daddy and sister and brother and confessor."

"Dick, I don't know..."

"You'll do it, Tyrrell. I know you. You're ambitious and talented and smart. It's the only way we're going to nail Grace Jacobs and you know it."

Greg sighed. "I know."

"Don't feel sorry for this girl. She got herself into this fix, eyes wide open. She can redeem herself, though. She'll be doing some good, some real good. For society."

"For us," Greg muttered.

"That, too." Dick nodded. "Listen, this is the best job she'll ever have. A free ride, nothing to do. Just sit and get fat and happy while we pay the bills."

Greg tried to picture the skinny B.G. growing fat. It was hard. He scowled.

"Don't be a jackass, Tyrrell. This girl sounds perfect. Don't scare her off. We need to stop Jacobs—it's been too long already. She's selling babies, Tyrrell, selling them for top dollar. She's breaking the law every day and thumbing her nose at us."

"Yeah, I know," Greg said. "But I'm a little worried. This girl seems so defenseless. If she does this for us and if Jacobs finds out..." He shook his head. "She could be in some danger."

"I know what you're thinking," Dick Mayer said. "That Jane Doe we found out in the desert. The hit-and-run."

"I guess I am thinking about that. She'd just had a baby, according to the medical examiner, and she'd been spotted at Jacobs's office on police-surveillance tapes. What in hell am I supposed to think?"

"That Grace Jacobs killed Jane Doe or had her killed," Dick replied coolly. "Yeah, we know that. No proof, though."

"So...what if something like that happens to this girl?"

Dick shook his head. "It can't. You're running her, Tyrrell. You're in touch with her. She won't make a move without checking with you, so how can she get in trouble?"

Greg scowled again.

"Okay, okay, your reluctance is commendable," Dick said. "Now that you've registered your objections, go get that girl."

"I won't coerce her," Greg said.

"You won't have to. Just use your charm, Tyrrell, and those good looks of yours. She'll be eating out of the palm of your hand." And Dick gave Greg one of his rare smiles.

Greg left work early that afternoon. He had to run by his oldest sister's house to firm up the plans for his mother's birthday party the next night, and then he had to be back at the jail by six.

Abby answered the door and hauled Greg inside, where he was instantly assaulted by her two kids. They hung on to their adored uncle Greg, rubbing sticky Popsicle fingers on his good gray suit.

"Sorry," Abby said, wiping at the spots with a cloth. "Darn kids."

"No big deal," Greg said. "Just tell me what to bring tomorrow."

"A date," Abby said without missing a beat.

"Come on, Abby."

"Bring some champagne then. A coupla bottles."

"Done. And how much do I owe you for her present?"

"It's fifty dollars from each of us."

"That's all?"

"Paul got the dishwasher wholesale, and Andy's going to install it." Paul and Andy were Greg's brothers. Paul ran an appliance store, and Andy was the head of maintenance for a ritzy golf resort in the foothills.

"So, everybody can make it?" Greg asked.

"Yup, we'll all be there. And you, Gregory, don't you fight with Sandy."

"No fights, I promise."

"Six o'clock, okay?" Suddenly there was a blood-curdling scream from the backyard, and Abby rolled her eyes and ran to see what had happened.

Greg left his sister's house in the southeastern part of Tucson and drove toward the county jail. The sun was low in the sky, setting behind the jagged gray dryland mountains that enclosed the city. He drove his Honda sedan automatically; his mind was on his meeting with Bettie Gay Bryson—B.G.—what he would say, how he would say it. The girl was ripe for someone to direct her, obviously, and if he didn't take her in hand, she'd probably hook up with some other no-good bum like the one who'd left her high and dry at the gas station. Greg frowned, driving along in rush-hour traffic, his elbow resting on the windowsill, his other wrist crooked over the steering wheel.

So, was he just rationalizing, convincing himself that this girl needed him to save her from herself? Or would he really be doing her a favor?

She certainly needed help, that was for sure, but he wondered whether she'd take advantage of it. And then, even if she decided to make the deal with him, she could still split, take off before the job was done, ruin the whole plan. She had asked if she'd have to pay back the money if things didn't work out.

He recalled what Dick Mayer had said that afternoon: *I want you to be her new best friend. I want her dependent on you.*

If she did consent to doing the job, he'd be babysitting her, for God's sake, and for how long? Five months. It was a helluva lot for Dick to ask of him. Of course, the plan had been Greg's in the first place, and so he'd been the natural choice to find the girl and handle her. He'd been working on the Jacobs case for six months, and so far there hadn't been a break, not one adoptive parent who'd testify against Jacobs, not one unmarried pregnant girl who'd complain on the record.

Except for that Jane Doe. Maybe she'd been going to complain, and Grace Jacobs hadn't liked the idea.

It was still light out when he drove into the county-jail parking lot, the sun down now behind the mountains, but the early-spring light was clear and golden, with the diamond-bright clarity typical of the desert. Details stood out starkly and distinctly, every shadow sharp as a pen-and-ink rendering. Tucson was a great town, Greg thought as he had so many times. A city of some sophistication, it drew its citizens from all over

the nation but was still, in a subtle way, a frontier
town, far from the center of things. Everyone who
lived in Tucson had a sense of adventure, as if they
were all inhabiting a kind of exotic colorful outpost.

Greg had been born and raised in Tucson and really hadn't traveled much—no time or money. But he
had plans. When he passed the bar and got his
$75,000-a-year job in one of the state's big law firms,
he was going to travel. Oh, yes. First-class. Paris,
London, Tokyo, Athens, the South Pacific.

He had no one to spend all that money on but himself, and he intended to spend it with panache. He deserved it after all these years of nose-to-the-grindstone
work and study. Ten years of going to law school at
night and working all day. He owed himself some
pleasure.

Sure, he liked his hometown, but he needed to see
the world. Hell, even B.G. had seen more of the States
than he had!

Greg parked his car, got out and slid the keys into
his pants pocket. This assignment he was about to
undertake was important. He wondered whether he'd
been too smooth, too nice that morning. B.G. would
suspect someone who was too nice; clearly she hadn't
had much experience with nice guys. But then again,
she couldn't be ordered around either. He knew that.

He'd have to be sincere, genuine, straight. *Just use
your charm, Tyrrell, and those good looks of yours,*
Dick had said. Without false modesty, Greg was well
aware that he could...well, influence people with a
smile and just the right word. He'd been doing it since
he was a kid. It wasn't for nothing that his mother had

called him Prince Charming all his life. Hell, Greg thought, you use what God gave you. Sugar got more smiles than vinegar.

He walked into the front door of the jail, showed his ID to the guard and asked that Bettie Gay Bryson be brought to one of the interrogation rooms. He went into the indicated room to wait for her and sat with one ankle resting on the other knee. There was a dust smudge on his tassle loafer; he rubbed it off, then drummed his fingers on his knee, waiting, rehearsing what he'd say to her.

When the door finally clanked open, he stood quickly, smiling, not too broadly, just enough.

"Here she is," the policewoman said. "You call me when you're done."

"Will do," Greg said, and the door closed behind the guard. He turned to B.G. "Well, how are you? Feeling better?"

She stood there in her same old clothes, but she looked refreshed. Her hair was clean, long and brown and shiny, and she appeared to be rested. "Yes, thanks," she said softly.

"Sit down, B.G."

She sat, both feet on the floor, hands on her thighs. She looked at him expectantly.

"Well, good, I'm glad you got some rest. I hope you've given some thought to my proposal. I'm here to talk about anything you'd like, answer any questions."

"I have thought about it," she said. "But I need to know a lot more. I can't promise anything until I know all the details."

"Of course, no one would expect you to. And I'll try my best to fill you in."

"Tell me about the lawyer, the one you want to get. What exactly is he doing?"

"The lawyer is a woman," Greg said.

"A woman?"

"A very smart woman. Very rich now, too. We figure she's hauling in three million a year, all from independent adoptions. See, there're two kinds of adoptions. There's the agency kind, where the social-services agency takes the baby from the mother and then places it. The second kind is independent. That's where the baby is placed directly with the adoptive parents by the natural mother. It's perfectly legal if done properly, but our lady lawyer isn't doing it properly."

He got up and paced back and forth in front of B.G. He felt her eyes on him, following every move he made. Big hazel eyes with dark lashes.

"In an independent adoption both the natural mother and the adoptive parents should get lawyers, because it's unethical for one lawyer to represent both sides. Our lady doesn't allow another lawyer to be involved. She takes care of everything herself. Now, it's illegal to give the mother any money above and beyond her living expenses, but we know this lady is doing that, charging the childless couples huge amounts—under-the-table cash payments. It's also illegal for anyone to collect a 'placement' fee. Legal fees are okay, but nothing more, and they shouldn't go over, say, a thousand dollars. These people are paying thirty, forty thousand for a baby. Some of it goes to the natural mother, but most of it goes to our lawyer friend.''

''Where does the lawyer get these babies?'' B.G. asked.

''She's got it all set up. Some come from doctors, word of mouth. Some are referrals from hotlines that advertise themselves as pregnancy or reproductive-information hotlines. And she also has a house full of young pregnant women. She pays their living expenses and takes their babies.''

He saw a grimace cross B.G.'s face. ''Yeah, it's real ugly. There's a shortage, you see, of healthy white babies ever since it became socially acceptable for single women to keep their babies. And there are a lot of desperate childless couples out there. We know of some who've mortgaged their homes to pay for a baby.''

He saw her serious expression, saw the way her brows drew together. He had her hooked, he was pretty sure. She was paying very close attention. And maybe, too, she was listening so closely because she was deciding what to do with her own baby.

''Why do you need me?'' she finally asked. ''What can I do?''

''We've had a big problem trying to prove this lawyer is doing something illegal. No one'll talk. The adoptive parents are too scared—they're afraid the adoption would be declared illegal and their child taken away from them. The natural mothers are young and ignorant of their rights and mostly relieved that they're rid of an unwanted baby.'' He stopped pacing and stood before B.G., meeting her gaze, choosing his words carefully. "This lawyer is breaking the law in a dozen ways. She's selling the custody of one person to another. It's slavery, pure and simple. And we need you to prove this for us."

"How?"

"You go to this lady lawyer, go through her whole procedure as if you want her to place your baby. You're perfect. You're what she's looking for. You report back to me."

"But my word against hers, how will that hold up? I mean, will that really help you?"

She was smart, he thought. He'd wanted to rope her in completely before going into this aspect of the plan, but she'd asked, so...

"It wouldn't be just your word, B.G—you're right. We do need more than that." He put his hands behind his back, leaned forward slightly, weight on his toes, and put on his most sincere expression. "You'd be recording your conversations with this woman."

Her gaze snapped up to his. He could see into the clearness of her hazel eyes, golden brown with dark circles around the irises. She reached a hand up and hooked a strand of hair behind her ear, a nervous gesture. "You mean," she began, "you mean I'd be... wired?"

He smiled reassuringly. "There's nothing to it. We have equipment nowadays that's incredible. Easy to use."

"Wired." She breathed the word.

He let it sink in, watching her, saying nothing.

"What if she searched me, found out I was taping her?" B.G. finally asked.

Greg let out a breath he didn't know he'd been holding. "I won't lie to you. There's a very small chance that could happen, but it's so unlikely I hesitate to even mention it. And if she did, well, I'd be on the other end listening to every word. Anyway, this woman has absolutely no reason to distrust you, and we'll see to it she never does."

"I don't know... What if I'm not a good enough actress? What if I'm not convincing?"

"You will be."

She tilted her head up at him. "You're talking like I already said I'd do it."

"I didn't mean to. It's your choice entirely."

"Okay, tell me more about what I get if I do this."

He took a deep breath. This was a good sign. "We'd provide you with a place to live. A house. Not fancy but quite acceptable. An allowance for your personal use. All your doctor bills, prenatal and postnatal. Delivery charges, hospital bills. You wouldn't owe a penny of that. And if there were complications, they'd be covered, too."

"And I wouldn't have to pay you back?"

"That's right. I told you that already."

"No matter what happens, say, if she finds the wire and the deal falls through?"

"No matter what."

"And what if I decided after a while I couldn't go through with it?"

"You're entitled to do that. We won't force you. Then the deal is simply terminated on both sides." Greg went to a chair on the other side of the table and sat down. He tugged at his suit sleeve. "I want to be totally honest with you, B.G. There is a small amount of danger here. It's unlikely that this woman would search you, but I suppose it's within the realm of possibility. And she's one tough cookie. She could turn nasty to protect her setup. You'd have to be careful, very careful. We'd establish a procedure—how to contact me and so on. A safe procedure. There are some things you'd need to learn. Pretty simple stuff. Plus, I'd lessen your exposure to her. You wouldn't even have to make the initial contact with her for several weeks at least." He felt the urge to tell B.G. about that Jane Doe, the dead girl who'd just had a baby. The one out of hundreds who'd probably caused some trouble for Grace Jacobs. Then he decided not to. There was no proof whatsoever Jacobs had anything to do with it. And B.G. would be warned not to threaten Jacobs or her organization in any way.

"That's all I'd have to do? Go talk to this lawyer, tape her?"

"Well, you'd be asked to testify in court," he said reluctantly. This was the one thing that had caused previous girls he'd interviewed to refuse the deal.

"Oh," she said, a little surprised. "Then I'd have to stay here in Tucson?"

"You'd have to be here for the trial, yes. But you could go wherever you wanted, as long as I knew where you were. I'd see that your travel costs were covered."

"And the robbery charges," she asked, "they'd be dropped?"

"As if they'd never existed. You could leave here with me right now, tonight."

She slumped back in her chair, thinking. Her hair fell like a shiny curtain, hiding her face. He could imagine the struggle, the decision she had to make. Did she still believe that bum would come back for her? Did she love him?

Greg sat there across from her and waited. She was the best one for the job so far, and he hoped she'd agree to do it. Putting Grace Jacobs behind bars was a good thing, a necessary thing. It'd also look good on Greg's record, which wouldn't hurt one bit when he sent his résumé to the big law firms.

B.G. looked at him then, frowning a little, studying him, as if he and he alone held the answer for her. He tried his best to meet her gaze with genuine concern and utter honesty. But he felt just a bit uncomfortable, like a specimen under a microscope.

She sighed and ran a hand across her face. "I don't know," she whispered.

"Do you want more time to think about it?" he asked carefully.

"I don't know," she said. "I want to get out of here. I can't stand it in here another minute."

She's going to do it, he thought, a surge of elation shooting through him, but he didn't show a glimmer of it.

She stood up then and walked to the corner of the room, head down, facing the wall. Her back was slender, the jeans creased like an accordion behind her knees, the ugly plaid shirt wrinkled, shapeless. From the back she could have been fifteen years old, even younger, so slight was she. Abruptly Greg felt sorry for her. Poor thing, stuck between a rock and a hard place. She had no real alternatives, not any decent ones. A lost lamb, vulnerable, completely alone—she and her unborn baby. Then he hardened his resolve. Hey, she'd chosen a real creep for a boyfriend, gotten herself knocked up. She had to take responsibility now. He was only offering her a good deal, probably the best thing that'd come down the pike in a long time for Miss Bettie Gay Bryson. Hell, yes.

Finally she turned around and fixed her gaze on him. "Okay," she said in a strong voice. "Okay, yes, I'll do it."

He didn't allow himself to smile. He nodded somberly. "You've made the right decision, B.G."

"There's one thing, though . . ."

"What."

"I want you, your office, to find a good family to adopt my baby when this is all over. I want my baby to have the very best."

"Done."

"Okay then," she said, standing there in the corner of the interrogation room, a skinny figure in old clothes, but a figure possessing a singular dignity.

That spurt of admiration shot through Greg again.

"You promise," she said, "about my baby?"

"Absolutely. You have my word."

She moved toward him and held out her hand. "We have a deal then, Mr. Tyrrell."

He stared at her for a moment, caught off guard, then he reached out and enclosed her hand with his own. How small and cool her fingers felt in his. How trusting. "Deal, Miss Bryson," he said.

CHAPTER FIVE

GREG TYRRELL'S white Honda Accord smelled new and clean and was as spiffy as the day he'd bought it. B.G. sat in the passenger seat and thought about the total orderliness of the car and of the man himself—never a hair out of place. It made her uncomfortable.

"Ever been to Tucson before?" he asked, shifting gears.

"No," she said. "This is my first time in Arizona really." And then she caught herself. "Some first time, huh?"

"Mmm," he said. "But things are looking up for you, I hope."

"Sure," B.G. allowed.

They were passing the downtown core, heading north, she thought, because the sun had set not too long ago on Greg's side of the car. But to B.G. it didn't much matter what direction they were going; she was in his hands now, and she felt safer than she had in a long time.

"This motel I've got in mind," he told her, "isn't a fancy spot, but it's clean and secure and you should be comfortable for the night. Tomorrow we'll get you set up in the house."

"Okay," she said.

"Any questions? I must have forgotten something."

"No, not for now."

B.G. supposed he was thinking she was an idiot, a puppet on a string. Well, maybe she was for the time being, but she didn't care. She had to do what was right for the baby. Then later, by the autumn, she could begin to worry about herself for a change. Right now she couldn't afford to care what Greg Tyrrell thought of her.

They drove by a strip mall or two, past dozens of Mexican restaurants and fast-food joints. Up ahead B.G. could see the interstate, but Greg turned into a motel before they got there. It was one of those Arizona-type places, called the Oasis. In the center of the U-shaped adobe building was an elevated area with a pool and plastic lounges, surrounded by tall Egyptian palms with colored spotlights tilted up from the ground, illuminating their long fronds. Pretty. The place was much older than the Days Inn or Best Western right next to the interstate, but this was homier. For tonight it would do just fine.

Greg parked next to the office and opened his door. "I'll be right back," he said, pausing. "Will you be okay?"

"Sure," she said, taken aback. Jay had never asked her that: *Will you be okay?*

He disappeared inside, and three or four minutes later he reappeared and climbed back in the car, room key in hand. "Room 201," he said, starting the ignition. "I thought you'd feel safer on the upper level."

"Sure," she repeated.

They parked and he walked her up, unlocked and opened the door to the room, went in and glanced around. "It looks fine," he said, tall and terribly masculine standing there next to a dresser, jiggling the key in his hand.

"It's okay," B.G. said, looking at her feet. "I mean, it's great. It's been a long time since I was in such a nice place. Thank you."

"You're very welcome," he said.

B.G. kept looking at her feet, her purse clutched in her hands in front of her. She felt stupid and shy and couldn't believe her reaction to being alone in a motel room with a man. Good Lord, she'd been in plenty of rooms with Jay. But, she realized, she'd never been in a room alone with a man like Greg Tyrrell. She thought in a flash that if only he was dressed down or something, stripped of his expensive suit, his perfect hair mussed, maybe she'd feel less . . . out of place.

She glanced up as he put the key on the dresser and then reached into his pocket. B.G. still clutched her purse, feeling small and awkward.

"Here," he said, holding money out to her. "There's a minimart right next door. I'm sure you need a few things for the night. Maybe they even have T-shirts or whatever, you know, to sleep in. The place is perfectly safe to go into up until midnight, anyway. Tomorrow we'll get you settled. We can at least get you some clothes."

She tilted her head. "You mean . . . you're going to take me shopping?"

He gave her one of those winning smiles. "Sure, why not?"

"Well, I..."

"B.G.," he said, his voice somber, "when you agreed to do this job, you became...my responsibility."

She stared at him, not understanding.

"You're very valuable to the county attorney. I have to—want to—keep a close eye on you. Whatever you need, I'll see to it. That's my job."

"But you don't...I mean...you don't have to, you know, tag along with me or anything."

"It's my responsibility," he repeated, and she felt the blood rush to her cheeks. This man didn't want to hang around with her; he was only doing his job. She hated that.

"You probably have something better to do," she said.

"Nope, not a thing."

She didn't believe it, but there wasn't much she could say. And then it occurred to her that he was afraid to leave her alone, that he didn't trust her.

"I'll let you get settled," he said. "Why don't I pick you up around nine or so in the morning?"

"That's fine," she muttered. Then, when he was half out the door, she said abruptly, "I won't run. I mean, I'll be here." And then she gave an embarrassed laugh. "Where would I go, anyway?"

In answer he stared at her for a moment, then nodded and left. B.G. let out a breath she seemed to have been holding for hours.

With the TV on in the background, she sat on the side of the king-size bed and stared at the telephone. Greg Tyrrell had not been gone five minutes and here she was, already going back on her promise to herself to have nothing to do with Jay Pearson ever again. Or, at least, she was thinking about it, contemplating calling Maverick's in Phoenix. She even put her fingers on the receiver and traced its smoothness for long minutes before she withdrew them.

"No," she said aloud, firmly.

She took off for the minimart shortly thereafter, the fifty dollars safely in her wallet. Greg Tyrrell had been right; she could buy a T-shirt for the night, toothbrush, toothpaste, that sort of thing. Fifty dollars. It had been a long time since she'd had that much to spend.

She spent sixteen. Twelve on a University of Arizona T-shirt and four on toiletries. Then, not admitting to herself why, she asked for the difference between the twenty-dollar bill she gave the clerk and the sixteen dollars she owed in coin. The whole time the kid counted it out into her palm, she told herself it was just in case. But just in case of what, B.G. didn't want to examine.

She left the store, the cool night air washing over her. She saw it then, out of the corner of her eye, the pay phone on the outside wall of the minimart.

Automatically her feet carried her over, and a part of her mind was telling her that if she was going to call him, do it from a pay phone and not the motel-room phone—maybe somehow a bug had been planted there. Another part of her railed against the whole thing. Jay was a no-good thief who'd abandoned her and their baby. If she never saw him or spoke to him again, it would be too soon.

Nevertheless she put a quarter in the slot and dialed information, asking for Phoenix. When she finally dialed Maverick's, she was positive he wasn't going to be there. He'd be a fool to have gone straight to a destination she could so easily have given the Tucson police.

"Pearson, Jay Pearson," B.G. said into the receiver. "He's with the group that's playing tonight. He plays lead—"

"Yeah, he's here" came the reply. "Hold on. I'll see if I can find him."

B.G.'s heart flip-flopped. He'd shown up for the gig! And then she wasn't sure if she was angry or relieved. Shouldn't he have been looking for her or something?

But he came on the line before she could think it out further. She almost hung up. She knew she should. But she couldn't.

"Yeah? Hello?" came his familiar voice.

"Jay?"

There was a long pause. "B.G.? Is that you?"

"Yes," she breathed, still not believing she'd contacted him. *Fool,* her brain said. *Fool.*

"Well, I'll be! Where in hell are you?"

"Jail. I'm in the Tucson jail," she shot back.

"No way," he said with a little laugh. "You're putting me on, baby."

"Where'd you think I was, then?" *Oh, God,* she thought, *hang up on him. Hang up now before you're lost.*

"Well, I—"

"You don't care where I am. You left me last night holding the bag and just drove off!"

"Hey, baby, I . . . Now look—"

"Look nothing. They took me to jail, Jay. They hauled me off to jail and raked me over the coals, for God's sake. How *could* you?"

There was silence again. Then, "Hey, I'm real sorry. I know I screwed up big time. I guess I panicked."

"You robbed that store, Jay. You held a gun on that poor kid and robbed—"

"Whoa," he said, and she could see him in her mind's eye casting around guiltily as if someone could overhear her. "Now listen—" his voice was a whisper "—I lost my head for a minute, that's all, B.G. For God's sake, all I got was sixty-five dollars! I—"

"Where'd you get that gun, Jay?"

"You don't need to know."

"Okay, fine," she said, trying to control the shaking in her voice. "Don't tell me. I really don't want to know, anyway."

"Listen," he said, calmer now. "I'm real sorry about the whole thing, baby. It was bad news. Hey, you didn't tell the cops . . ."

"I didn't rat on you, if that's what you're getting at."

"Thanks. I mean it. But how did you—"

"I'll tell you sometime," she cut in.

"Okay," he said, "okay. Listen, as soon as I get a few bucks and dump the Caddy, I'll, like, send you some money, you know, so you can head up here. Okay? The gig's going pretty good. It won't take long."

"I see," she said, realizing he hadn't asked where she was staying, how she was eating, how she felt. He didn't care.

"Hey," he said, "this looks like the break we've been waiting for."

"That's nice. Look, I've got to go. I'll . . . I'll call again." She paused, waiting for him to ask if there was a number where he could reach her, anything. But he didn't.

"Well," he said, "hang in there. It'll all work out, you'll see, B.G. And what happened last night . . . it won't happen again. I just lost it there. Okay?"

"Okay, Jay."

"I gotta go, baby," he said, his voice a little distant, as if he were signaling someone that he was getting off the line. "They're calling me. Show's gotta go on, you know."

"Sure."

"Stay in touch," he said, and then the line went dead.

B.G. stood there in the cool desert night holding her bag with the U of A T-shirt and toothpaste and toothbrush and sighed so heavily she thought her chest might tear. And then she squared her shoulders and turned toward the motel.

Well, at least she knew where she stood with him now, she thought as she took the stairs to the second floor, letting herself into room 201—totally unaware of the white Honda across the street and the man sitting inside it, who'd been watching every move she'd made.

GRACE JACOBS was up and showered by six. By six-thirty she'd had a cup of coffee, juice and cereal and now stood at the vanity in her master bath putting the finishing touches on her makeup. She didn't use much makeup. At thirty-eight she still didn't need it. Grace was blessed with a classically beautiful face and a figure to match. Everything about her bespoke breeding. Even the manner she wore her blond-streaked hair combed back into a rather severe knot displayed that same good breeding.

She'd been educated in Boston, received her law degree from Brandeis. She'd moved to Tucson and passed the Arizona bar shortly thereafter, and in the ten years since she'd lived in the desert Southwest, she'd amassed a fortune.

Grace slipped into the double-breasted jacket of her three-thousand-dollar silk-and-rayon beige suit and pushed the sleeves up. For jewelry she wore a gold watch and several gold chain bracelets, a single gold chain showing at the V neck of the jacket and gold stud earrings.

After buttoning the jacket over her slip and the above-the-knee skirt, she slipped into a pair of very high-heeled shoes of butter-soft Italian leather, also beige.

She glanced at her watch—six-forty-five—and quietly crossed the plush carpet toward the bed. Dirk Bernman was still sleeping. She reset the alarm for him—an investment banker, he didn't have to be at work till nine—then coolly studied his lean dark frame contrasted against the peach-colored silk sheets. There was something very primitive about Dirk, something that brought out the animal in her. Maybe it was the hair that covered his back and chest, that grew up his neck, almost meeting his gray-flecked beard. Grace herself was very white, her skin smooth and hairless.

Within minutes she left her sprawling fashionable foothills adobe home, pulling her silver BMW out of the garage, noting that the sprinkler system had just shut off.

She loved her new house with a passion, had selected every item in it personally, from the brass hardware on the doors to the bronze sculpture on an end table. The place was truly hers, not some overpriced interior decorator's.

For all Grace Jacobs's femininity, she drove like a man, confidently, easing the BMW in and out of lines of traffic like a race-car driver. Men always let her in, too, grudgingly but smiling, wondering if she was somebody's wife and why their wives didn't look like that at seven in the morning.

She pulled into her private parking slot at the office building on Broadway and slid out of the soft leather interior, straightening her skirt. Across the street a construction crew was just starting up, and, as usual, a few of them whistled. And, as usual, without looking in their direction, Grace waved over her shoulder.

Debbie was already at her desk when Grace walked into the office. Debbie was paid an extra hundred a week for keeping such early hours; she also received frequent and large bonuses for keeping her mouth shut.

"Good morning, Ms. Jacobs," she said, looking up from some notes she was transcribing. "Beautiful night last night. Cool."

"Yes, it was," Grace said, pouring herself a second cup of coffee before going into her private office.

"Oh, there are several messages still on your machine. I left them because I thought you'd want to listen to the one from the Levys out in La Jolla. You know." Debbie made a face.

"Yes, I know," Grace said.

The Levys were driving her nuts. Not because Grace didn't want to deal with them; quite the opposite actually. She simply had not been able to provide them with a baby yet. What she wouldn't have done for a hundred fat healthy infants. A thousand. She could place each and every one.

Well, she'd just have to call Mel and Sarah Levy this morning, keep them on the hook. After all, they were desperate—and filthy rich.

Pushing aside some court documents on her desk, Grace sat, coffee mug in both hands, and listened to her messages. There was one from Trey's Gallery—a new Charles Pabst was in. There was one from the dry cleaner—oops, she'd forgotten about that. One from her mother—they'd never gotten along—and three from total strangers, husbands and wives, always the woman's voice, tentative, anxious, sickeningly sweet, as if Grace gave a damn what kind of parents they'd make. As long as there was money, she'd place a baby with the devil himself.

Then the Levys' call. "Hello, this is Sarah Levy from La Jolla, California," the woman said in her baby-doll voice. "I'm just touching base, Miss Jacobs, just in case something's turned up. You understand." *Uh-huh,* Grace thought, *sure do.* "Oh," Sarah went on, "I almost forgot to tell you—we finished the addition on the house, so the baby and nanny's rooms are all ready. And I have very good news—Mel is selling his half of the business to his partner. We're almost retired! I hope this helps in your decision, because we'll have all the time in the world for the baby now. Well, I'm sorry I missed you at the office. If you get a minute, please give us a call. In case you need it, our number here is—"

Grace reached out and shut off the machine. Originally, six months ago, she'd told the Levys her services could run as high as thirty thousand. But now... well, Mel was selling his business. And babies were so very hard to come by.

Grace picked up a pen and made a note on her calendar: call Levys. She also wrote down dry cleaner, underlining it.

No sooner had Grace done that when Maureen Stonehocker telephoned. Fifty-year-old Maureen was, to all intents and purposes, a den mother to the pregnant girls being sheltered at the house Grace rented. Currently six girls in various stages of pregnancy were living there. Most were in their late teens. They received room and board and a very small allowance. When their babies were born they finished signing documents—all legitimate—and turned their infants over to the adoptive parents. At that crucial stage, Grace gave them a small bonus—illegal hush money— and collected huge sums from the deliriously happy new parents. Grace had always figured no one was harmed, and everyone got what they desired.

Then that one girl had threatened to blow the whistle...

Grace dragged her thoughts back to the moment and listened to Maureen on the phone. "Oh, hell," the den mother was saying, "it's that little snit Kathleen and her buddy, Jackie. They actually got into a knockdown drag-out fight this morning over a pair of jeans, if you can believe that."

"So handle it," Grace said.

"I did. But Kathleen's threatening to leave. She says she's going back to her parents up in Kingman."

"Stop her. If I recall, her father beats her on a regular basis. She's terrified of him. Ask her what she thinks he'll do when she gets home and he finds out she's six months pregnant."

"I'll try."

"Don't try. Do it, damn it. I won't let these little twits think they have any say at all when they're under my roof."

"Yes, Ms. Jacobs."

"I mean it, Maureen. If you can't control them, I'll find someone who can."

"Yes, I hear you."

"So don't call me again today. I'm getting fed up with the endless nonsense." Grace did not wait for a reply. She hung up.

Damn, damn, she thought. But then, as always, she collected herself quickly. A little bit of hassle was worth it. If she wasn't in this business, she'd be a regular contracts or wills attorney for a fraction of the money. It was worth a little trouble.

And as for the so-called Jane Doe, that had been . . . unfortunate. The girl had been so upset, had threatened to blow the whistle if Grace didn't return her newborn baby. Well, Grace had taken her for a drive to calm her down, reason with her. They'd gone out into the desert. But instead of calming down, the young woman had screamed and cried and jumped out of the car, then began banging with her fists on the hood. Grace had lost it—just for an instant—and somehow the car had leapt forward.

She certainly had never meant for that to happen. She'd hit the wrong pedal with her foot. Horrible, horrible. But then it was over, done, and Grace couldn't have brought the girl back even if she'd wanted to.

It was regrettable. An accident.

She could have told the police. But that wouldn't have brought the girl back, either. So she'd driven home, put her car in the garage, washed it the next morning, checked to see if there were any dents or missing paint.

Grace steepled her fingers beneath her chin and cleared her mind. It had just been one of those things.

After a moment she looked at the clock on the wall. It was almost nine, eight o'clock in California. She thumbed through her Rolodex and got the Levys' number, dialed it. Sarah answered.

"It's not too early to call, is it?" Grace asked.

"Oh, no. No, we're always up early. Is there any news? A baby?"

So much hope, so much desperation. "Well," Grace began, "there could be. I don't want to get your hopes up too high."

"Tell me," Sarah said.

And Grace made up a story. It didn't matter. Eventually she would find them a baby. The thing was to keep them hooked. After the fabrication, she said, "There's a little problem, though."

"Oh?" Disappointment.

"The girl would like a little more monetary help than usual. She's hoping to go back to college..."

"Oh," Sarah Levy breathed, "is that all? Well, that's no problem, Ms. Jacobs. Whatever she wants."

"Good," Grace said, "that will facilitate things, I'm quite sure. I always hate these vulgar money matters, but you understand."

"Oh, yes, yes, of course I do."

When the conversation was over, Grace took a pad of paper out of her desk and began a grocery list. She felt super. She'd cook a perfect meal for Dirk, some wine, too, and then the night was theirs. The *world* was theirs.

CHAPTER SIX

GREG PULLED into the parking lot of the Oasis at nine sharp. He turned his car off, got out and climbed the stairs to the second floor. He was raising his hand to knock on the door when the window curtain was pulled aside and B.G. looked out, smiling.

She opened the door and stood there, purse over her shoulder, ready to go. "Good morning," she said.

"Morning."

She looked better, her hair in one thick braid down her back, tendrils escaping around her face. She had on the same shabby clothes, but that was going to change soon.

"Did you sleep well?" he asked.

"Oh, yes, I feel much better. I seem to get real tired lately. I guess it's the... you know, the baby."

Any mention of her pregnancy had the bizarre effect of embarrassing Greg. He hoped she didn't want to discuss it in detail. It might be the reason he was here, but he really didn't want to dwell on the intimate physical aspects.

"All ready?" he asked.

"I sure am. I'm sort of hungry, though."

"We can stop someplace on the way, okay?"

"That's fine, but on the way to where?"

"To your new house. Well, it isn't new, but it'll be yours."

"A house," she said, as if savoring the thought.

They stopped at a Denny's and he had coffee while she ate. Greg had already had breakfast with Dick Mayer that morning, filling his boss in, getting the keys to the house. Dick had congratulated him on his coup, and he was still basking in the glow.

Greg drove north up to the highway called Miracle Mile, then turned left onto a dead-end street not far from where Interstate 10 left Tucson on its way to Phoenix. It was an older neighborhood, very quiet, no gangs or crime to speak of. A typical Tucson mixture of retirees, Hispanics, new families. Children in the streets on tricycles, a small Vietnamese grocery store, dusty front yards, a palm tree in each narrow fenced backyard.

"Where is it?" B.G. asked.

"Next block," Greg told her.

"Is it like these houses, the ones we're passing?" she asked.

"Pretty much. They must have built this area up in the forties or fifties, and all the houses are alike. I sure hope you won't be disappointed—it's no mansion."

"I won't be disappointed," she said. "A house. I haven't lived in a house since I left Mayport."

"No one's ever stayed in this place for long. It belongs to the county, and it's been used mostly for witnesses. I hope it's in decent shape."

She sat with her hands clasped tightly in her lap, her ankles crossed. Tense, expectant. Was she reconsidering the deal?

He pulled up to the curb in front of 345 Navaho Street, turned off the ignition. "Well, this is it." A beige stucco bungalow.

B.G. looked out the window for a moment, then opened the car door and got out. Greg followed her up the cracked cement sidewalk, through a gate to the front door that was shiny with too many layers of paint, the last being brown. He stepped in front of her and unlocked it, pushing it open. Hot musty air hit him in the face.

B.G. walked past him into the living room and looked around, while Greg crossed to the windows, opening the blinds and pushing them up. "Needs airing," he said.

"Sure does."

"There are two bedrooms back past the kitchen, one bathroom. There should be linen. I'll check," he said.

She turned slowly, looking at the worn carpet, stained velvet couch and chair, TV set on a stand, rickety tables, the scratched old-fashioned wainscoting, steam radiators and chipped paint on the door and window frames that showed the numerous coats. It was a pretty ugly place, Greg thought, all brown and dull. "It certainly could use a decorator's touch," he said with false joviality.

"It's fine," she said, then walked past him, through the kitchen with its worn gold-and-brown linoleum and white-painted cupboards, to the bathroom off the hall beyond and the two bedrooms, one after the other. Greg wandered into the kitchen and turned on the faucet in the sink. Rusty water came gurgling out, spat, chugged, then flowed more strongly, clearing. He opened a cupboard. A few unmatched dishes were stacked there, some spotted glasses. The refrigerator door was propped open. The plug lay on the floor in the dust behind the fridge. He plugged it in, and it began to hum.

B.G. came into the kitchen, smiling. "It's a cute little house," she said. "The backyard has cactus in it."

"In Tucson everybody's backyard has cactus in it," Greg said dryly.

"I'm not used to it," she said.

"I have to tell you one thing—there's no air-conditioning."

"There's a ceiling fan," she said, pointing.

"It gets hot here in the summer. A hundred and ten."

"That's hot," she said soberly.

"But it's a dry heat," he told her, repeating the age-old mantra of desert dwellers.

"I'll manage okay."

"So," Greg said, "the house works for you?"

"It's wonderful. I can live here all alone, for free?"

"That's the deal."

She turned her big golden eyes on him. "You wouldn't back out now, change your minds?"

"Us? No. Absolutely not. In fact, I have some papers for you to look over, B.G., kind of a contract, so that you're protected and so are we."

"Papers." She considered. "Do I need a lawyer?"

"To all intents and purposes, I *am* a lawyer, and I can assure you the papers will protect you. I made certain there was a proviso for adopting out your baby when the time comes.''

She turned away from him and stared out the window. "I guess I better read them.''

He took the envelope out of his inside pocket and handed it to her. "Take your time.''

B.G. sat down on the fat brown chair and unfolded the papers. Her brow puckered as she read, her lips moving slightly, nicely shaped, pale pink lips, the upper one deeply bowed, the lower one round.

"What does this mean?'' she asked. "In event of injury in the line of duty, um, subject is covered according to previous stated addenda I, II and III.''

"Just legalese. It means you're covered for any medical problem you might suffer while working for us. Say, if you broke your leg. Aside from the pregnancy.''

"Okay.'' She read on, then looked up sharply. "I have a checking account?''

"We'll set one up for you. You'll have to go in and sign the signature card. Five hundred a month.''

"Wow.''

"That's not very much, but if you have any additional expenses, I can probably get you more.''

"It sounds like a lot to me.'' She finished reading the pages. "Do you have a pen?'' she asked.

"Of course.'' Greg handed her the ballpoint in his pocket, watched as she signed. Then he scribbled his name below hers. "There,'' he said, "all done. I'll keep the papers, because they could be incriminating if our lawyer friend ever had this place searched.''

"Do you think she would?" B.G. asked quickly, alarmed.

"No, but we don't want to leave anything to chance. Every detail of your life has to be convincing. We have a cover story all planned for you—where you get your money, whose house this is. But that'll come later when you're all settled in."

She sat there in the homely overstuffed chair and looked up at him. "Am I really worth all this trouble?"

Greg sat down on the couch across from her. He leaned forward, elbows on his knees. "The answer is definitely yes. Think about it this way. We'd have to pay the salary of a full-time investigator if we didn't have you, and then we wouldn't be assured of putting a stop to Jacobs's operation."

"Is that her name?"

"Yes, Grace Jacobs. A real bad lady."

"And you're sure you'll get her—with me?"

"We have a much better chance."

"I feel so guilty. All this—" she gestured with her hand "—and I haven't done a thing."

"You will, B.G. You'll earn your keep, believe me."

"I sure hope so. I don't want to take charity. I couldn't."

Greg laughed. "The way the county budget is these days, I wouldn't worry about that. If my boss didn't think you were worth it, you wouldn't be here."

She nodded thoughtfully, and Greg wondered what was going through her head. She was a pretty easy read actually, a straightforward sort of person, a bit naive, as he'd told Dick Mayer, but honest, a nice lady.

It remained to be seen if she was clever, too, sharp enough to fool Grace Jacobs. It wasn't that she had to be trained in any specific skills, because she was already the perfect bait. It was more her frame of mind, her toughness, that concerned him.

"Can you give me an idea what I'll be doing?" B.G. said. "I keep wondering and wondering."

Greg leaned back on the couch. "First of all you'll get your cover story straight down to the last detail. She'll ask, and you need to be real sure of everything. Then you'll put in a few calls to some clinics and a couple of the reproductive counseling hotlines, ones my office suspects are referring pregnant girls to Ms. Jacobs. You'll hear from her—she'll call to feel you out. It might take a while, but she'll call. You'll play hard to get, put her off, say you're not sure what you want to do."

"Why?" Her eyes were on him, that frown back. Unconsciously one hand rested on her stomach as if to shield the baby, protect it from this subterfuge.

"I want to put off the meeting as long as possible. There'll be less exposure for you, less chance for Jacobs to get suspicious." He watched B.G. very carefully as he said this, testing her reaction. If she was too nervous, too afraid, she wouldn't work out; Grace Jacobs would suspect her in a second. But B.G. only listened, concentrating on his words, nodding. Good.

"Eventually you'll have to meet her and actually contract with her to sell, uh, place your baby. That's when you'll need to be on your toes. We're going to tape all those conversations, but first you have to earn her trust."

She nodded again, solemnly, and he was struck once more by how young she looked, how her dark lashes made fans against her cheeks when she glanced down, how her lower lip had the slightest pout to it when she frowned. Now that she was out of jail, rested and well fed, she had a kind of serenity, and he wondered if it was because of her condition.

Grace Jacobs was bound to fall for her story, hook, line and sinker.

"The Tucson Mall is just up the road a little ways," he went on. "There's a bus you can take there, and the place you catch it is just a short walk from here. If you need to get someplace you can't reach by bus, take a cab and we'll reimburse you. Today I'll take you."

"I better look around and see what I need," she said, rising. "Do you have time to wait?"

"That's what I'm here for, B.G."

She checked out the cupboards and closets, walking through the house, that small frown of concentration on her face.

"Wow, I need lots of things," she finally said. "Stuff to clean up with, food."

"Don't forget things for yourself. Some new clothes, whatever you want."

"How much can I spend?" she asked.

"Don't worry about it."

She smiled. "I don't know how not to worry about money."

He drove her to the Tucson Mall. She was quiet in the car, not a chatterbox like other women he knew. He thought that they were getting along all right, that she was beginning to trust him, to depend on him. The way Dick Mayer wanted.

He glanced at her profile as he drove, and it occurred to him to ask her who she'd called from that pay phone last night. Of course, he already knew who she'd called. The boyfriend, the father of her baby, the jerk. He could ask her, but at this point it would be counterproductive. He needed her to like him. *Let it go,* he told himself. But the knowledge rankled in him; she still cared for the bum who'd left her holding the bag. And she had a secret she was keeping from Greg, which wasn't what he or Dick Mayer had in mind. She had to be completely under his control for this plan to work.

It made it hard for Greg to respect her, too, a woman who'd still feel loyalty to a man like that. Grudgingly he had to admit that if she'd felt no loyalty, he'd consider her fickle. Hell, she couldn't win. But then, she'd made a bad choice, and now she had to deal with the consequences.

Greg had made sure his choices were always right. There was no room in his life for mistakes. He wouldn't settle for mediocrity, never had. And he'd worked hard to get where he was, so he knew it could be done. He'd pulled himself out of the blue-collar class of his family and was on the brink of a successful law career. Just a few months till he sat for the bar. If you had a plan and held to it, you could accomplish anything. Maybe B.G. needed to learn that.

"Is it a big mall?" she asked.

"Pretty big, I guess."

She was quiet for a moment, and Greg had a feeling she wanted to say something. He waited.

"Uh," she began, "this is embarrassing."

"What is it, B.G.?"

"I can't call you Mr. Tyrrell."

He smiled. "It's Greg."

"Greg." She had a way of savoring words, saying them slowly as if testing out their properties. "Okay."

"We're going to be working together very closely. May as well get used to me."

"That shouldn't be hard," she said softly.

He glanced at her, then away.

The Tucson Mall was bustling. Southwest style predominated, although the usual chain stores were well represented. What Greg noticed right away was that nobody was dressed like B.G. It was a warm eighty-degree day, pretty normal for March, and everyone wore cotton shorts or skirts, or lightweight linen slacks. Hardly anyone wore jeans, fewer still flannel shirts. And B.G. must have noticed it, too, because he saw her glance around and then duck her head the way he'd seen her do before, as if to diminish herself.

"They're dressed for summer here," she finally said.

"Well, it *is* almost summer here. Isn't it in Florida?"

"Well, maybe in the Keys, but up around Mayport, well, I guess it's warm by now. But I've been in California, and it wasn't that hot there yet, at least not in Santa Monica."

"Get yourself some summer clothes then," Greg said. "Anything you want."

"I *would* like a few things. Not too much. I'm starting to outgrow these jeans, and this shirt—" she plucked at a sleeve "—is really gross."

"Do you, uh, need to find a . . . a maternity shop?" he asked carefully.

She blushed and ducked her head. "I don't know. I've never done this before."

They walked by Southwest Souvenirs, with a display of Kachina dolls, howling coyotes, Spanish-style candlesticks, pottery with Indian designs, Navaho rugs. Sporting-goods stores, stores with silver Indian jewelry sparkling under the lights, department stores, kitchen shops, toy stores. B.G. lingered at the clothing stores, studying the displays, then moving on.

"I bet you're bored silly," she finally remarked.

"Not at all."

"Liar." She cut him a sidelong glance that held the first hint of humor he'd seen in her. "You hate it."

"I wouldn't say that."

She laughed, the first time he'd heard her do so. "You're a bad liar, too."

"Do you want to forget shopping for today?"

"Not on your life. If I don't get these clothes off, they're going to crawl away."

"Well . . ." He wasn't sure how to handle this.

"I'll make it as fast as I can," she said.

By the time she'd been to the second store, it hit Greg with some force that everyone there, no doubt everyone they passed in the mall, assumed that this badly dressed waif was his wife. He was buying her clothes, wasn't he?

It made him feel acutely uncomfortable, but he couldn't let B.G. know that, not for an instant.

When he'd first handed his credit card to the salesclerk, B.G. had touched his arm, stopping him. "Uh, is that your personal credit card . . . Greg?"

"Yes, of course," he said, then realized what she meant. "Don't worry, I'll get reimbursed."

"They won't question anything?"

"Nope."

She fixed him with lambent golden eyes. "I really appreciate this."

The third stop was a department store. B.G. led him straight to the lingerie department. "I won't make you watch this," she said shyly. "Do you mind just waiting right here for a bit?" He was in the aisle between lingerie and costume jewelry.

"God, no. Just give me a shout when it's time to pay."

He was carrying all the bags for her; he could have been a husband for sure. Luckily it was a weekday and he'd be unlikely to meet anyone he knew. He thanked his lucky stars for that.

He'd noticed that she was a determined but shrewd shopper. She'd examined every item carefully, buying mostly simple things. And although she'd studied the display in the window of a maternity shop, she'd blushed and hadn't gone in. But everything she'd bought was big and loose or had an elastic waist. He'd kept eyeing her surreptitiously when she was occupied, and there'd been times he could see the small bulge in her belly. He tried to imagine B.G. in the coming months, grossly swollen, but couldn't. He tried to imagine the baby that was growing in her, but couldn't do that, either. His mind shied away from such images.

Her voice intruded into his musings. "This bathrobe is sort of expensive. What do you think? I mean, I could look somewhere else if. . ."

The tag read $39.95. Expensive? His ties cost more than that. "It's fine, B.G. If you like it, get it."

He felt ridiculously oversensitive as he walked beside her down the wide corridors of the mall, the shoppers' glances crawling on his skin like a million tiny insects. He was sure that every woman they passed smiled fondly at B.G., instinctively recognizing her condition, and then turned their gazes on him, measuring him as a man, as a husband, as a father. He shrank mentally.

She stopped at a small shop that carried Western-style clothes—blouses and skirts embroidered with cacti and horses and cowboy hats, swinging with fringe, brightly colored.

"Oh, that's such a cute outfit," she said wistfully.

"Do you want to go in and look at it?" he asked, subduing his impatience.

She looked up at him. "It'll be really expensive."

"Go ahead." *The bond,* Dick Mayer had told him this morning. *Create the bond. Be her best friend, her big brother, her mentor.*

She ended up trying on an oversize pale blue denim camp shirt with colorful cowboy boots dancing across the yoke and matching leggings. She came out of the dressing room wearing the outfit, a determined look on her face. "I'm throwing away my old jeans and shirt,'' she told Greg. "I can't look at them another second. They smell like that jail." She pulled at the hem of the new shirt. "I'll wear these."

"Fine, sure," he said. "I don't blame you." She looked real cute in the new clothes. Her legs were shapely, with strong rounded calves. She was thin, though. He'd better make sure she ate well; he needed to keep her and the baby healthy.

They made one more stop—a shoe store. She bought a pair of tennis shoes and a pair of huaraches, which she kept on, putting her scuffed loafers in a bag. She had slender feet with high insteps, and Greg couldn't help staring at them while she walked around the store. She had pretty feet, he thought, wondering why he'd even notice such a thing.

Lunch was Greek gyros in the food court of the mall. The spicy meat, served on pita bread with a garlicky yogurt-cucumber sauce and washed down with iced tea, was delicious. She ate every last bite, then wiped the sauce off her fingers.

"I'm always hungry," she said.

"Uh-huh," he said, but he was thinking that she was eating for two, as the old saying went. Why did everything she said or did remind him of her pregnancy?

"I think we should go to a grocery store now. I can get everything else I need there," she said. "Is that okay? I mean, do you have time to do that?"

"I have as much time as you need."

"Is that what the county attorney pays you for?" she asked.

"Not usually, but you're a special case."

"Baby-sitting," she said with a wry twist of her lips.

"Not at all," he lied. "Just getting you all set up."

"I've never taken charity," she said. "I'll repay you somehow."

"I told you before, it's not charity. You're being paid to do a job. And it's not for me. It's for the citizens of Pima County."

"I'm just worried, I guess, because I'm afraid I won't be able to do the job right." She rested her chin on her fist, staring unfocused into space.

"Don't worry about that. You'll do fine. It's going to be a piece of cake."

"Who're you trying to convince," she said with a smile, "you or me?"

They stopped at a giant grocery store on the way back to her house. She filled the shopping cart with groceries and all the basic necessities of a household—detergent, sponges and scrubbers, a mop and broom.

"I'm afraid I'll forget something," she said apologetically as she rolled the cart down the aisles she'd already covered. "And it'll be harder for me to get things when you're not here."

"All you have to do is call," he said.

"I'd rather not bother you so much."

"I'll be talking to you just about every day, anyway, B.G."

"I know, but, well, I do have to learn how to take care of myself. I'm on my own now. I've never really been on my own before. There was Grandma and then—" She stopped abruptly and became very busy reading the labels on cereal boxes.

The jerk, Greg thought. *Yeah, B.G., he really took good care of you.* And then he knew he had to reassure her. "You're not on your own, B.G. There's me and my whole office behind you. You can call me anytime, and if you can't reach me, there's my voice mail. I'll leave all the numbers with you. You'll never be on your own, not as long as this job lasts."

She flashed him a brief smile, but he saw wariness in it. There was time, though, plenty of time to win her over completely. What he didn't want was for her to become too independent. That would be dangerous.

B.G. gasped as the checker totaled her purchases. "Wow, that's a lot."

"Don't worry, it'll last a long time."

He wheeled the cart out to his car, unlocked the trunk and began transferring bags into it. He'd taken his suit coat off, loosened his tie. He could have been a suburban husband on a weekly shopping trip with his cute young pregnant wife, he supposed. God forbid.

And yet there was a certain cozy feeling to this expedition. He and B.G. got along, which was a good thing, and he was performing a necessary duty to get his plan rolling. It was just this one day, after all. And he realized, too, that he was rather enjoying the feeling of taking care of B.G., transforming her from a disheveled jailbird into a respectable young woman with her own house and responsibilities. He was like a sculptor, forming a clay statue, molding it, smoothing it, carving features into it that were pleasing to him. Wasn't there a story like that, an old Greek myth? Pygmalion and Galatea. Sure, it had been in one of his humanities courses.

While he was driving back to her house, he called into the office on his cellular phone, checking on another case he'd been working on, a series of robberies. Someone, probably a gang of punks, had been burglarizing homes in the foothills area, taking jewelry, CD players, VCRs. He was aware of B.G. listening to the conversation, her face turned away to give him the semblance of privacy. Polite. But there was nothing said that she couldn't hear, just routine questions. There wasn't anything new on the case, anyway. The lead he'd thought would pan out hadn't.

The small beige bungalow looked seedier than ever when he pulled up in front of it. It needed painting and landscaping. Oh, well, B.G. seemed happy with it.

She unlocked the door with the key he'd given her, and they started carrying bags in. He helped her put things away, like a dutiful husband, and he wondered if she was tired or hungry, but she worked away, not complaining.

"There," she said, closing the last cupboard door, sinking onto a kitchen chair. "Whew, that's the most work I've done in a long time." She smiled. "Are you thirsty? I am. Let's have something, the first in my new house."

"Sure, why not?"

"Let's see, I have orange juice or that bottled iced tea. I could make some coffee, but it'd take a while. Did I remember filters? Yes, I did."

"Iced tea," he said. "That'd be fine."

She took down two glasses, peered at them, rubbed the glass with one of her new dish towels, then filled them with lemon-flavored iced tea.

She sat across the Formica table from him and sipped her drink. "I should have bought some beer," she finally said. "I bet you'd like a beer. I'm not supposed to drink alcohol, but I should've gotten some. Darn."

"This is fine, B.G."

"You're sure?"

"Yup."

"Would you think I'm silly if I propose a toast?" she said, then she laughed. "With iced tea."

"Sure, propose away."

She raised her glass. "To our new venture," she said solemnly. "To success."

"I'll drink to that," Greg said, and they clicked glasses.

It was very pleasant and relaxed sitting at B.G.'s kitchen table. It was getting late, though, and when he left here he'd have to go straight to his mother's party. Amazing. It had taken the whole day to get B.G. set up.

"Now," he said, "I'm going to give you all the numbers you need. The phone's been turned on and I have your number." He handed her a card from his wallet. "This is my home number, my work number, my cellular phone, my voice mail. Anyone at the office can help you if you can't reach me—that's this number."

She held the card, reading it, nodding.

"And another thing. Have you been to a doctor about the, uh, your pregnancy?"

She shook her head.

"Okay, we'll set you up with an obstetrician. Grace Jacobs will require proof that you and the baby are healthy. But I'll take care of it, okay?"

"Okay."

Greg finished his drink, got up and put the glass in the sink. He was mentally framing his exit lines when B.G. spoke up.

"I could cook you dinner," she said. "I'm starving, and I'll have to make myself something, anyway..." She let the words hang in the air, awaiting his reply, expectant.

God. "That's nice of you, B.G., but I can't stay. I've, well, I've got another commitment tonight." He glanced at his watch. "Soon, in fact."

He could see her face fall, and then realized that when he left, she'd be alone, totally alone, in a new house in a strange city, where she knew not a soul—except him.

She ducked her head. "Oh, I'm sorry. I didn't mean to keep you. Go on. You've spent enough time with me today, that's for sure."

She pulled at his heartstrings, an unfamiliar sensation, but then he'd never had to run an undercover agent before. She was, in the end, wholly his creature, his creation, and thus his responsibility.

"Look," he said, fumbling a little, "you're tired. It's been a long day. How about—" he put a smile on his lips "—you come with me to dinner?"

Her eyes widened. "Oh, I couldn't."

"It's my mother's birthday party, that's all."

"No, that wouldn't be right," she said, her cheeks turning pink. "A family thing like that."

"It would please me if you came," he said. "Honestly."

"I don't think...I couldn't..."

"Sure you could. It'll be a casual affair, a barbecue. Lots of Tyrrells, lots of kids, nothing fancy."

"No, Greg, please..."

"You don't want to stay here by yourself, not this first night. I'd feel bad leaving you on your own."

"I'd be intruding," she said painfully.

"Go on, brush your hair or whatever you need to do. I have to get moving, got to buy some champagne to bring to the party."

"Can I go like this?" She looked down at her new outfit.

"You sure can. You look great, perfect."

"Can I have a minute then?"

"Go ahead."

He waited for her in the living room, already regretting his impulsive invitation. It wasn't that Nana would mind, but he'd have to explain. "Bring a date," Abby had said. She hadn't meant someone else's pregnant castoff. Good Lord, what had he gotten himself into?

CHAPTER SEVEN

DESPITE GREG'S ASSURANCE that no one in his family was going to ask her any awkward questions, B.G. was as nervous as a teen on a first date when they pulled up in front of the modest Tyrrell house.

Surely everyone was going to notice she was pregnant. They'd notice, too, that she was a newcomer to Tucson, and they all had to at least wonder what on earth Greg was doing with her. Maybe they'd figure he was on a case, but they'd have to think it was a pretty strange relationship—Mr. Perfect and a down-on-her-luck cracker from Florida.

When he turned the car off they sat for a moment, and B.G. firmly told herself to quit putting herself down so much. He'd told her they were nice plain folks. She had nothing to worry about, for Lord's sake.

"Ready?" he said, opening his door, pulling out the sack with the champagne bottles from the back seat.

"Sure," B.G. said, shrugging.

And then he laughed a little. "You do that a lot," he said.

"What?"

"Say, 'Sure,' as if everything's no big deal."

"Mmm," she said. "I guess it's just a habit. I am a little nervous. I mean, are you really okay with this?"

"Absolutely."

It was an unpretentious neighborhood, dating from before the Southwest's craze for Spanish mission-style homes and rustic territorials and adobes. The homes nestled snugly on this quiet road were ordinary wood-frame ones—two and three bedrooms with one-car garages facing the street. All of them had fenced yards, most planted with cactus and desert flowers, some even with green lawns. All of them appeared to have backyards. It was a real family community, kids' tricycles sitting in driveways, neighbors chatting on the sidewalk. And the fact that it was so ordinary lent B.G. a measure of comfort. Greg had grown up here, played on the street, shot basketballs into the hoop above the garage door.

Next to the front door was a palm that drooped onto the walk, and behind that was an orange tree, the last fruit of the season still on its branches. He held the door open for her.

"Be prepared for a lot of noise," Greg told her as they entered the hallway. "I'm the middle of five kids, and God only knows how many nieces and nephews I've got. Last count it was nine, I think."

"Wow," B.G. said. "I was an only child. I can't imagine—" But before she could finish her sentence, three tykes tumbled down a set of steps, shrieking, laughing, tripping over one another. They flew by Greg and B.G. without apparently even noticing them.

And then a woman's voice came from the back of the house. "I'm not telling you kids again—you play outside. You're driving Nana crazy."

"Oh, they're fine" came another voice.

"I warned you," Greg said as he and B.G. headed through the living room toward the kitchen.

It was a huge family, and as B.G. was introduced around, she repeated everyone's name over and over in her mind in the hope of remembering them all.

There was his sister Abby and her husband, Martin—Marty—and their two kids. There was another sister, Sandy, who also had two children, one of which was a two-month-old boy. Adorable.

It seemed that Sandy and Greg sparred a lot, because no sooner had B.G. been introduced, when Sandy eyed Greg and said, "Couldn't you at least have changed clothes before you came over? God, Greg, you're so...stuffy."

"Well, here," he said, tossing his suit jacket over the back of a kitchen chair, loosening his tie, rolling up his shirtsleeves. "Is this more to your liking?"

"God, he's obnoxious," Sandy said to B.G. "Always was. Mr. Big-Shot Lawyer."

There was Sandy's husband, Art, a tall good-looking carpenter, who absolutely doted on the new baby.

Greg's dad, Ray, was also a tall man, with a full head of graying hair and bright blue eyes. He was a retired miner, on disability from a leg injury. He limped a little.

And then there was Greg's mother, called Nana by everyone, although her name was actually Kathryn.

"My grandma's name is Kathryn," B.G. said when introductions were made. Nana was a sweet-natured, easygoing woman, who didn't seem to mind in the least if the grandchildren raced through the house, banged the screen doors, spilled soda on the living-room carpet. Of course, she'd had five children of her own.

Right now she was busy making potato salad, while Sandy made a green salad and Abby worked hamburger meat into patties.

"Can I do that?" B.G. asked, nodding at the bowl of cut-up potatoes. "I worked in my grandma's restaurant for years."

"You sure can," Nana said, handing her a jar of mayonnaise.

B.G. was glad to have something to do. While she cut up celery and onions and spooned mayonnaise into the huge bowl, Greg disappeared outside to help with the charcoal fire in the backyard. Men outside drinking beer and women in the kitchen cooking and sipping on blush wine—all but B.G. She felt embarrassed when she declined the wine. The women had to realize she was pregnant. But to their credit, no one mentioned it or asked a thing about her relationship with Greg.

At one point B.G. felt she had to say something. She cleaned the cutting board in the sink and casually mentioned, "Greg and I are going to be working together. I'm new in town actually, and this was so nice of him to ask me over here. I really appreciate it."

"Hey," Sandy said as she reached into the fridge, "anyone who can cook is welcome here."

It must have been a minute later that the rest of the Tyrrells arrived, Greg's two brothers and their families—wives and five more kids. Then a great racket came from the front door, and the women left the kitchen to see what the heck was going on.

Nana's hands flew to her cheeks and she gasped, seeing Greg's brothers, Paul and Andy, wheeling a brand-new dishwasher toward the kitchen. There was a big red bow tied around it.

"Omigosh!" Nana kept saying. "Omigosh!"

As B.G. soon learned, Paul—who in the family most resembled Greg—was the manager of an appliance store, and Andy was the head of maintenance at a foothills golf resort. Their wives worked, too, one at a grocery store, the other as a dispatcher for a private security outfit.

It was very much a working-class family, and B.G. felt quite comfortable in their midst. Except for one of them, that was, the one who'd really made it—Greg, the prodigal son. It was obvious that everyone looked up to him, because in the space of an hour, he must have answered a dozen legal questions from his family, little things, such as the question from Paul, who'd just bought a new pickup truck on time payments.

"So, I've got three days to change my mind, right?"

"That's the law," Greg told him as they tended the burgers on the grill in the fading desert light. "And if you take it back and they give you any guff, simply leave it there and tell them your lawyer will be in touch."

"You'd call them for me?"

"Of course I would," Greg said.

B.G. even held Sandy's baby, sitting out back on a lawn chair, letting the women's gossip and the men's discussion of local politics flow around her. She held the baby—Will—even as she ate, marveling at the little fingers and the translucent eyelids that fluttered in his sleep.

"He's so beautiful," B.G. said to his parents, not aware of the wistful tone of her voice or of Greg standing nearby, listening.

She held Will for a long time, and once she felt the tiny stirrings of her own baby deep within her womb. She couldn't think about it, though, she simply couldn't. Not here, not now, not with these people who all had families and such normal lives. It was a bittersweet relief when Sandy finally took him from her arms and put him down for the night.

"You're a great baby-sitter, B.G.," Sandy said. "Anytime you want, feel free."

Soon there was birthday cake, champagne and ice cream, and all the little presents from the grandchildren.

The whole time, Andy and Paul were busy hooking up the new dishwasher, Greg occasionally helping when he wasn't serving hamburgers. Nana put the first dishes in and announced that she almost hated to use it, it was so new and shiny, but she did, anyway, and was delighted with the result.

The younger kids were put down to sleep in the bedrooms, the four older ones allowed to stay up and watch TV in the living room. The adults collected outside for coffee, wearing sweaters and jackets as the temperature dropped. Greg insisted that B.G. put his jacket around her shoulders.

"But you'll be cold," she protested.

"I'm fine. I'm tough," he said.

"Yeah, right," Sandy put in.

So B.G. sat in a lawn chair and listened to the family chatter. They were a lively group, some very opinionated, all far from shy. Such a large close family, and handsome, too, though in B.G.'s eyes Greg was by far the best looking. There was something about his carriage, the pitch of his head when he was listening or thinking, the way he leaned against the side of the house talking to his father, one shoulder casually against the clapboard, arms folded across his chest, one knee flexed. And that deep almost gravelly voice that reached inside her and awakened an emotion she was afraid to name.

"It was very sweet of you to help out tonight," Nana said to her, and she patted B.G.'s arm. "Next time you can just sit and be a proper guest."

"Oh, I like helping," B.G. said. "Honestly, I do."

"Well, this crowd can get underfoot in a hurry."

"I think it's wonderful," B.G. was quick to say. "All I ever had were my grandparents."

"Oh, I'm sorry, honey," Nana said, and nothing more. No probing questions.

For a time B.G. talked to Greg's oldest sister, Abby, whose kids were watching TV. They spoke about living in the desert, Tucson in particular.

Abby declared she couldn't abide Florida. "I was there once in July," she said. "Thought I'd die of the humidity."

"It does get bad," B.G. concurred.

"Well, maybe you'll settle here," Abby said.

"Maybe," B.G. replied, and then she had to wonder what Abby must think of her—obviously alone here, doing some sort of work with Greg, and pregnant.

The whole time they were outside after dinner, B.G. had been sitting in the same chair, Greg's jacket over her shoulders. As the conversations around her ebbed and flowed, she relaxed, looking beyond the roof of the neighbor's house to the foothills in the east. The stars had risen above them, brilliant jewels in the desert sky, and a slice of moon was just now showing.

She thought about Abby's asking her if she might settle here. Maybe she would. There was nothing for her in Florida—Grandma was in that home, comfortable, surrounded by women her age who all played cards incessantly. And there was no place else B.G. had been to long enough to get to know. She'd be here for five months, anyway. Until the baby was born.

The baby. If B.G. had learned one thing tonight, it was that her baby deserved at least this much—a stable loving family. And more than ever, she knew she could not provide one. Even if things had worked out with Jay and he hadn't robbed that store, she knew instinctively he'd be a lousy father, gone all the time on gigs, out till all hours. Yet she still held that faint spark of hope, deep down inside, that Jay could change. People changed, didn't they?

Only if they cared enough about something, was the answer she gave herself.

She couldn't help thinking about Jay then, picturing him, wondering exactly where he was at that minute, who he was with.

She felt a pang, remembering that he'd robbed that store. It was so inconceivable. As she sipped her coffee, she examined her feelings about him, probing them the way you would a sore tooth, very deliberately, slowly. Only two days ago she'd believed she and Jay had a future. Could she forget that so easily?

"That's the cutest top you're wearing," Abby was saying to B.G., and she had to shake herself mentally. "Marty and I just took up line-dancing and that top would be perfect."

B.G. told her where she'd bought it. She didn't mention the circumstances.

"You must be pretty tired" came that deep voice a few minutes later, and B.G. looked over her shoulder. "How about a ride home now?" Greg asked.

She smiled. She *was* tired.

"Sure."

And then it was time to say good-night to everyone. B.G. remembered all their names and they declared that amazing, a first. She was invited back again, anytime she wanted, with or without Greg.

"Who needs him, anyway?" Sandy said at the front door, and she gave Greg a punch in the arm. As Greg turned to say something to his father, Sandy put her hand on B.G.'s shoulder. "You take care of yourself," she said in a quiet voice. "I don't know and I don't care what Greg's up to, but you stand up to him, hear? And if you ever need an ear, I'm in the book. Call me."

"Sure," B.G. said, her usual noncommittal reply.

"I mean it."

"Okay, I will."

It wasn't until they were in the car, halfway back to her bungalow, that Greg said, "Sandy's my nemesis in the family. You probably gathered that, though. All I'm saying is, be careful what you tell her, she's... Well, we've been at each other since birth, just about."

"I didn't tell her anything, Greg. She didn't ask and I didn't offer, and besides, except for you, I'd never tell a soul anything about what we're doing. I promise."

"I know that," he said, but B.G. wondered, and then suddenly she realized how much she wanted him to trust her.

She sat quietly, staring out the car window at the passing lights of the city. Somehow she knew if she said any more it would be like the lady who protested too much. After a time she let her head rest against the back of the seat and closed her eyes.

It had been a long day. It seemed like a million years ago that she and Greg had headed off to the Tucson Mall.

The sounds of the traffic and the city surrounded her, but in the interior of the closed car they were only a muffled din. Greg's jacket was still around her shoulders, and the cool softness of its lining caressed her bare arms. It was as if Greg were all around her, a faint scent of after-shave and male. It was...pleasant, comforting, though B.G. put the notions from her mind with a stern admonition. Greg Tyrrell, for all his apparent kindness, for all his fine education and good looks, was using her. Just like Jay had used her. She'd go along with Greg, though, because she believed in her heart he'd keep his word and find the best possible home for her baby. But after that, it was time for herself, time to get in gear and make a better life. She could finish her education, find a really good job. Maybe, if she believed enough in herself, find a good man, too. Because she'd made this one monumental mistake didn't mean the end of everything. She could make a new beginning, learn from her mistakes.

She gave Greg a surreptitious glance. As always, her breath caught, and she thought that maybe even a man like Greg might be in her future—if she could just turn things around.

B.G. settled back again into the seat, snug in Greg's jacket. She began to feel each moment in the car and to isolate them, to hold on to them, because she knew that somehow, at some distant point in the future, she'd look back on this time spent with Greg Tyrrell as very special.

They arrived at her little house on Navaho just after ten, and Greg used his own key to let her in.

"Well, good night, B.G.," he said. "Tomorrow we'll meet and go over a few things. How about I see you around two?"

"Two? In the afternoon?" she said. What was she going to do all morning?

"I've got a couple of cases I have to get caught up on first. Is there a problem?"

"No. No, of course not."

"Fine," he said, standing just outside the door. "We'll get that checking account opened, too. Okay?"

"Sure."

"You'll be okay?"

"Sure . . . yes, I'll be fine, really I will." She smiled, trying not to duck her head.

And then he was leaving.

"Greg . . ." she said quickly.

He turned and stopped.

"I . . . Look, thanks a lot for tonight."

"My pleasure."

"You know," she said, "they're all very proud of you. You could just tell."

A corner of his mouth lifted shyly. "Yeah," he admitted, "I guess they are." And then he left. B.G. stood at the window until his taillights disappeared. She'd been alone a lot in her life. But not until this moment did she feel so utterly lonely.

CHAPTER EIGHT

BY THE BEGINNING of April the weather in the desert Southwest took its usual turn. Spring arrived. The trees and brush turned a subtle shade of pale delicate green; it wasn't cold that made the vegetation go into hibernation here, it was dryness. The rain came at intervals, but this wasn't the wet season. That would come in late summer, when the thirsty desert was parched and brown once again.

The cacti, dozens of varieties, flowered. Huge bizarre blooms with fleshy petals appeared on the ends of prickly woody stems. Red and yellow and white, indecently sensuous flowers. The hillsides were dotted with color.

No longer did men wear winter suits and long-sleeved shirts. Now the temperature was in the high eighties, and even Greg had switched wardrobes to lighter cotton slacks, short-sleeved shirts and summer-weight suits or blazers. Air conditioners were on for the long, seven-month stretch.

B.G. had taken on a new look, too. She'd bought several oversize T-shirts in an array of colors and for the most part wore them over tights. She was approaching her fifth month, and it showed. Greg was amazed at how quickly she'd gone from having that slight telltale bulge in her belly to a fuller roundness. From the back she didn't look in any way pregnant; but from the side . . .

It was time to get the ball rolling now, Greg knew. Time to set up B.G.'s cover story and make those initial calls to the pregnancy hotlines. He sure as hell hoped this was going to work.

He met B.G. at the Tucson Mall, rather than at her house. They sat in the food court, ate and talked.

"I want you to have every aspect of this cover story down pat," he told his protégée, then he launched into it, aware that she'd stopped eating and was listening intently. He explained that she'd keep her own name—after all, she had no record with the police now or, for that matter, any history whatsoever in Arizona. "And the best lie is always the one that's closest to the truth."

"So I'm not some totally different person?"

"No, you're exactly right as you are," Greg said. "We're taking care of all the details. Even the house you're in is registered in Pima County to your grandmother. We've called her by her real name, Kathryn Bryson, to make it easy for you. The story is that she spends the hot spring and summer months up north in Colorado. You're house-sitting. She even gives you a monthly allowance to keep the place up. Ergo the monthly deposits into your checking account."

Greg saw her lower her eyes, thinking this over, her long dark lashes lying like miniature fans against her pale skin. Then she looked up. "But what if this Grace Jacobs checks me out? You know, really tries to call my grandmother in . . . Colorado?"

Greg smiled. "All taken care of. If Jacobs asks for a number—which I doubt she will—but if she does, it'll ring in the county attorney's office right here in Tucson."

B.G.'s eyes widened. "You can do that?"

"You bet," Greg said. "And the lady who will answer is named Rosemary. She'll handle everything."

"Wow," B.G. breathed. Then, "But have I always lived in Tucson? I mean . . ."

Greg shook his head. "No. You don't know enough about it to be convincing. You're to tell Jacobs you lived in Florida and Southern California. You moved around with your parents. Navy brat."

"Um . . ."

"Is there a problem?"

"No. It's just that I never really had regular parents. I mean, after Grandpa died, my grandma raised me. I don't know much about being a navy brat, either."

"Improvise. Say the usual things. We'll work on it."

"You mean like I changed schools a lot and moved around?"

"Exactly. There's a navy base in Mayport and one in Long Beach, California. You've been there, to Long Beach?"

"Uh-huh," she said. "Through there, anyway."

"Jacobs won't ask for details, not unless she becomes suspicious about something."

"So I just won't let her get suspicious, right?"

"Right. And in the meantime we'll practice your story over and over. I'll grill you. Okay?"

She smiled, a shy smile, and Greg was suddenly struck with the notion of how very pretty she was.

Maybe it was the nebulous thing people called the bloom of pregnancy, but she did look lovely today.

He cleared his throat, took a drink of his soda and went on, "The one area Jacobs might question you about is staying in the bungalow. In fact, she might really squawk about that. She'll want you under her thumb. Warehoused with her other pregnant girls. We want you to be really firm about that. You'll have to tell Jacobs you're no sixteen-year-old and you want your privacy. After all, you are twenty-six."

"How old are you?" B.G. asked abruptly, catching him off guard.

"Thirty-four," he said. "But we're talking about you, B.G., not me."

"I know," she said, and she ducked her head.

They talked about her boyfriend. The county attorney and Greg had decided B.G. would be firm with Jacobs about this issue, too, giving the woman very little info on him, as if protecting him. Greg almost said aloud how true that was, but he figured B.G. knew it as well as he did. Best let that one lie, he thought.

All he said at this point was, "Jacobs will want the father of your baby to sign documents relinquishing his parental rights. You're to tell Jacobs you don't have any idea where he is. He left you at your grandmother's here and just took off. You don't even know how to reach him. Okay?"

Slowly, avoiding Greg's eyes, B.G. nodded. They met three more times that week, never in the same place and never at her house. And each time, Greg went over the details of her cover story, until he was satisfied she had them down pat. And then they'd part, and Greg would worry about her getting home, but she'd always assure him she was perfectly capable of taking care of herself. He'd watch her walk away, see the slight sway she was developing as the baby grew; he'd wonder how capable she really was, and he was unable to stop from worrying. She looked so damn innocent and young to him. Could she handle this whole thing? Had she been a good choice? Had he prepared her adequately? He felt the responsibility of her weigh on him.

Finally she was ready to make the first telephone calls to the pregnancy hotlines. She did well, speaking to the counselors with a tone of slight desperation, telling them she hadn't made up her mind yet whether or not she was going to keep her baby. She telephoned three different hotlines in all.

A week later, however, there'd been no contact from Jacobs.

B.G. was concerned. "Maybe she won't contact me at all," she said to Greg on one of his rare visits to her house.

"She'll get in touch," Greg said as he looked around the bungalow, marveling at all the personal touches B.G. had added: a flowerpot here, a coat of paint there, white lace valences above the windows. She'd even bought a pastel Indian blanket to cover the dull brown couch.

"Well, what if she doesn't? I mean, maybe I could call her directly."

Greg turned and faced her, his hands on his hips. "Absolutely not, B.G. We want her to think she's in complete control. She'll call. We know a lot about how Jacobs operates. It might be a week, two weeks, but she will call. Believe me, she's probably already gotten your name and phone number from one of the hotlines.''

''You're sure?''

''Of course I'm sure,'' he replied. The truth was, he was quite concerned. Why hadn't Jacobs called? Was she already checking B.G. out from the information she'd given the hotlines? Had he covered all the bases? Oh, he was concerned, all right, but he wasn't going to let B.G. know it.

Jacobs still hadn't called three days later when Greg met B.G. at the crowded mall. It was seven o'clock in the evening, and the first thing he did was lead her out to his car.

''Where are we going?'' she asked.

''My condo. I want to start teaching you how to use the wire.''

''Why your place?'' she asked.

He shrugged as if it was no big deal. The truth was, he'd been going to rent a motel room for the night, show B.G. how to use the wire, drive her safely home—or near to her home. But he knew she was going to have to strip down to her bra, and somehow the idea of having her do that in some strange aerosol-scented room seemed tawdry.

''The wire equipment's there'' was all he said.

He drove the familiar winding road through the clustered town homes of his development. The landscaping was ''mature'' desert growth, which meant the desert vegetation had had time to grow back the way

it had been before the bulldozers had ridden rough-
shod over the ground. They drove past the community pool, where at this time of the evening lots of
people were gathered, men home from work, mothers with kids. B.G. looked out the window at the
crowd. All Greg could see was the side of her cheek
and her heavy dark hair where her ponytail spilled over
her shoulder.

It was almost dark when he pulled into his carport.

"This is your place?" she asked. "You live here all
alone?"

"Yes. I bought it last year. It's not much, two bedrooms. Needs some fixing up." He led the way
through the carport door into the kitchen, switching
on lights.

B.G. stood in his small kitchen and looked around.
It was neat of course. Greg couldn't live in a mess, too
much of that when he was a kid crowded into a bedroom with his two brothers.

She walked slowly through the hallway, with its
floor-length window showing his shaded patio and the
desert beyond, and into his living room. It had white
walls and off-white carpet, white blinds on the windows and simple light-colored furniture. He liked the
clean look of it.

"This is nice," she said, studying the room.
"Very...stylish."

"Uh...thanks. I'm not here much." He shrugged,
embarrassed at the obvious comparison B.G. must be
making.

"It's cool in here," she said.

"I leave the air-conditioning on. Bad habit, but otherwise it takes so long to cool down, you know." She didn't know.

"Want something to drink?" he asked. "I have lemonade, I think."

"No," she murmured. "No thanks. Let's just do this wire thing."

In his living room they talked about the importance of the wire. Greg had told B.G. all this before, but he couldn't stress it enough.

Sitting on the couch, he fooled with the wires, untangling, straightening them, while B.G. stood near the coffee table watching him, eyeing the tiny battery-powered transmitter and microphone.

He said, "What we're after is for Jacobs to offer you something clearly illegal. The more you get out of her the better." One of the wires was tangled, and Greg swore, then said, "Excuse me," and fiddled with it. "Once she's incriminated herself on tape, we could, theoretically, go to a grand jury for an indictment. We want her to line your baby up with the adoptive parents, get them to promise a lot of money, and then, when we indict Jacobs, maybe we can talk them into testifying, too. We want everything we can get on her."

"If she calls," B.G. put in, still watching him.

"She'll call," he said.

"So, this is all there is to the wire?" B.G. nodded at the table.

He shook his head, still concentrating on the equipment. "No," he said. "The big stuff is in our van, but you don't have to worry about that. It'll work like this: When you meet with Jacobs, you alert me. I wire you, then I'll be nearby, outside her office build-ing, say, with a radio receiver and a small earphone. Also, the van will be parked nearby, with a team in-side listening and doing the actual taping. We'll all hear every word you say."

"It makes me nervous. What if you can't hear me? Static or something."

"Yeah, that could happen. If it does, we just try again, maybe plan to meet her somewhere outside her office where the reception is better. But it usually works well." He glanced up and gave her his most re-assuring smile. "And remember, we have time. She's going to want to see you several times. We'll tape every meeting no matter where it is."

"What if she searches me?"

He shook his head. "Unlikely. The chances are less than nonexistent. Why would she?" Carefully he kept his tone light. *Don't exaggerate the danger,* Dick Mayer had said.

B.G. chewed on her lower lip. "I hope I can do this."

"You've done great so far, just great. You'll do just as well when you meet her."

"I sure hope so," she whispered.

"Okay," Greg said, "I think we're ready to show you how to do this." He stood up and eyed her, try-ing to keep things businesslike. "You'll have to take off your T-shirt." And then, to put her at ease, he said lightly, "Don't worry, I've done this before."

"You mean with a woman?"

He laughed. "No, I haven't wired a woman before, B.G. I meant, I've wired people before."

"Oh, sure, okay," she said, and put down her purse.

He helped her out of her peach-colored T-shirt, and he tried awfully hard not to pay any attention at all to the slimness of her arms and back and the disproportionate size of her breasts in the lacy white cups—and the heavy swell of her belly.

He turned, bent, picked up one of the wires and the roll of tape. He faced her again. Her cheeks showed two bright red spots. Something inside Greg stirred, shifted uneasily.

He brought her closer, smiled reassuringly, his hands cool on her warm flesh. "We start the wire here," he said, his tone impersonal, totally professional.

"Uh-huh," she said, as he ran the wire along her rib cage to her armpit, then followed the seam on the underside of her bra.

When he got it to the front he looked down at her. "The mike has to be clipped," he said, "here." With his finger he indicated the center of her bra where it dipped down in a V.

"Oh," B.G. said, and she helped him, pulling the bra away from her skin, clipping the mike to the fabric.

"That's right," he said, nodding, unable to keep from noticing the full blue-veined swell of her breasts, the nipples dark through the flowered lace. Despite himself, a fine sheen of sweat broke out on his body.

He turned her around, hands on her arms, and ran the wire around her back, along the waist of her shorts, taping the transmitter into the small of her back. Her skin was pale and soft and warm. He could feel the slightest quiver of her beneath his touch, as if she were a nervous filly.

"There," he said, and he picked up her T-shirt and handed it to her. She quickly pulled it on. "Let's take a look at you." He walked around her slowly, eyeing his work. "Good, good, can't tell a thing."

In the end B.G. took the apparatus off herself, pulling at the tape, then holding up the tangle of wires. "What do I do with this now?" she asked, not meeting his gaze.

"You'll keep it," he said. "Put it someplace safe in your house. Most likely I'll be wiring you myself. But in case of an emergency, you'll know how to do it. Okay?"

"Okay."

"Didn't hurt a bit, did it?" he asked, his tone casual, but the image of her breasts under airy lace flowers refused to leave him, taunting him. And even after he'd driven her to a spot close to her house and she'd disappeared from view, he could still see the fullness of her body in his mind's eye. Even just the thought made him sweat.

THE DAYS GREW HOTTER and the weeks of April slipped by, and still Grace Jacobs didn't call. Greg worried a lot about that, trying to second-guess the woman. He knew she was smart and very cautious, but this was overdoing it.

B.G. began to pester him, too, wanting to know when she was going to earn her keep.

"You are," he told her. "You will."

"Yes, I know," she said. "But when?"

"Don't be so ready to jump out of the frying pan," he said, his tone curt.

B.G. murmured, "I've always earned my own way." And her words made him feel like a heel.

There was another subject, too, that crept up more than once, B.G.'s concern that the county attorney keep his promise to provide the very best home for her baby.

She said to Greg, "If Grace Jacobs never calls me, if something goes wrong with this sting of yours, I expect your boss to live up to our agreement. I mean, that's why I'm doing this, Greg. My baby's got to have every chance...every chance I didn't have. I'm serious about this."

They were sitting in Greg's car down the street from B.G.'s house, and he reached over and covered her hand with his. "You have my word."

"Okay," she said, her gaze lowered, and carefully, awkwardly, she slipped her fingers from his and got out of the car. He watched as she walked down the sidewalk in the heat, her gait changed with her growing pregnancy, her long dark braid swinging.

Though he told himself it was natural—when you ran an agent that was what happened—he still wondered why he thought about her so much, worried about her, why she consumed him so totally. He'd see a slip of a girl with long brown hair and he'd think of her. Or a pregnant woman, and he'd wonder if B.G. could ever get that big. He'd read an arrest report on an armed robbery, and he'd immediately wonder if B.G. was in contact with her boyfriend. She knew her telephone line was tapped for the sting, but that wouldn't stop her from using a pay phone to reach him. Or maybe the guy was in Tucson, close by, and they met on the sly. Greg couldn't imagine she'd be that stupid. But who knew? Regardless, the idea of her having anything to do with the jerk made him unaccountably angry.

Dick Mayer questioned Greg daily on the progress of the case.

"You sure you can keep control over Bettie Gay?" he'd ask.

"Yeah. No problem," Greg would always answer.

"I hope so. I really want to nail Jacobs" was Dick's unchanging reply.

Sometimes Greg felt pangs of discomfort about his role in the Grace Jacobs operation. Sure, it had sounded simple at first, straightforward, morally right. But now he was running B.G., and she was a real person who could conceivably face some danger, and he had to ask himself from time to time just how much he really wanted to play Pygmalion.

He told himself often that he was doing her a favor, that she was better off, and he could see that she was indeed making a home for herself. He could also see that she was lonely and bored and that her face lit up too much when she saw him, that her tone was too happy when he phoned her. She was dependent on him, utterly and completely, for the roof over her head, her food, her clothes, everything. That was the plan, and Greg had made it come true. It was a good thing. Wasn't it?

He was soon to learn how badly he'd misjudged Bettie Gay Bryson.

It was a hot ninety-degree day when he left his office and headed over to the little house on Navaho. His intention was to drop off her monthly allowance check and to discuss the possibility of her contacting the pregnancy crises centers again. He parked down the street, left his jacket in the car and went on foot up to her bungalow. He was positive no one was watching, but caution was his middle name. There was no one on the street, however, no out-of-place man sitting in a car, drinking coffee and watching.

Greg knocked. After a while, when there was no answer, he took out his key and let himself in. The place was neat and clean, all the dishes washed and drying in a rack, her bed made.

He stopped back one more time that afternoon, figuring she'd gone shopping, taken the bus or whatever. But she still wasn't home.

A seed of alarm sprouted in him. That evening, early, he telephoned her. Finally she answered.

"Hey, I was starting to get a little worried," he said from the pay phone outside the law library at the University of Arizona. "Is everything all right?"

"Everything's fine," she said, but he detected a hesitation in her voice.

"You positive?"

"Sure. Well, I do have some news."

"Jacobs called," he said.

"No, not yet."

"Then . . . ?"

"I took a job, Greg."

"You what?"

"It's just part-time. Right down the way, on Miracle Mile."

"Goddamn, B.G.!" He ran a hand through his razor-cut hair. "I don't get it. A job. Why on earth…?"

"I just couldn't sit and do nothing. It's no big deal, really. I—"

"No big deal?" he shot back, surprising even himself with his anger.

"Greg," she said, her voice even and controlled, "it's a part-time job at a little Mexican restaurant a few blocks away. I'll only work three days a week and only the lunch-to-dinner shift."

"Swell," he said. "And you can carry a bunch of heavy plates of beans and burritos in your condition. That's really smart, B.G."

"I'm only going to hostess. I know what I'm doing. I've worked in restaurants all my life. My grandma's, a couple of other spots until I met…" Her voice trailed off, and he knew exactly who she'd met—the guy who'd dumped her out on the highway.

"Look," she said, "I'm only going to be seating people, working the cash register—"

"Busing tables when it's busy," he cut in sharply.

She let out a sigh. "It won't be much money, I know. But I'm going to do it, Greg. You won't talk me out of this. At least it'll be my money. I'll earn it fair and square."

"You *are* earning money. I told you—"

Again she sighed. "If we're going to argue, I'm hanging up, Greg."

"I am not arguing," he said tightly, and she hung up.

He couldn't believe it. He stood there in the warm desert evening and stared at the phone in his hand and simply could not believe she'd done that.

It drove him nuts all night. He'd honestly thought he had a measure of control over her. Well, damn, he'd sure misjudged her.

By the following morning his anger, at least, had diminished. Now he felt only frustration and no small measure of anxiety. In order for this plan to work, Dick was right. B.G. had to be under the thumb of the county attorney—and that meant under Greg's thumb. And now, well, now he didn't know how much control he still had. First it would be this job. Then she'd want to take a vacation or something, and next thing any of them knew, she'd be gone.

As much as Greg hated to do it, he had to tell Dick about this development. He thought about downplaying it, but Dick was no idiot. As far as the old army man would be concerned, B.G. was a soldier who'd gone AWOL.

Greg was not wrong.

"She took a job?" Dick exploded.

Greg tried to explain, telling him it was the boredom, coupled with her need to be self-reliant.

"Well, damn it, didn't you tell her this job for us was going to take a while to develop? We can't push it. We don't dare push Jacobs one inch. She'll smell a rat. Damn."

"I'll talk to B.G. again. Maybe I can reason with her."

"Hell, what are you going to tell her? That if she gets independent we lose control over her?"

"Uh, well, no, that's not quite it," Greg said.

"I don't know what you're going to tell her, Tyrrell, but make it good. You told me this woman was pretty much beaten down. You said she was smart but could be manipulated. Well, hell, Tyrrell, guess you missed this aspect of her. And by the way," Dick said, "how come you haven't charmed her to death yet?"

"Beats me," Greg said.

"Go talk to her." Dick came out of his chair impatiently. "Offer her a boost in her allowance. Try that."

"I don't think it'll work, but I'll try."

"You do that."

"You know," Greg said, "no matter how this job thing comes out with her, she's the only game in town. I'll just have to make it work, won't I."

"Yeah," Dick Mayer said. "I guess you will."

Greg telephoned B.G.'s house from his own office a few minutes later. "Morning," he said. Mr. Congeniality.

"Hi," she said. "Hey, look, I'm sorry I hung up on you last night. I was only afraid you'd keep trying to talk me out of my job."

"I do want to discuss it some more, B.G. Why don't I take you to lunch today? There's this very nice place over on—"

"I have to work today," she broke in, and Greg felt a muscle tighten in his jaw.

He said nothing for a moment, then, carefully, "I see. Well, then, maybe I could pick you up after work, and—"

"Please don't try to talk me out of this. You can pick me up, I'd like that, but please . . ."

"Okay," he said, "okay. Now where is this join . . . uh, this restaurant?"

She gave him the address. "It's called the Casa del Sol. I'm supposed to be off at six."

"Six it is, then."

"Greg," she said, "don't be mad at me. Please. This won't interfere in any way with my job for you."

"I'm not mad," he said, lying through his teeth.

All day he mulled over in his mind his relationship with B.G. At first, when he'd seen her through that one-way glass in the interrogation room, he'd been convinced he could run her like a Swiss clock. He'd misjudged her, he knew now. She apparently had a core of strength he'd failed to see. And that could work against him.

Still, she'd done what he'd asked so far. She'd called the hotlines, she'd seen the doctor—twice now—she knew her cover story, and she'd learned to use the wire. So, as far as it went, she was doing her job.

Why, then, was he feeling such a loss of control over her?

Greg got to the Casa del Sol a few minutes before six. He'd dressed down—blue jeans and a polo shirt—because anyone noticing that he was picking her up might wonder. He parked his car in the small lot and eyed the joint through his sunglasses. It was vintage

Tucson, an old salmon-colored stucco building that
needed painting. There were neon beer signs in the
windows, and the cactus gardens on either side of the
front walk were untended. That didn't mean the food
was bad of course, but it wasn't the sort of place he
frequented.

He got out of his car, locked it and went inside. The
cash-register stand was just to his right, but no B.G.
He spotted her near a swinging kitchen door, setting
a heavy stack of plates into a gray tub. Aha, he
thought.

She looked...cute. He had to admit she looked very
cute in a bright lavender oversize T-shirt with a raised
gold sun god motif across her breasts. Her tights were
black, showing off her trim shapely legs. She was
wearing her hair in a French braid, a pen stuck behind one ear. Her cheeks were flushed. When she
wiped her hands on a rag and checked the door, she
saw him, and her face broke into a smile.

"Hi," she mouthed.

"Hi." Suddenly he felt stupid standing there, twirl-
ing his sunglasses in one hand.

While B.G. went into the back, presumably to
punch out, Greg looked around. There were maybe
twenty tables covered with brown oilcloth. On every
table was a small cactus plant and four or five bottles
of various hot sauces. Three ceiling fans whirled
overhead, blowing the aroma of beans and cheese and
posole, Mexican-style grits, into his face. Smelled
pretty good, too. On the walls were the worst works of

art Greg had ever seen—black-velvet paintings, children with big eyes, desert scenes. Godawful.

After a few minutes B.G. reappeared, carrying her purse. Alongside her, saying something to her that was causing her to duck her head, was a young Mexican dressed in kitchen whites over jeans. He was a pretty good-looking guy, Greg could see, a real Latino stud, in fact. It struck Greg with a curious forcefulness that he was actually flirting with B.G.

He wondered if B.G. realized just how attractive she must be to this young macho guy, glowing with the full bloom of pregnancy. "Hi," she said to Greg, her face even more flushed. "This is Santino. He's the cook."

Greg introduced himself and shook Santino's hand. The handshake was strong, the cords in the man's brown forearm tightening.

"Well," B.G. said, "guess we better go. See you on Wednesday, Santino."

"Adios, Señorita Bettie Gay," the stud said with a twinkle in his black eyes.

"For crying out loud," Greg said when they were out the door, "it's a good thing I came when I did. That dude was drooling over you, B.G., and you didn't even know it."

"Don't be silly," she said. "He's very sweet. Young, but—"

"Young? You mean *your* age?"

"Well, I suppose."

Greg unlocked the doors and they climbed into his car. He didn't say anything else until they were practically at her house.

"Okay," he finally asked, "how much are they paying you, anyway?"

She shrugged. "Five-seventy-five an hour."

"Trust me," he said tightly, "it isn't enough."

CHAPTER NINE

A WEEK AND A HALF LATER the telephone pulled B.G. from a sound sleep. Her first muddled thought was that it was Greg, calling to argue about her job again.

She picked up the receiver, trying to wake up, steeling herself.

"Miss Bryson?" came a well-modulated woman's voice. "My name is Grace Jacobs. I'm an attorney here in Tucson."

B.G.'s heart began to pound. "Hello," she managed. "Do I...um, do I know you?"

"No, you don't, but I was given your name by one of my colleagues."

"You were?"

"Yes, you made some calls a few weeks back."

B.G. tried to judge just how dumb she should sound. *Don't lay it on too thick,* Greg had warned her. "Some calls... You mean, about my being pregnant?"

"Exactly. I'd like very much to talk to you about your situation, Miss Bryson. I think we can be of great assistance to each other."

"Well, I don't know. How do you mean?" B.G. pushed herself up so that she was sitting. This conversation was being taped. *Don't blow it,* she told herself. God, they'd rehearsed this so many times.

"I can't go into details over the phone, but I would very much like to meet you. Could you come to my office? At your convenience of course."

No. Not at her office, not yet. "I don't think so, I'm afraid I'd be wasting your time," B.G. said.

"Not at all. Please, let me be the judge of that."

"Well, before I went to your office, I'd have to know what you could do for me, Mrs. Jacobs."

"*Ms.* Jacobs," the woman said, then reluctantly, "I do so hate to talk on the phone, Miss Bryson, but I can tell you that I would be able to place your baby with a wonderful handpicked family, and that all your living expenses would be paid up to and including delivery costs."

Nothing illegal there, B.G. thought. Funny, her deal sounded the same as Greg's.

"Miss Bryson?"

"Uh, sorry, I'm listening. But I don't know... I haven't decided whether I'm going to give my baby up or not."

"I understand completely. It's a hard choice and, God knows, I'd be the last one to try to influence your decision. I do realize what a spot you're in and how very difficult it will be for you with an infant."

"I don't know what I'm going to do yet," B.G. said. "I just don't know."

"Of course, dear. Let me give you my office number and address. That way you can call whenever you feel like it. Or stop by. I'll be available to you whenever you want. Call just to talk if you want," she said sweetly. "I'll always have time for you."

"That's awfully nice of you, Ms. Jacobs."

"Thank you, Miss Bryson. I try my best for my clients. I've helped a lot of people, girls like you. And families who aren't able to have children, too. That's my job."

"Okay, I'll write your number down, but I'm not promising anything."

"Of course not. I wouldn't want you to promise anything on the spur of the moment. Now, here's my number."

B.G. wrote it down, along with the address. As if Greg didn't have it in his head! "I've got it," she said.

"Good. Now don't lose it and, truly, call me, please."

"Okay," B.G. said and hung up.

She sat there in her bed and put her hand on her chest to still her heart. Grace Jacobs had called!

Had she handled it all right? Had she said anything wrong? She thought back over the conversation. No, she'd said nothing to raise the woman's suspicions. As a matter of fact, she'd handled it pretty well, she thought.

Greg. She had to tell Greg! It was starting. At last she was really doing the job she'd waited all these weeks to do. Grinning like an idiot, she got up and went into the bathroom. Her bladder was sending her distress signals.

But when she picked up the phone to dial Greg's number, she realized it was Sunday. Grace Jacobs had called her on a Sunday morning. How odd. And maybe Greg didn't want to be bothered on a Sunday. Sure, he'd told her to call him anytime she needed to, but this wasn't an emergency. It could wait. Maybe Greg's Sundays were precious to him. She knew how busy he was at work. And studying for the bar.

B.G. brushed her teeth and wondered if he might have a date. He'd never mentioned anyone, but then, why would he? It wasn't any of her business. She'd figured all along Greg must have a girlfriend, a good-looking guy like him. Maybe lots of girlfriends. It could be that at this very moment on a lazy Sunday morning he was asleep in some gorgeous woman's bed—or some woman was in his.

B.G. brushed and rinsed, and the image of Greg in bed, tousled and naked and twined in expensive perfumed sheets, wouldn't leave her. She imagined what he'd look like naked, a muscular arm flung casually, a taut lean leg lying flexed, his chest bare, his belly flat. Tanned.

Jay. She remembered his body. Lanky and long. The greatest buns on earth, and his shoulder-length sun-kissed hair. Gorgeous. Jay. Greg. So different, yet both very attractive. She shook her head, angry, sad. She couldn't have either of them, could she? So what was the use of dreaming or imagining or even hoping?

Get real, she told herself, making a definite decision that she'd wait till tomorrow to call Greg.

She had all day to herself. She didn't have to work, and she had very little to do. Tidy up her house. She could take some things to the Laundromat, but it wasn't really necessary. Maybe she'd walk to that nursery on the Mile and get those flowers she'd been looking at. And some pots and soil. Maybe they'd deliver. Santino had told her she could call him if she ever needed a ride, but she hated to be dependent. And she was wary of owing Santino too much.

She'd seen the obstetrician Greg had set her up with twice now. She liked the doctor's bright new clinic, full of pregnant women and mothers with babies. Dr. Resniak had told her get exercise, to walk.

So, she'd go for a walk. Soon, before it got too hot.

She ate breakfast, with the radio on for company. Her house was too quiet. She kept the windows open all night now and in the morning, but she'd learned to close everything up tight when it got really hot, around noon. The ceiling fan didn't do much good, and she wondered how it would be in the midsummer when it was over a hundred degrees every day. Already the hot weather enervated her, made her feel ill. Dr. Resniak had told her that pregnancy made a woman very sensitive to the heat.

Well, at least she didn't have swollen feet yet, or toxemia or varicose veins or any of those other things she'd read about in the pamphlets the nurse at the clinic had given her.

She got dressed in shorts, real maternity shorts, because she couldn't fit into ladies' large sizes anymore. A sleeveless scoop-neck cotton top, her tennis shoes. Her hair back in a ponytail.

Before going on her walk she telephoned her grandmother in Florida, keeping in mind as always that the conversation was being taped. It didn't matter, though. She always talked to Grandma when the rates were low on Sunday, and they pretty much said the same things every time. The idea was to keep in touch.

But when Kathryn Bryson said, "Are you still with that man, that Jay?" B.G. felt the blood drain from her face. She squeezed her eyes shut and prayed her grandmother would let it drop.

"B.G.?" Kathryn was saying.

"Uh, no, Grandma, he's gone." Then, quickly, "What did the doctor say about your swollen ankles, Grandma?" *Oh, please, please don't say anything more about Jay!*

"Well, he put me on diuretics. I have to get up and use the bathroom every two minutes, and my card partners are getting sick of it."

"A nuisance, Grandma," B.G. said, "but you do as the doctor says."

"Oh, I do, honey, I do."

They talked for a few minutes longer and, thank the merciful Lord, Grandma said only that she was real glad B.G. had a job and was rid of that man.

When B.G. was off the phone, she assessed the damage. Greg would have the name Jay. That was all. "Phew," she breathed. There had to be a couple of million Jays in America.

She smiled, chided herself for almost blowing it and left the house.

She walked briskly, swinging her arms. She still felt energetic, fine, except for the hottest afternoons. Work would be no problem. She could work for months yet.

She was getting to know her neighborhood, even nodding hello to some of the women she saw most often. Once she'd helped a toddler who'd fallen on the sidewalk, and his mother had thanked her.

Out on the noisy highway near the Casa del Sol, she went into the greenhouse of the Miracle Nursery. It was open on Sunday of course, its busiest day.

The woman who helped her said they'd be glad to deliver, since her house wasn't far. "This afternoon, no problem," she told B.G. "That's six ceramic pots, two dozen geraniums—mixed color—potting soil."

"Yes, that's right," B.G. said, counting out her cash carefully. And the money was hers, from her restaurant job, not her allowance from Greg's office. It made her feel better somehow to spend the county attorney's money only on absolute necessities such as food.

On the way home she felt good. She was going to be busy this afternoon planting her flowers. It was something to do at least, something worthwhile. She'd have loved to go to a movie, but she shied away from going alone. If only she had a friend, someone to hang around with. Sandy, Greg's sister, had told her to call, but B.G. didn't feel entirely comfortable with the idea.

Just around the corner from her house, a movement caught her eye, a streak across the yard of the place she was passing. With furious barking and snarling, two dogs were in hot pursuit of a cat. She stopped and turned to see what was going to happen. In seconds the cat leapt onto a fence post, where it arched and puffed up, hissing and spitting, the two dogs leaping and barking.

B.G. waded right in. "Go on!" she shouted at the dogs, walking right up to them, waving her hands. "Go on, shoo! Leave that poor cat alone!"

The dogs ignored her. She looked around and saw a stick lying on the ground. Grabbing it, she advanced on the dogs. "Get out of here, shoo!" She poked at one, and the dog whirled on her, then cowered. "Shoo! Go home, you bad boy!" B.G. said, waving her stick.

The dog slunk away, and the second dog, realizing it had no backup, followed.

Then there was only B.G. and the bristly cat.

"Okay, you're safe now," she said. "Go on home yourself."

The cat's fur subsided slowly, and B.G. could see it was a scrawny tatter-eared thing.

"Poor kitty." B.G. walked up to the fence and held out her hand. The cat flinched but didn't run, just fixed her with its green eyes, vigilant.

She shrugged. "Okay, I did my good deed for the day. See you around, kitty."

B.G. was thrilled when the nursery delivered her flowerpots and soil and flats of pink and red and white geraniums. The day had grown very hot, but she put on the sunglasses she'd bought and a baseball cap that read Casa del Sol and located the rusty trowel she'd found behind the house.

She was busy filling pots with soil and sticking a geranium in each when she happened to look up and see the cat sitting in the shade of her lacy gray-green mesquite tree.

"Well, well," she said softly, and she rocked back onto her knees and stayed there a minute, watching it. The cat sat with unfailing patience, its tail curled delicately around its black toes. It was a dark gray tortoiseshell, and it blended into the shadows like a chameleon.

Carefully B.G. rose, which was not as easy as it had once been, stepped inside her front door and poured a shallow bowl of milk. She set it halfway between her front door and the cat, then went back to work.

It took fifteen minutes, but the cat finally moved, silently and stealthily, stalking the bowl. It sniffed and looked around, flicking its tail, lowered its head, jerked it upright at some imagined danger, then lowered it and began to lap.

That was the beginning. By that evening, the cat was sitting on the windowsill of B.G.'s open bedroom window. By morning it was curled up on the foot of her bed.

She reached out and scratched its ears. "If you're going to sleep with me, you better have a name, sweetie. How do you feel about... Whiskers? Yes, that's it."

The cat seemed to grant consent with a purr. Then B.G. smiled and reached for the phone. It was time to call Greg with the news.

She got him just as he walked into his office. "She called," were B.G.'s first words.

"Who? Jacobs, you mean? She called you? When?" Greg said.

"Yesterday morning."

"Sunday morning?"

"Yes, I thought that was sort of strange."

"She called yesterday and you didn't let me know?" B.G. could hear the restrained anger in Greg's voice.

"It was Sunday. I didn't want to bother you. I mean—"

"You wouldn't be bothering me, B.G. That's my job."

"Don't you get days off?"

"Not for the Jacobs case, I don't. Next time, you call me right away, understand?" She heard him take a deep breath. "Okay, what did she say?"

"Nothing much, just that she could help me and that she wanted to talk to me."

"Yeah, okay, I'll listen to the tape. You put her off?"

"Just like you told me to."

"Good. Did it go all right?"

"I think so."

"Well, I'll listen to the tape and see how it sounds. This is perfect, B.G. She's taken the bait."

"The bait. Me," B.G. said dryly.

"I didn't mean—"

"Yes, you did. I'm the bait, right? Isn't that what I'm being paid for?"

"You're not bait, B.G.," he said in an injured tone.

"Well, if it doesn't bother me to be bait, then it shouldn't bother you."

He was silent for a moment. "Hey, this is a little early for me to be getting into it with you."

"I'm not getting into it with you. I'm just being realistic," she said.

"Listen, B.G., I'm coming over after I hear the tape."

"How come?"

"We need to talk."

"Okay. I'll be here."

"See you then. I'll be over on my lunch hour."

After B.G. hung up she wondered why she'd been so prickly with Greg. Maybe it had been his tone of voice when he'd told her she should have called him. As if she were a child. Maybe he deserved it. Then again, maybe he didn't.

He arrived with a box under his arm.

"What's that?" she asked.

"An answering machine. I didn't like not being able to reach you the other day when you were at work."

"Oh wow."

"I'll hook it up. It'll only take a minute."

"The phone's in my—"

"I know where it is."

He was short with her, and she found herself alternating between defiance and distress. She followed him into her bedroom and watched for a minute as he lifted the answering machine out of the box. "Have you had lunch?" she finally asked the back of his head.

"No, I'll grab something on my way back to the office."

"I have some burritos from the restaurant. I was going to heat them up. There're plenty for both of us."

"No, don't bother." His hands were busy, running wires, plugging things in.

"I was going to fix them anyway for myself. You may as well have some."

He stopped what he was doing and looked at her. "I said—"

"Greg, for goodness sakes!"

He ran a hand through his hair. "Okay, sorry, I'll have some."

When he finished hooking up the answering machine he had her record a greeting on it, then showed her how to use it. As he was demonstrating how she could leave alternative messages on it, Whiskers appeared at her open window and landed soft as a feather on her bed.

"Whoa, what's this?" Greg said.

She stroked the cat's head, and the animal closed his eyes and lifted his face to her, purring. "This is Whiskers. He sort of adopted me."

Greg's eyes switched back and forth between B.G. and the cat, a small frown etched on his forehead. "You sure are settling in here, aren't you?"

She smiled, a complacent calm sort of smile. "Sure, I like it here."

They ate the burritos at her kitchen table, which now had a cheerful cloth on it to cover the chipped Formica.

"Good?" B.G. asked, her mouth full.

"Uh-huh, real good," Greg said, and she thought he admitted that a bit grudgingly.

She watched him in the bright light that spilled in the kitchen window. As always, he was dressed in a jacket and tie, white shirt, neatly pressed trousers. So very businesslike, so much more formal than she was used to. And handsome. She thought she'd always remember his face—the strong lines, the blue of his eyes, the sensual curve of his lips, the golden tan beneath a perfect shave. Only once had she seen a five-o'clock shadow on him, the stubble almost blond. It had taken her breath away, as if she'd been given a forbidden peek at him before he'd gotten out of bed.

He took a long drink of iced tea and met her gaze over the rim of the glass. Her heart skipped a beat.

And then he mentioned the tape. "I listened to your conversation with Jacobs," he said, putting down the glass. "You did just fine."

"Oh," she said, and she rose quickly, remembering that her conversation with her grandmother was on that same tape. Jay's name. Would Greg mention it? "I didn't lay it on too thick?" B.G. asked as she scraped the bits of food left on their plates into a bowl for Whiskers and set it on the floor.

Greg watched her. "Yes, I thought you sounded just right." Then he frowned as the cat dove into the scraps. "You're going to make that animal sick," he remarked.

"No, I won't. He loves Santino's cooking," B.G. said, hoping the conversation was off the subject of the tape now.

There was a moment of silence, then, "Does Santino... has he met your cat?"

"No, he hasn't been here. Besides, I just got Whiskers yesterday."

"Santino is the owner of the restaurant?"

She looked at him questioningly. "No, his mom and dad own it. He and his sisters work there. He's the cook, like I told you."

"What's their last name?"

"Fuentes. Why?"

"Oh, no special reason."

B.G. washed the two dishes and the two glasses, set them in the rack and dried her hands on a towel. When she turned around Greg was rising, doing a basketball shot with his paper napkin into the trash can by the back door. Then he walked over to the door, turned, folded his arms and leaned against it. He looked very, very serious.

Uh-oh, B.G. thought. *He's was going to ask about Jay.*

"Listen," he said, "I know you don't want to hear this, but Dick, my boss, wants me to offer you a higher allowance. He wants you to quit that job." Greg pinned her with his gaze.

"No," she said, squaring her shoulders. "You tell him no. I can handle it and your job, too. No."

"I told him you'd say that."

"You were right."

"He's only concerned about your commitment to us."

"As long as you find that home for my baby," she said, and she placed her hands on her stomach, "I'll do whatever you ask."

He studied her for a long moment and then slowly nodded. She knew, she just knew, he'd been ready to say something about Jay, about how his boss, Dick, was worried she might still run off with the man. But the moment slipped by and Greg let it go. She felt a fine sheen of sweat break out all over her body.

"Let's talk about your next contact with Jacobs," he said then. "Let's talk about how to play it out."

"Okay," B.G. said, "okay, sure."

BY THE TIME Greg left it was almost three o'clock. They'd gone over a dozen scenarios on how to handle Jacobs, but in the end they stuck to the plan: B.G. was to act undecided, play hard to get for a while longer. Greg wanted Grace Jacobs to be champing at the bit.

B.G. sat on the couch with Whiskers in her lap and absently stroked his head, thinking, the baby in her womb stirring. And then she found herself crying, silently, the tears rolling down her cheeks and dropping unchecked onto the cat's fur.

If only there was some way she could keep her baby. She had a job now...but if she worked—and it would have to be full-time—who would take care of the baby? And how would she pay for it? What kind of a life could she offer her child?

Jay. If only, by some miracle, things could be worked out with him. Maybe he could go to Dick Mayer and explain how sorry he was about the robbery. Maybe they'd let him off if she insisted, said she wouldn't go through with the sting unless they dropped charges against Jay.

That hadn't been the deal, but maybe she could change it. It was underhanded, but she could try. And then, after the baby was born, she and Jay could somehow make things work out. If Jay would just settle down, get real about life, at least get a steady paying job. Jay was the father of her baby, after all.

She knew she was just dreaming, though. Jay Pearson would never turn into the man she wanted.

That evening, when the temperature finally dropped into the low eighties, B.G. walked the few blocks to the Seven-Eleven store on the highway. The telephone number of Maverick's in Phoenix was clutched in her hand. She had no idea if Jay was even still there.

A part of her desperately needed to hear his voice. Another part cried out for her to stop and turn around and let him go for good. And all along, in her mind's eye, she couldn't quite keep Greg's face from superimposing itself over Jay's.

Despite the warning signals in her brain, she put the coins in the pay-phone slot.

He was there.

She almost hung up. Almost.

"God, baby, I couldn't believe when we talked I forgot to get your number. Man, was that dumb or what?" he said.

"Yeah," she said, "I meant to give it to you. My address, that is," she hastily corrected. "I, uh, don't have a phone."

And so he wrote down her Navaho Street address.

"How's your gig going? You've been there awhile now," she said.

"It's going pretty good. We've got some crowds coming in, anyway. And the lead singer, Al, says he might be able to line up this other gig here for a two-month run. Money in the bank, baby."

"That's great," B.G. said. "Do you have a place to live?"

"Well, I'm kinda crashing on this dude's couch. He's our drummer. I'd have you join me, B.G., but you know, the dude might get uptight."

"Sure," she said. "I understand."

"You working or something?" he asked then.

"Yes." She told him about the Casa del Sol.

"That's good," he said. "I was worried, you know."

"Sure."

"Maybe I could drive on down to Tucson, visit. You know."

B.G. thought quickly. "I wouldn't do that," she said. "The cops... Someone might recognize the Caddy. You still have it, don't you?"

"Still do. I guess you're right. But maybe I can trade it in soon, get something newer. Then I'll be on down to see you, baby. You know I will."

"Sure," she said.

They hung up shortly, and B.G. realized that, as before, he had never once mentioned their baby or how she was feeling.

She turned and walked home, her head bowed as she went. She couldn't imagine ever loving someone as selfish and callous as Jay. On the other hand, the sound of his voice stirred so many memories in her, the good times, the laughs. He was the father of her child, for God's sake. She had loved him once, hadn't she?

CHAPTER TEN

GREG SAT in the county attorney's conference room and stared at the screen of the monitor, clenching his jaw hard.

Jay. Her grandmother had called him Jay on the taped phone conversation, and now Greg was watching this Jay character on the security-system videotape from the convenience store. Stan Manzanares had finally thought to send it over to the county attorney's office with a note that they might want to watch it "just for the hell of it."

He sat there and studied the jerky grainy image on the screen; he saw the young clerk raise his hands, scared half to death, then Jay moved into the picture, his face twisted in desperation and, yes, fear. An amateur.

The guy was young and dressed like a slob. His hair was long and blond and swung around his face when he jerked his head at the clerk. Good-looking. Very good-looking, with the kind of pouty, pretty-boy looks you saw in a youthful movie star. The jerk.

As Greg watched the reenactment of the robbery that night two months ago, all he could think was that this boy was the father of B.G.'s child. She had loved him, left her home to go with him, protected him from the police.

Greg got angry watching the tape, felt a kind of hard cold rage that was like a knife in the gut. And he was ashamed of his anger, confused by it. Why in hell should he get so worked up over this penny-ante kid who'd shacked up with a pretty girl, stolen a few bucks and then dumped her? It happened every day, a thousand times every day.

He'd have to give Stan Jay's name, not that it would do much good. How many million Jays were there in the world, after all?

B.G. was certainly aware that Greg reviewed all the tapes of her phone conversations, and it was clear she'd wanted to get her grandmother off the subject. He'd heard the tension in her voice. She must be nervous, waiting for him to ask her about Jay. Well, he wasn't going to.

But at least now he knew what the guy looked like. And his first name.

He turned off the monitor, rewound the tape and put it back in the manila envelope. He was not going to tell B.G. he'd seen it, and he wasn't going to press her for Jay's last name. Even if it ticked Stan off, he wasn't going to do it, because it would endanger the bond he was establishing with B.G. And right now, with her job and her dangerous new streak of independence, he wasn't about to compromise the relationship.

He left the conference room, weighing the envelope in his hand, trying to clear himself of the unproductive anger that still seethed inside him. B.G. and that silly posturing boy. God!

He put the envelope on Rosemary's desk. "File this with the Bryson stuff, I guess," he said.

"Sure thing, Greg."

"And give a call to Stan Manzanares over at the sheriff's department, will you, please? Tell him thanks for the film and that the perpetrator's first name is Jay. J-a-y. No other info."

Rosemary was writing it down. "Okay, consider it done." She looked up at him over her half glasses, the gold chains looping down on either side of her neck from the earpieces. "How you coming with the girl?"

He grimaced. "She's showing some signs of independence."

"Tsk, tsk," Rosemary said, "that's almost as bad in an undercover agent as it is in a wife, isn't it, Greg?"

"What's that supposed to mean, Rosemary?"

"It's a relationship, that's what I mean. Like a marriage. You have to work at it. It doesn't come easy, I can tell you from experience. Put yourself in the girl's position and try to understand where she's coming from."

"Did I ask for a lecture?"

"No, but you got one," Rosemary shot back.

At his own desk, two floors below, Greg tried reading some police reports. He couldn't concentrate, his mind sliding back to the videotape of the robbery. He was swearing under his breath, reading the same sentence for the fourth time, when his phone rang.

"Greg?"

It was B.G. He sat straighter, resting his elbows on his desk. "B.G.? What is it?"

"Is this a good time for you? Are you busy?" she asked.

"No, it's fine. What's up?" He felt her hesitation, sensed the nervousness in her voice.

"Well, I wanted to ask a favor. Oh, I hate this, I hate to ask you, but there's no one else..."

"What is it, B.G.?"

"I, um, I have an appointment this afternoon with the doctor. I—"

"Are you all right?" he interrupted.

"I'm fine. It's just that, I had some...a little spotting, and I called, and they told me to come in right away for an ultrasound to see if everything's okay," she said breathlessly.

"So you need a ride," he said.

"Well, the nurse said I shouldn't exert myself just in case. Oh, I hate to ask."

"No, you did right. What time's the appointment?"

"Three."

"I'll pick you up at two-thirty."

"Should I meet you at the corner?"

"No. For God's sake, B.G., you just told me you were supposed to take it easy."

"Okay." Her voice was soft, uncertain, more like the girl he'd first seen in the interrogation room than the one who'd argued with him about keeping her job at the Mexican restaurant.

"I'll see you then, okay?"

"Greg," she said then paused. "I'm scared. What if...?"

"Nothing's wrong. I'm sure it'll be fine," he replied with false assurance.

"But—" he heard her swallow "—Greg, would you come into the doctor's with me? Would you, please?"

"Well, I—"

"There's no one else I can ask, and I'm scared." She sounded like a lost kid, her voice breaking, her defenses down.

Greg felt his insides twist in a most peculiar way. She sounded so panicky. "All right, sure, I'll go with you," he said gently.

"Thanks, Greg. I mean it. I really appreciate it."

"You take it easy till then, B.G., you hear me?"

"Sure. I mean, I promise."

"See you at two-thirty," he said.

The first thing that flew into his head was that if B.G. lost the baby, the Grace Jacobs sting was off. The next thing was that B.G. would be free then to do whatever she wanted, to leave Tucson, to go back to Jay. The third scenario that popped into his mind was that there could be something really wrong and B.G. could be in danger, and that was the thought that stuck with him all morning, the thought he worried like a dog with a bone.

He drove out to Navaho too fast and got there early. But B.G. was ready, meeting him at the door when he knocked.

"Hi," she said, trying to smile.

"Are you okay?"

"Sure." She shrugged.

She looked very pretty, wearing a loose sundress in a bright orange print, like some young professional's wife. He took her arm to lead her to the car, but she stopped and withdrew it. "I'm not crippled, Greg," she said, feigning levity.

She was quiet on the way to the doctor's, only speaking once just to say that the air-conditioning felt good, but he knew she was nervous. She kept chewing on her lip, and her fingers played with the seat belt that lay across her stomach.

"I'm sure everything will be fine," Greg said at one point, but she only gave him a swift pained smile and said nothing.

He dropped her at the entrance to the clinic, then parked the Honda in the lot. When he entered the building, she was standing at the counter talking to one of the nurses.

"They're ready for me," she said.

"So *here* he is," the nurse said, smiling at him. "It's nice to meet you. This way, please."

"But..." Greg wasn't sure what was happening.

"Greg..." B.G. said, her eyes pleading.

"Dr. Resniak is happy to have you watch," the nurse said. "It's a very simple procedure. Not invasive in the least."

He turned to B.G. and said in a low voice, "You don't want me to be in the room with you, do you?"

Her eyes were big, frightened. "Please."

Oh, God. "I don't think—"

"Dr. Resniak is waiting," the nurse said apologetically.

Greg took a deep breath. B.G. was his creature, his responsibility. "Okay," he said, not meeting B.G.'s eyes, "lead on."

He waited while she went into a changing room. She came out in one of those paper gowns and got up on the examining table while the nurse fussed with a big machine that had a panel of buttons. Above the machine was a screen on an arm. Greg realized the equipment must be for an ultrasound. He looked at B.G. sitting there on the table, gave her a smile and thought how small and vulnerable she seemed just then, her slender arms and legs so pale, wisps of dark hair escaping from the ribbon tying her hair behind her slender neck, making her skin seem all the paler. And the bulge in her belly...she suddenly seemed far too little to carry such a burden. Maybe everything *wasn't* all right...

Dr. Resniak came in a moment later. He was a slim man, short, with a receding hairline. He greeted B.G. and shook hands with Greg.

"Let's see that chart," he said. "Hm, spotting yesterday. And you're, let's see, approximately twenty-four weeks along."

"Yes," B.G. said.

"Any pain? Cramps, backache?"

"No."

"Okay, let's take a look."

The nurse turned on the machine, and Dr. Resniak picked up something that looked like a microphone, which was plugged into the machine. "This is called the transducer," he told B.G. "It sends sound waves into your abdomen. Like sonar. They bounce back, and what they've hit is transmitted onto the screen as an image."

Greg lowered his gaze as B.G. lay on her back and the nurse pushed up her gown. Sure, he'd seen her when he wired her, but not like this....

The nurse rubbed gel all over B.G.'s stomach. "This helps the sound waves get through easier," Dr. Resniak explained.

Greg felt his cheeks flush, and suddenly the room seemed unbearably close. He couldn't stop looking at B.G., at the blue-veined swell of her stomach, the hint of dark growth just below the thin paper sheet that did a poor job of covering her. There was something so…intimate to the sight, intimate and seductive, and he was shocked by his reaction.

He thought again that this was certainly no place for him to be. He wasn't her husband, for God's sake. It was too private, too personal. How could he have let himself get dragged into this? Jay should be here, he thought, then almost laughed. Jay, the jerk, the coward. Right.

Greg was afraid to look up again. He felt his heart slamming against his breastbone. He wanted to leave, bolt out the door, but he knew he couldn't. He had to stand there and pretend he wasn't a wreck.

"Okay, we're going to start. Bettie Gay, Greg, watch the screen," Dr. Resniak said.

B.G. reached out her hand and touched Greg's arm. He glanced at her, and she grasped his hand. Hers was cold and damp and shaking a little. He stood there and held it and hoped he could get through this. What if there really was something wrong with the baby?

The doctor was running the transducer back and forth across B.G.'s stomach. She had her eyes closed and was squeezing Greg's hand so hard his fingers were going numb.

"There," he heard the nurse say, and he looked up.

"Oh," he heard B.G. say wonderingly.

On the screen was an image, a white image on black, like the negative of a photograph, a grainy blotchy negative. A head, a curved back, bent legs, arms, two tiny hands. And the image moved—a knee, an arm, the beat of the heart in the tiny rib cage. A head.

"Oh, my goodness," B.G. said.

Eyes, nose, mouth, ears. There was a madonnalike smile on the baby's mouth, and while Greg watched, a tiny arm moved and a miniature thumb went into the diminutive mouth. It was sucking its thumb.

B.G. gave a sob, and Greg saw a tear run down her temple to wet her hair. She still held his hand in a death grip. "My baby," she whispered, and something broke inside Greg.

"Looks good," the doctor said, then he pressed buttons on the machine, and an arrow moved on the screen. "I'm measuring the baby's head and femur. It'll go into the computer in this thing and give us the baby's exact age. How you doing, Bettie Gay?"

"Okay," she managed.

"I'm looking for a problem with the placenta," Dr. Resniak said. "It's called 'placenta previa.' That's usually the cause of bleeding. Often it migrates back to a safe spot, though, and that's what it seems to have done here. I see no sign of it positioned wrongly."

"That's good?" B.G. said.

"Yes, it means you're fine. There's no danger for the baby or you."

"Thank God," she said fervently.

Greg stared at the image, the tiny body that moved and sucked its thumb. The snub nose and closed eyes, the fingers and curled-in feet with perfect little toes. A live human being, growing there inside B.G., floating inside her in a dark warm ocean. Growing. A miracle. And he could actually see it.

"Do you want to know the sex?" the doctor asked. "If you haven't already seen for yourselves."

"I don't know," B.G. said. "Maybe..."

"Sure," Greg said, surprising himself. "We want to know."

"Yes, then," B.G. said.

"It's a girl."

"A girl." B.G. smiled for the first time. Then she turned her head and looked at Greg. "I wanted a girl."

"Congratulations," Dr. Resniak said, and Greg realized the doctor was talking to him. "You're going to have a beautiful little girl."

Shock hit Greg like a blow in the solar plexus. He opened his mouth to object, to tell the doctor he was wrong. It was all a mistake, the baby wasn't his! No words came. How could he tell them? How could he even begin to explain?

He cleared his throat, avoiding the doctor's eyes. "Thank you," he muttered, and he felt B.G. press his fingers.

"Do you want me to print out a copy of this for you?" Dr. Resniak asked. "You can take it home. Show it to your daughter when she's grown."

"Yes," B.G. said. "I'd like that."

But B.G. wasn't going to have this daughter when she was grown, Greg thought, and for a second he felt the loss she would feel. It might be the only picture B.G. ever had of her daughter.

The machine hummed and printed out a picture, but Greg kept staring at the screen where the baby moved its arms and pushed one tiny foot out, stretching. He'd never before felt the awe he felt right now, not for anything, and it was a revelation to him, an almost humbling experience. Then the nurse turned the machine off, the image faded, and Greg exhaled a lungful of air, as if he'd been holding his breath for a long time.

"Well, that's it," the doctor said. "Greg, will you come into my office for a minute while Bettie Gay gets dressed?"

"I, uh..."

"I just want to have a word with you."

Greg cast about, slightly desperate, for B.G. to tell the doctor who he was, but she'd already disappeared into the changing room.

"Right this way, Mr. Bryson," the nurse said, and he couldn't start explaining to her that he wasn't Mr. Bryson, that he wasn't the father of this child.

Then he was sitting across from Dr. Resniak, his mind whirling furiously with explanations. But the doctor was saying something, and Greg had to listen, pretend he was interested.

"I did speak to Bettie Gay about Lamaze classes, and I wondered if you two had started them."

"Lamaze classes?" Greg said blankly.

"Natural childbirth, breathing techniques, that kind of thing. They're very helpful."

"Well, I, uh . . . we haven't really talked about it," he fumbled.

"There's plenty of time. I recommend taking the classes, though."

"Okay, sure, I'll mention it to her."

"Good."

Greg squirmed inside. He was getting deeper and deeper into this ridiculous charade. Why had he ever started it?

Dr. Resniak folded his hands on his desk and gave Greg a very serious look. "I just wanted to make sure you understood that Bettie Gay's bleeding is not your fault. Lots of husbands feel very guilty when this happens, because they're afraid it was caused by their having intercourse with their wives."

Greg was as mute as if his tongue had been cut out.

"It's not your fault, believe me. I'd wait a couple of weeks, and if there's no more bleeding, it's perfectly all right to continue to have intercourse." The doctor unfolded his hands and leaned back. "In fact, it's safe to have intercourse all the way through her term. Now, do you have any questions you'd like to ask?"

Greg couldn't think of a single one.

CHAPTER ELEVEN

THE NEXT WEEK, as spring progressed toward summer, the weather turned unusually hot, and one midafternoon the thermometer reached a hundred degrees.

Everyone told B.G. it was a rare hot spell. "It never gets this bad in May," the others at the Casa del Sol told her.

"Sure," B.G. replied. "That's what we always told the tourists in Florida, too."

At work she'd given everyone the same story she was to tell Grace Jacobs: she was a navy brat, born in Florida, moved a few times, and now she was house-sitting for her paternal grandmother. No one questioned her past. Why should they? No one ever asked about the father of her baby, either. But then, plenty of single women had children these days.

Santino was starting to become a problem, though. Despite the growing bulge in her belly—or maybe because of it—he was flirting with her more and more, sometimes even walking her home after work. She never let him in, though. But she did tell him he was crazy.

He walked her to the painted gate in front of the house on the hottest evening so far, and then he stopped her, reaching for her hand. "Let me take you out tonight, B.G.," he said, his dark eyes shining in the dimming light.

"You really are nuts," she told him, and she laughed. "Look at me! I'm a cow."

But he shook his head adamantly. "No, no, you're beautiful. If you would let me, I would take care of you forever, fill your belly many more times because you are so beautiful like this."

A true Latin lover, she thought. Still, she couldn't help blushing all the way down to her toes. She reached up and put her fingers against his smooth cheek and told him how sweet he was. "But I can't... be with you, Santino. I can't."

He looked ineffably sad. "There is another for you? The father of your baby perhaps?"

"Perhaps," she allowed.

"My heart is broken, then."

"Santino—"

"No, it is. Because no one would love you as much as I do."

"Oh, stop," she got out. He couldn't be serious.

"But I do love you," he insisted.

"And I bet you love a dozen others, too."

He lowered his head. "None as much as you, Bettie Gay."

That evening, as she watered her geraniums and gave Whiskers his dinner, she couldn't help wondering if Greg found her attractive in any way. But maybe to Greg she *was* a cow. She'd seen his face during the ultrasound and was certain he'd looked at her differently afterward; she just didn't know exactly how. She knew only that the way he felt was beginning to mean a lot to her. It shouldn't, and maybe she was as crazy as Santino, but it mattered. Oh, how it mattered!

She thought about Jay, too, later when she sat out back on an old lawn chair and watched the first stars brighten over the foothills. Jay had always made her feel good. Well, almost always. When they'd been together in the beginning he'd had this way about him, a way of looking at her and listening to her as if she was the only person on earth. As if she was truly beautiful. She'd spent so much time in her life putting herself down that Jay's attentiveness, his boyishly gentle compliments, had made her feel like a million. At first.

But then he'd starting taking her for granted. She should have left him then, she knew now, but at the time it was impossible for her; she'd grown too emotionally dependent on him. The next thing she knew she was pregnant, and the whole process of convincing herself that she still loved Jay had taken over.

Whiskers wandered lazily out the back door, sniffed the air, stretched, then hopped up into her disappearing lap. B.G. stroked him absently and wondered if Greg ever said sweet things to his girlfriends—or one particular girlfriend. She was sure he must, but she wondered nevertheless, almost able to hear the caress in his deep voice. She stroked Whiskers and closed her eyes and conjured up his voice, the way his hand had felt in hers when she'd been on the examination table, the look in his blue eyes. Someday Greg would marry, and his wife would share those moments. Would she appreciate how lucky she was?

The next day the temperature soared to 104. Greg called, too, and B.G. knew it had been more than a week since they'd spoken. Since the ultrasound. She wanted to curse him. Didn't he know how nuts he made her? But how could she tell him that? She didn't dare let him even glimpse her infatuation. Not ever.

"I'm sorry I haven't been in touch," he said. "I got hung up investigating this other case...but I won't go into that. How are you? Is everything okay?"

"I'm fine," she said, gripping the receiver, her fingers damp.

"I do check up on the phone tapes," he said. "And I assume if anything was wrong you'd call in immediately."

"Greg," she said, swallowing, "you don't have to make excuses for not calling. I know you're busy. I know I'm not your only case."

He laughed tightly. "You may not be my only case, B.G., but you are my most important one."

"That's nice," she said lightly.

"The heat getting you?" he asked then.

"Kind of. I feel better at work, to be honest. At least it's air-conditioned there."

"Yeah," he said, "I'm sure." Then, "What I really called for was to give you the go-ahead to get in touch with Jacobs. It's time you met her."

"Okay," B.G. said, and her heart gave a lurch.

"Of course we'll go all over everything again," he said. "And why not practice with the wire? I'll probably be hooking you up myself, but just in case. Okay?"

"Sure," she said.

"Look," he said after a pause, "I'll stop by tonight when I'm through work. We'll plan out that call to Jacobs."

"Okay."

"I'll, uh, pick up some chicken or something at the store. Already cooked. Okay? We can eat and talk."

"Sure."

"You didn't have any other plans or anything?"

"No. No plans."

"I'll be there around seven, then."

"Okay," she said, and hung up. Her hand was trembling.

She told herself not to bother. She told herself how silly and childish she was being. But nonetheless she bathed for more than an hour and did her hair and put on one of her favorite outfits—a bright red top and white shorts—all for him. She even put on lipstick and a dab of perfume, chiding herself, thinking what an idiot she was to believe he'd even give her the time of day if it wasn't for this sting operation. But, oh God, she couldn't help it. Couldn't help it any more than she could cease to breathe.

At a quarter to seven, B.G. started glancing out the window, looking for his familiar figure to come down the street. She must have looked out the window five or six times, her nerves thrumming, the baby stirring within. She was a fool, an absolute fool.

He arrived right on time. But instead of parking down the street and checking out the neighborhood before coming to her door, he pulled up right in front. B.G. peeked through the blinds and watched as he opened the trunk of his car, lifted out a heavy box and then had a heck of a time getting it through the gate.

She swung open the front door. "What on earth...? Here, let me help."

But he would have none of it. And then he was inside and she could read the writing on the box—an air-conditioner!

"Oh, Greg," she said, "is this for me?"

He was sweating as he set the huge box onto the kitchen table. "No, it's for the cat, B.G. You still have that ratty-eared thing?"

"Of course," she said, beaming, her hands on her cheeks. No one had ever bought her a gift like this. It didn't even matter that the money came from the county attorney's budget. Greg had done this for her.

"Well," he said, catching his breath, "do we put it in the bedroom window or in the living room? Your decision."

She had a terrible time deciding. But in the end Greg hooked it up in the bedroom and switched it on. B.G. stood with the icy-cold air fanning her face for at least five minutes. "Oh, it's wonderful," she said over and over.

"Glad you like it," he said, standing quietly at the bedroom door, watching her.

He'd brought the chicken, too, as well as a macaroni salad and two pieces of cheesecake. They ate every bit at her kitchen table, and she felt so happy she was near tears.

After dinner they sat in her living room in the dim light from the single lamp and talked about when she was going to call Grace Jacobs.

"Early next week," Greg said. "I really want her champing at that bit. But we can't wait too long. Might make her wonder."

"Okay," B.G. said. "Whatever you think's best."

Then he wanted to go over her story again, but she begged off. "I will, I promise," she said. "I'll even practice with the wire. But not tonight."

"Why not?" he asked.

"Because tonight's special," she said, giving him a shy smile. "Tonight I got the best present of my whole life."

"An air-conditioner?" He leaned forward and clasped his hands between his knees.

B.G. colored. "We never had much when I was growing up. With what Grandma made in profits at the restaurant, she paid off the mortgage at our house." B.G. stared off into the distance now. "I don't ever remember going shopping for school clothes like my girlfriends did. I always wore stuff from used-clothing stores."

"It must have been rough," he said gently, and she almost closed her eyes to let his voice wash over her, that low-pitched, resonant, very masculine voice she was coming to know so well.

"Oh, lots of kids grow up with not too much. You learn to make do. It's just that, well, sometimes you feel like a second-class citizen."

"I guess that's true," Greg said. "God knows I wore a lot of castoffs from my brothers. We weren't exactly...rich, B.G. My folks still just make do."

She nodded. "But you decided to make a better life for yourself. My gosh, Greg, you're going to be a full-fledged lawyer soon. Think of it."

"I do, all the time," he said. "And I admit it, I want it all. House, swimming pool, cars, country-club membership. The whole nine yards. I'm not ashamed to want the best."

"You've worked for it," she said. Then, "I'm going to go back to school, too. I'm not going to live like this forever. I know I can do better. As soon as the baby... well, as soon as this job's over, I'm going to start taking classes again."

"And what do you want to be when you grow up, B.G.?" he asked, giving her a lopsided smile.

She waved a hand in the air. "Oh, maybe I'll be a manager or something at a restaurant. Or maybe I'll manage a restaurant at a country club—yours—and I can cater and do weddings and all that. I mean, I could do that stuff now, really I could, but nice places always want to know if you have a college degree. They couldn't care less whether or not you can actually do the job, as long as you've got that degree."

Greg nodded.

She studied his face. "What sort of lawyer do you plan to be?"

"I'm thinking of practicing strictly criminal law."

"What you're already used to."

"That's right," he said. "I think I'd be bored with run-of-the-mill law, doing real-estate contracts or writing up wills all day long."

"That'll be great," B.G. said. "You'll do well."

He cocked his head. "And how do you know that?"

"Because," she said, lowering her gaze to her lap, "I just do."

When Greg left that night, B.G. lay on her bed with the air-conditioner blasting and pictured him in her mind, the way he sat in a chair, the way he'd squatted on his haunches to hook up her air-conditioner, the width of his back under his clean white shirt, the curve of his thighs. She knew she was obsessed with him. She couldn't stop craving his touch. Even his voice on the phone was enough to make her knees go wobbly and sweat break out on her upper lip. How could she be so dumb? Almost seven months pregnant—with another man's child—and falling in love with the most unattainable man she'd ever met.

That night B.G. also thought a lot about her baby. A desperation was building in her to keep her child and raise her the best she could—no matter what. And yet every time she played the scenario out in her mind it just didn't work. At this stage of her life there was nothing she could offer the baby, only her love, but that was not going to put a roof over their heads or food in their stomachs. She had to give the baby up. She had to stop dwelling on the impossible and do what was best for the child, for Kathryn, she thought, giving the baby a name despite the pain she felt. Kathryn—after Grandma and ironically, she realized, after Greg's mother, too.

B.G. DIDN'T SEE or hear from Greg the next day at all. While at work in the restaurant, she kept expecting to glance up and see him there. It never happened.

The weekend was coming right up. She knew she'd hear from him then, because he'd want to go over her cover story one last time.

What B.G. didn't expect was the message waiting on her machine when she got home that Thursday night from the Casa del Sol.

It was from Greg. "I assume you're at work," he said. "Anyway, if you aren't busy this Saturday, I'll pick you up at eleven in the morning. I'll meet you at the corner, if that's okay. There's a place I'd like to show you. Dress comfortably—it's outdoors. If you can't make it, let me know. Otherwise, I'll see you Saturday."

If B.G. listened to the recording once, she listened to it a dozen times over the next day and a half. It was as if she couldn't get enough of his voice, and the invitation... Well, it boggled her mind. This couldn't be a date, not a real date, she told herself. Still, she barely slept a wink on Friday night and was dressed casually, her hair all neatly French braided, by nine on Saturday morning.

Greg picked her up punctually a block from her house. She knew he worried about the neighbors. If Grace Jacobs actually had her checked out, it wouldn't do to have a man constantly stopping over, especially the same man.

"I hate making you walk like this," he said when she got into his car.

B.G. smiled. "I don't mind a bit. The doctor said walking's good for me." She looked at Greg as he pulled away from the curb. He was dressed in shorts and a salmon-colored polo shirt. "Wow," she said,

"I've never seen you dressed like this. Where on earth are we going?"

"Would you believe on a picnic?" he said.

They stopped at a deli in a strip mall on Tanque Verde, got sandwiches and chips and bottled sparkling waters. Greg tucked it all into a small backpack he'd brought along, and then they were on their way again, heading north into the foothills of the Santa Catalina Mountains.

B.G. sat there next to him feeling absolutely wonderful. She never asked why he was taking her on this picnic or where they were going. She only knew that she was with Greg.

They drove along a winding stretch of road flanked by upscale houses, adobes and Spanish-mission-style homes. Most of them were beautifully landscaped and had swimming pools. B.G. imagined that this was what Greg had in mind for himself.

Finally the road ended at a parking lot filled with open-air buses picking up passengers. The sign said: Sabino Canyon. No cars. "We take the bus from here," Greg said, pulling out the pack and locking the car. "I think you'll get a real kick out of this spot.

Sabino Canyon was a place you'd never expect to find in the desert, a ragged cut in the mountainside made by a stream that tumbled down over boulders and broke into deep clear pools and rushing rivulets.

At the base area where the open-air buses loaded, the desert plants were labeled for the benefit of the tourists, and B.G. read the signs: tall saguarolike sentinels with their bent arms, ocotillos that looked like clusters of dead thorny sticks, prickly pears with round spiked paddles, chollas and organ pipe and barrel cactus. All strange, woody, covered with spines.

"Watch out," Greg said, "those are called Jumping Cholla cactus and they hurt like the dickens."

"They don't jump," B.G. protested.

"Actually they fall and bounce," he said, "but they still hurt."

He paid the fee to go into the preserve, then took her arm and climbed onto a bus. It was crowded, everyone in shorts and sunglasses and baseball caps. Greg had brought along a cap for each of them, as well as sunscreen, which they slathered on their arms, legs, faces.

There were lots of families, fathers pushing strollers, mothers grasping toddlers' hands, babies carried in backpacks. Children everywhere. And there were young couples walking hand in hand, other pregnant women, too. One of them sat behind B.G. and Greg, with her husband, and he had his arm around her shoulders.

It occurred to B.G. that everyone must assume she and Greg were a married couple expecting their first child, and she wondered if Greg realized that. Would he be embarrassed if he knew what other people thought?

B.G. sat on the bus beside Greg with the warm air washing over her, hearing the hum of conversation and shrill children's voices, and she decided to pretend, just for today, just for this one precious afternoon, that she was Greg's wife and it was his baby who kicked inside her, and that when they went home after their picnic, it would be together, to his condo in the prosperous foothills...

"You okay?" Greg asked.

"Sure."

"You haven't said a word. Is it too hot for you?"

She shook her head. "No, it's fine. Really."

Then they were off, up a winding narrow road that followed a shallow stream into the mountains northeast of the city. B.G. was struck by the beauty of the place, the sheer rock walls, the clear running water, the surprising greenness of it, the stream leaping the tumble of rocks between feathery silver-green mesquite trees. It was cool in the canyon, too, a verdant wonderland in the midst of the Sonoran Desert. A Shangri-la.

"This is great," she said to Greg. "I love it."

"Yeah, kind of neat for practically being in the city," he replied, and she was aware of his arm behind her on the seat back and his strong leg pressed to hers. His legs, sprinkled with fine blond curling hair, were golden brown. B.G. realized how tanned he was and surmised that he must spend a lot of time outdoors on the weekends. What did he do? And who did he do it with?

He nudged her arm as the bus stopped along the way, letting some picnickers off, taking more on who were headed to the top of the canyon. All along the way people walked or sat on big boulders in the shade and kids splashed in the stream.

"Right over there," Greg said, pointing, "my brothers and I used to jump off that rock into a pool. You never knew how deep it was, either." Then he twisted his leg for her to see a long scar that ran across his kneecap. "A memento from one of my jumps."

"Ouch," she said, and she could see the whole Tyrrell family coming up here on weekends, all the kids and his mom and dad. A real family. Like the families she was seeing right now. It was so...normal. And she wondered if she was ever going to lead a normal life.

They got off the bus a mile or so from the top of the canyon. At this particular point the canyon was wider, the stream lazier. Lots of spots to sit in the shade and eat.

Together, carrying their shoes, they crossed the shallow stream to the far side of the canyon. Greg kept hold of her arm, saying, "Don't slip on these rocks. Maybe this wasn't such a good idea."

But she was loving every minute. She kept alive in her mind the fantasy that they were happily married, a real couple, just like all these other couples. A man and a woman and a small child were walking along the far side of the stream. The woman looked at B.G.'s stomach and smiled, and she smiled back. She could pretend, couldn't she?

For a time they walked down the stream, ducking between the long thin arms of the mesquite trees, Greg pointing out the variety of cacti that dotted the canyon floor. Then they stopped and sat on a large flat boulder in the sun, the stream trickling past, the sound of children's laughter close by.

"Hungry?" he asked.

"Starved," she admitted. "'Course I'm always hungry now." Then she blushed a little, aware of his pensive gaze resting on the ever-growing swell of her stomach before he shifted his glance away.

Everything that warm Saturday afternoon seemed new and special to B.G. It was as if she was seeing things for the first time. Seeing things and smelling things and feeling things. Why hadn't she ever noticed how light Greg's hair was? Or seen how crooked his smile was, or how strong his neck was?

She smelled the fresh dry air and wondered if it was possible to smell the sunlight. She was sure she could. And she could feel the sun on her bare arms, feel the warmth of the rock beneath her. When Greg's hand brushed hers, or when he reached out and flicked a sandwich crumb from her chin, were moments isolated in time. And the way he laughed. Always a little reserved, perhaps a little shy. He was so in control, of this life, his emotions, his future. She admired that in him, but once in a while she wondered what he'd be like if he let go, really let go, did something on the spur of the moment, got sweaty and dirty, messy. She'd like to see that.

When the food was gone, she sat on the edge of the boulder and dangled her feet in the water. Greg took out a Swiss Army knife and whittled on a stick.

B.G. cocked her head, watching him. "Before he died, my grandfather used to do wood carvings," she said. "He had a whole room of them at the back of the restaurant, in fact. You know, ships and boats and stuff." She laughed. "Grandma used to get so mad at him. He was supposed to be helping in the restaurant, but he'd say he'd be back in a minute and he'd disappear into his carving room and that would be that."

Greg was watching her now. "They were all you had, your grandparents?"

"Uh-huh. My mom, well, basically she disappeared."

"And you went to high school in Mayport."

She nodded. "When I graduated I worked full-time at the restaurant until Grandma had to sell it. I worked for the new owner, but I didn't like it much anymore. I worked at a couple of other places then, in Jacksonville. Then I met..." She looked down and swallowed. She'd almost said his name again.

"So you left Florida," Greg finished for her.

"Yes. I traveled around the country for a while." She shrugged and looked up. "You know, I never gave my real folks much thought. Not till junior high, anyway. Then I guess I started noticing how everyone else had at least one parent."

"It must have been rough."

"Oh, I got along. But I suppose that's why it's so important for my baby to have a real home." Darn, B.G. thought. Somehow their conversation always came back to the baby or Grace Jacobs. There was no avoiding it.

Later, they walked down the canyon for a mile or so until B.G. said maybe that was enough. "It's the heat. It really gets to me now." So he took her elbow and steered her back across the stream and they rested, waiting for the tourist bus.

"You know," she said, "I'll never forget this day."

Greg was leaning against a tree, arms folded, staring across the canyon. He said nothing.

"I'm sorry—I embarrassed you," B.G. said, wishing she'd kept her mouth shut.

"No, no, you didn't," he said. "I won't forget today, either. I'm glad you came with me."

So she pushed it a little further. "You probably had a million other things to do, I bet."

"Actually," he said, "nothing important. I wanted to show you this place, get you out a little."

"I get out."

"To work."

"Well, it's better than not working."

"If you say so."

And then she couldn't stop the question from tumbling out of her mouth. "Greg? Have you... Well, is there someone? I mean, I don't even know if you're engaged or anything."

He was quiet for a long moment. She knew she'd gone way too far, gotten too personal. She wished a hole would open up and swallow her. "It's like this," he finally said, weighing his words. "I set goals for myself a long time ago. I'm about there, too, B.G. I'm afraid marriage and relationships are at the bottom of the list."

She tucked a stray hair behind her ear and adjusted the baseball cap he'd given her. "I don't know why I asked. It's none of my business."

"No problem," he said, and his voice was curiously gentle. "My life's no secret."

That might be true, she mused, still mortified that she'd asked him such a personal thing, but the fact remained that she still didn't know if there was someone special.

The whole way down the canyon and back to her house, B.G. could not get it out of her head that Greg had wanted to be with her. There'd been no ulterior motive today. He'd never once even mentioned Grace Jacobs, let alone what she, B.G., should say when she called the woman. He'd just wanted to show her Sabino Canyon.

That evening, after Greg dropped her off down the street, B.G. couldn't stop thinking about him, fantasizing, picturing Greg with her and the baby, a house of their own, all those nights together, forever in Greg's arms.

She thought about Jay, too, knowing she could always run back to him, raise the baby with him somehow. Her brain spun with the images of the two men: Jay, Greg, Jay, Greg. And the truth was that neither of them were right for her. Jay had robbed that store and abandoned her, and he'd be the worst, absolute worst sort of father and husband. And Greg . . . Sure he'd been nice, nicer than any man had ever been to her. But it was clear that nothing was going to get in the way of Greg Tyrrell's goals, especially not her.

What she had to concentrate on was the job she was to do for him. And when it was over, they'd keep their word and place Kathryn in the best of homes. That was what mattered. Kathryn mattered, and she couldn't afford to let anything stand in the way of her child's welfare.

CHAPTER TWELVE

GREG INSISTED on being there when B.G. finally made the call to Grace Jacobs. He came over on Tuesday morning and drank coffee and picked at a cheese Danish while he coached her.

"Okay," he said. "Go over it again."

B.G. sighed. She leaned back against the kitchen counter, folded her arms over her stomach and repeated her story. "I decided to give my baby up because I have no money and no job. The father's gone, and I have no idea where he is. Once the summer's over and my grandmother comes back, I have no place to live."

"Now, remember, we want something incriminating from her, but you can't push too hard. For God's sake, don't initiate anything. Just ask normal questions when she offers something. Nice and easy, conversational. She won't talk much on the phone, but when you meet her in her office she'll feel safe, and that's where you'll be wired."

"I know, Greg."

"If you can get anything about how she files the legal papers, how much she pays the hotlines, the referring doctors, how much the prospective parents pay—"

"I know, Greg."

"Don't push her too hard, though. You'll have to find that fine line."

"Greg . . ."

"Okay, okay. I just want to cover all the bases, B.G. I like to be prepared."

"You're making me nervous. I already know what to do."

"You feel comfortable with this?" He looked at her questioningly. "You're ready?"

"I'm ready."

"Then make the call."

B.G. went into her bedroom and sat on the edge of the bed. Greg stood in the doorway, leaning a shoulder on the frame, his eyes on her. She reached her hand out and picked up the receiver, her gaze meeting Greg's. He gave her a quick go-ahead smile, and she dialed the number.

The phone rang in her ear—once, twice, three times. What if Jacobs wasn't there? Should she leave a message?

"Jacobs Law Offices" came a voice.

B.G. sat up straighter, her eyes locked with Greg's. "My name is Bettie Gay Bryson. May I speak to Ms. Jacobs, please?"

"One moment please."

Grace Jacobs came on the phone instantly. "Bettie Gay, how good to hear from you."

"Oh, you remember me, Ms. Jacobs?"

"Of course I do, dear."

"Well, I've decided to give my baby up for adoption."

"You're absolutely sure?"

"Yes, I'm sure."

"Can we talk? I want to meet you as soon as possible. Can you make it tomorrow, Bettie Gay?"

"Tomorrow. That's fine. When?"

"Say, ten in the morning? You have my address, don't you?"

"Yes, I do. Ten's okay."

"You've made a wise decision, dear. I'm looking forward to meeting you."

"Me, too. See you tomorrow, Ms. Jacobs."

GRACE JACOBS knew her office impressed the girls the first time they entered it. Stucco walls, dark beams overhead, subtly colored art on the walls. Touches of Spanish-style wrought iron, a refectory-style desk of hand-finished pine, a very old, very fine *santo,* a Spanish holy painting, next to the window behind her. All in all the decor reflected her taste.

When Bettie Gay Bryson walked in promptly at ten, Grace saw her look around, her eyes widening.

Oh, yes. Grace thought. *This one's very nice indeed. Perfect for the Levys in La Jolla.* She rose and held out her hand. Her smile was absolutely genuine; she was thrilled to meet Bettie Gay Bryson. Miss Bryson was going to net her at least twenty-five thousand dollars.

"Hello, Bettie Gay," she said in her warm contralto. "It's so good to finally meet you." The girl's hand was damp. She was nervous, but then, they all were the first time. "So, you've decided to give up your baby for adoption," Grace began.

"Yes, I have."

"It's a good decision, Bettie Gay. There are so many people just desperate for a healthy baby. You'll be making a couple very happy."

"I want my baby to have a good home," the girl said.

"Of course." Grace put her hand on a stack of papers. "See these applications? There are dozens of them, and they're all from people who want a baby. Your baby, Bettie Gay."

The girl ducked her head, shy. Endearing, Grace thought.

"Uh, my friends call me B.G.," she said meekly.

"Well, I'm glad you count me among your friends, B.G., because I know we're going to have a wonderful relationship." She folded her hands on her desk. "Now, I have some papers for you to fill out, but first I'd like a little background. When's your due date, B.G.?"

"August nineteenth."

Grace studied her. A pretty girl, nice coloring. Beautiful hazel eyes. You couldn't tell what their figures were like while they were pregnant, but this one certainly had good legs. "And the father—where is he?"

"He's gone. I don't know where."

"Is he likely to come back? That is, could he, uh, complicate the arrangements?"

"What do you mean?"

"Well, legally, both parents must sign the relinquishment papers in an adoption. There have been some cases lately, awful cases, where the father's signature was never obtained and the adoption was reversed. It's devastating. Of course, if the father has truly abandoned you, we can have the court terminate his rights."

"Oh," B.G. said, "I get it. Well, my boyfriend's gone, all right. But if by some chance he came back, don't worry. He'd sign the papers. He doesn't want this baby."

"All right, that sounds fine, then. And, B.G., if he contacts you, I'd be careful about telling him much regarding our arrangements. They're between you and me."

"What arrangements, Ms. Jacobs?"

"I have a house where you can live for free until you deliver. I'll pay all your expenses—well, the prospective parents actually will do it through me. All your doctor bills will be covered, and you'll get an allowance."

"Uh-huh."

"You don't sound sure, B.G. Is there a problem?"

"I'm really broke, Ms. Jacobs. I thought... well, I kind of wanted to be able to start out with a little nest egg once I have the baby," she said hesitantly.

"Of course you do. There will be compensation for you, certainly." Grace hated to talk numbers, especially so early in the game.

B.G. cocked her head and regarded her. "Like, uh, can you give me an idea how much?"

Grace waved a hand. "I'll have to talk to the adoptive family about that. But I'm sure they'll be amenable."

"Do you know yet who would get my baby? Do I have any say in it?"

This was a sharp one, Grace thought. Careful. "I'm not sure yet. I'll have to see your papers when you fill them out, try to match your baby to the best family. But yes, you have a say to a certain extent. You can even meet the people if you want."

"I can?" B.G. seemed stunned. "They'd want to meet me?"

"Oh, yes. Most of my clients are very interested in meeting the birth mothers."

"Oh." B.G. looked at her hands and spoke softly. "There is something. See, I already have a place to live for free. I'd like to stay there. I hope that isn't going to cause trouble."

"Ah." Grace preferred the girls under her thumb, where Maureen could keep a close eye on them. She liked to isolate them, especially from family members, who might try to persuade them to keep their babies. Still, this one was too good to quibble about details. "Give me an idea of your living arrangements."

"I'm in my grandma's house. It's up off Miracle Mile. She goes to Colorado for the summer. I mean, Ms. Jacobs, I'm no teenager. I want my privacy, you know."

"I understand. You live alone?"

"Yes. I'm new to Tucson. I don't know a soul here. Well, that's why I came here, to tell the truth."

"Parents?"

She ducked her head again. "Divorced. I was a navy brat. God knows where they are now."

"Do they know about the baby?"

"No." Her voice was sullen.

Better and better, Grace thought. She was all alone. Oh, the Levys were going to love this one. "One more thing. Have you been to a doctor? I have a very good one I recommend to my girls."

"Yes, I've been. I like the one I'm going to. I'd rather not change."

"That's fine. As long as the baby's healthy. Eventually I'd like to see your medical records. You can ask your doctor to send them to me."

"Okay."

Grace stood up and walked around her desk to put a hand on B.G.'s shoulder. "Now, B.G., how are you managing financially? You mentioned you were broke."

"I am. My grandma sends me money for the house, but I'm really hurting. I can't even buy any clothes, and I outgrow everything."

She did look shabby, dressed in shorts and a big T-shirt that had seen better days. "I can certainly help you out there. Tell you what, you start working on the papers you have to fill out, and once you're done, I'll write you a check to hold you over for a while. How's that?"

"Can I have five hundred dollars? I need some clothes, and I owe the doctor."

"I don't see why not." This girl was no dummy, Grace thought. She'd have to be handled carefully. She went back around her desk and found the correct file, pulled out a set of papers. "Here we go."

The papers were very thorough, a biography of the girl—age, height, weight, eye color, hair, ethnic background of her and the father, religion, health, drug use, school history and activities, jobs, siblings and health, their own and their parents. It usually took the girls quite a while to fill them out. Grace busied herself at her desk, glancing up from time to time to study her newest catch.

B.G. stopped and looked up as she came to a form letter. "I have to sign this?"

Grace glanced at the paper B.G. held up. "Yes, that's routine. It starts the whole process, the whole legal process. I'll sign it, too."

B.G. read out loud: "'This letter is to confirm agreement with regard to placing my as yet unborn child for adoption. The adoptive parents will pay expenses...' and so on. But this part—" she pointed "—says I have to pay back all the expenses if I fail to surrender the child."

Grace said offhandedly, "Oh, that's just a precaution. It never happens."

"No one ever decides to keep her baby after it's born?"

"I try to screen my girls very carefully, B.G. It's a very serious thing to make a promise, to sign a legal contract, and then break it. I want all my girls to be sure before I take them on. You do understand, don't you?"

B.G. was looking at her. "Oh, I won't change my mind, if that's what you're worried about. I've had six whole months to decide."

"That's what I like to hear." Grace smiled. "So go ahead and sign the letter, then I'll sign it and give you a copy to keep."

B.G. signed the letter and put the stack of forms she'd filled out on the desk. "Whew, that's a lot of paperwork."

"I'm very thorough, dear. We're talking about people's lives here, so I have to be careful."

"When will I find out who the family will be?" B.G. asked. "The one who'll get my baby?"

"Very soon. I'll let you know the minute I decide." Grace cocked her head and said sweetly, "They have to get ready, too, you know. Buy a crib and baby clothes. They get so excited it's as if they're going through the pregnancy themselves. These people have waited so long, you know. Years, some of them."

"Uh-huh. Well, I wish I could give my baby to them right now and not have to worry about it anymore. It's easy for them to get excited. They don't have to walk around like a cow and look forward to going through labor. I mean, it's a really hard thing to do, and here I am broke and not a friend in the world."

"I know, dear, I know. But you'll see, I'll work very hard to make it all worthwhile. You are, after all, in possession of a very precious commodity."

When Bettie Gay Bryson was gone, five-hundred-dollar check stashed in her purse, Grace turned her swivel chair and gazed out toward the ragged gray silhouette of the Santa Catalina Mountains north of the city, a self-satisfied smile curving her lips. Then she turned back to her desk, pressed the intercom button and asked Debbie to get the Levys on the phone.

"Good news, Sarah," Grace said, "the best news. By mid-August you're going to be a mother."

"Oh, my God," Sarah said, her voice breaking. "Oh, my God."

B.G. FINISHED her morning cup of coffee and stared out her back window at a wren pecking at something on the ocotillo cactus. Whiskers purred on her lap, and she stroked his tattered ears. She mulled over yesterday's happenings, remembering Greg's reaction with a mixture of pleasure and regret.

He'd picked her up as arranged several blocks from Grace's office, and he'd been grinning from ear to ear. "Good work, B.G.," he exclaimed. "You got more than I ever expected."

She hadn't answered for a minute, only reached under her T-shirt and unclipped the tiny microphone, then tugged, pulling the tape and wires off. "Boy, am I glad to have that stuff off. I kept thinking she'd notice it any second!"

"I told you she wouldn't be able to tell," Greg said smugly.

"I was scared, though. She has X-ray eyes."

"You did great."

"Thanks." She felt absolutely worn-out.

"We got every word without a hitch, clear as day. I could even hear you breathing," he said.

"I didn't sound nervous?"

"No, you're a pro, B.G., a real pro. Cool as a cucumber."

"I was sure nervous at first," she said, luxuriating in his approval.

"Well, we've got her now," Greg said.

"You mean that's it? I got what you need?" B.G. had asked, suddenly alarmed, her bubble burst. He only wanted her for what she could do for him, after all. She had to keep reminding herself of that.

"No, of course not," he said. "We need more. We need numbers. We need names. The more we get the better."

She sat here in her kitchen now, her baby, Kathryn, moving inside her, Whiskers vibrating against her in his pleasure, and she wondered if Greg would have dropped her like a hot potato if she hadn't come through for him yesterday. Well, terrific, so she was good at something in her life—acting out a lie, deceiving a smart lady like Grace Jacobs. No, she was good at two things—the second was getting pregnant. What career options did those talents leave her?

She sighed and stood up, Whiskers jumping to the ground soundlessly, and took her breakfast dishes to the sink. Greg. He only thought of her as a tool, just as Grace Jacobs did. She wasn't a person to either of them; she was a commodity to buy and sell. She tried to remind herself that what Grace was doing was immoral, not to mention illegal, and what she herself was doing was helping to put a stop to Grace's activities. She was on the side of the good guys. But when it came down to how she really felt, all she could think of was Greg and how he was only using her. How he didn't give two hoots about how she felt or what happened to her after her job for him was done.

She washed and stacked the dishes, and when she turned away from the sink she thought she heard a

knock at her front door. She listened. Yes, definitely
a knock. Greg? Had he come this early in the morning to see how she was? But no, he'd said he wouldn't
be coming here anymore now that she'd contacted Jacobs.

A neighbor?

B.G. went to the door and pulled it open, and there
on her doorstep, between her pots of geraniums, stood
Grace Jacobs.

"Oh," B.G. said, her heart leaping into her throat.

"Good morning, B.G. I didn't wake you, did I?"

"Oh, no, I was... Uh, come in."

Grace smiled, very fresh-looking at this early hour,
very beautiful in her cool blond elegant way. "I'm an
early riser. I like to get things done in the morning. I
hope you don't mind."

"No, I don't mind." B.G. tried to smile. All she
could think was that this wasn't being recorded; there
was no way she could get it on tape without the van.
And, my God, what if Greg *did* show up?

Grace was standing in the middle of her small brown
living room, perfectly relaxed, not the least self-
conscious. She wore a steel blue gabardine suit, tai-
lored but feminine, and her ash blond hair was pulled
back into a French twist. Small pearl earrings adorned
her earlobes. B.G. felt utterly tacky next to her. And
scared to death. What was Jacobs doing here?

"Please sit down," B.G. said. "Can I get you
something?"

"No, nothing, dear. I just stopped by for a minute.
I like to keep a close eye on my girls. I want to make
sure your surroundings are...comfortable. Healthy.

After all—'' she shook a manicured finger at B.G. ''—I have an investment in you now.''

''Oh,'' B.G. said, trying to gather her wits.

''And I have good news for you, B.G.'' Grace sat and put the briefcase she carried on her lap. She snapped it open and reached inside for some papers. ''I have a family for your baby. A wonderful family.''

''Already?'' B.G. asked.

''Oh, these people have been pestering me for months, calling and calling. When I saw you yesterday I just knew you were perfect for them. So I phoned, and they're, well, they're just ecstatic.'' She handed a folder to B.G. ''Here's their application. Read it, and you'll agree with me that these are the best parents your baby could ever have.''

B.G. took the folder and opened it. There was the application, filled out in neat printing: Mel Levy, Sarah Levy, 10375 Monte Vista, La Jolla, California. Income, education, jobs, personal descriptions, hobbies, sports, associations they belonged to, elected positions held. Everything. And then, on the third page, a typed letter describing how the Levys lived and how much they wanted children, saying they had a room set aside, a college fund started.

It was all there, the ultimate misery of a couple who couldn't conceive a baby, their hopes and dreams, their desperation.

B.G. read the letter, her eyes filling with tears, burning. These people, Mel and Sarah, would make wonderful parents. They'd give a child a real home with all the advantages, so much better than B.G.

could ever provide. How she wanted a couple just like this for Kathryn!

"Aren't they terrific?" Grace finally asked. "Wealthy, cultured. A stable marriage. You see where Sarah is head of her local art museum fund-raising drive? And he's in the Young Presidents program. Very special people."

"Yes," B.G. whispered.

"They want to meet you," Grace said. "They're very anxious to talk to you."

B.G. steeled herself and looked up at Grace. "What do they want to say?"

"Oh, nothing specific. They just want to see you. They're willing to talk support, anything you need. I've seen to it they understand your situation."

"You mean money?"

"They want to help you, B.G.," Grace said firmly.

"I hope they're not stingy," B.G. said, hating what she was going to do to these people.

"I assure you they're willing to pay almost anything to get a baby, dear."

"Good."

"I'm going to make arrangements for them to come here to visit you. I'll let you know exactly when."

"You mean here, at my house?"

"No, no. I mean Tucson. They'll come here and probably take you out, say to dinner or something. It's best to meet on neutral ground the first time."

"Okay."

"Well, I'm so happy for all of you. I get a real kick out of getting people together like this." Grace stood, brushed imaginary wrinkles out of her skirt. "I better get to the office. Now, don't forget to have your doctor send your records to me. The Levys asked for them. And the father—they're worried about him not being available to sign the papers. I assured them it'd be no problem, but if you hear from him, let me know." She picked up her briefcase and started toward the door. "Keep the Levys' application. It's a copy." She stopped in the center of the living room and glanced around. "It's a nice little house, your grandmother's. What did you say her name was?"

"Kathryn Bryson."

"Can't take the heat, I suppose," Grace said.

"No, she hates the summers here."

"It takes some getting used to, it's true, but you know, I've come to really like the heat. It can be overwhelming, but it's, I don't know, powerful." She smiled. "Well, take care of yourself, B.G. I'll be phoning you soon. About the Levys."

B.G. sank onto the couch after Grace left. Wow. The woman was smooth. She'd shown up without warning to check her out, just as Greg had warned her. Was Grace suspicious? B.G. thought back, going over every word she'd said, every nuance of Grace's conversation. Asking her grandmother's name. Testing, probing. Sweet as pie but calculating. B.G. was sure she'd said nothing to arouse the woman's suspicions. She'd have to be careful, though. And Greg was right about not coming to her house anymore. Grace could make another surprise visit anytime.

She let out a breath and pushed herself off the couch. She had to call Greg and tell him. Right now.

She got him on his cellular phone as he was driving to work. She could hear his car radio blaring until he turned it off. "Tyrrell." That deep resonant voice.

"She was just here," B.G. said. "Grace Jacobs."

"At your house?"

"Yes. She showed up. Big surprise. I almost fainted."

"What'd she want?"

"To check me out, Greg. I know it."

"How'd it go?" His voice was tight, his words clipped.

"Okay, I think. No, I'm sure it was okay."

"Damn, and nothing on tape."

"No." She hesitated, then, "Greg, she has a family for my baby. They're going to come here to Tucson."

"Uh-huh. Listen, B.G., we better get together. I need to know every word you said. I'm real tied up today, but tonight . . ."

"Okay, but you can't come here."

"Obviously not a good idea. So, my place, then. Meet me at the mall, the usual spot. Six, no, six-thirty."

"Okay."

"See you then. Gotta go, B.G."

SARAH LEVY hung up the phone and turned to her husband. She was crying. "We're going to meet her, honey. We're going to actually see her and our baby."

"It's not ours yet, Sarah," Mel said.

"But it will be, won't it? Promise me, Mel, no bargaining, no arguing. Whatever she wants, however much, just pay it."

"It's illegal, Sarah."

"I don't care. I want a baby. I have to have a baby. Mel, honey, please, you know how desperate I am."

He took his petite red-haired wife in his arms. "Shush now. You know I'll do whatever it takes. I want a baby, too."

"Grace Jacobs told me we could meet her, go to Tucson and see her."

"Is that a good idea?"

"It's done all the time. Don't you want to see if she's pretty or ugly?"

"When do we do this?" Mel asked.

"Grace will make the arrangements and let us know."

"I wish we could get a baby the old-fashioned way," he said.

"We tried, honey, and it didn't work," Sarah said in a bitter tone, surprising in view of her little-girl voice. "So we'll just have to do it this way. But no matter what, I'm going to get a baby."

CHAPTER THIRTEEN

GREG HAD A PROBLEM. He'd had lots of them in his life, and he'd always found a solution. But this time he couldn't see a way out.

The problem was his mental preoccupation with Bettie Gay Bryson. It was making him crazy. She was pretty, sure, but certainly not the most beautiful woman he'd been around. True, she had a quick mind, a natural intelligence he admired, but she wasn't the brainiest woman he'd ever known certainly. And obviously it wasn't money that attracted him. She was penniless. Broke and seven months pregnant with that jerk's baby.

She was all wrong for him and for the goals he'd set himself, yet she captivated his imagination. She was innocent and naive and in some ways a victim of life. But on the other side, she was tough and resilient, brave and a true scrapper. Life had thrown her a lot of curves, but she'd survived. He thought about her declaration that once her job was finished with the county attorney, she was going to continue her education. She would, too, Greg knew it. She was that kind of person, and he admired her no end for that.

He drove toward his folks' after work that early-June day and couldn't stop thinking about the many facets of Bettie Gay. What was it that made him want to hold and protect her and punch out Jay's lights, while at the same instant he could appreciate that she was as strong and able as anyone he'd ever met?

His mom was out back watering the yard when he got there.

"Oh, Greg," she said, holding the hose, "I didn't expect you tonight. What a nice surprise."

He kissed her on the cheek. "I just stopped by. Can't stay."

"Not even for dinner?"

"Not even for your chicken. I smelled it when I came through the kitchen."

"That's too bad," she said. "Sandy and her family are coming over."

"What's the occasion?" he asked, helping her roll up the hose.

"No occasion. We just don't see enough of each other it seems, and we decided to get together no matter what once a week."

"Maybe I'll try to join the once-a-week crowd when I'm done with the bar exam," he said.

"How's the studying going?"

"Long and slow. I've been putting in a lot of time at the law library."

She smiled warmly as they walked back inside. "You'll do fine."

"I sure hope so," he said.

While Greg snacked on a couple of homemade cookies, his mother fussed at the stove. Then, in a neutral voice, she said, "How's your friend, B.G.? She's such a sweet girl. Everyone's asked about her."

"She's fine," he said. "In fact, I'm picking her up in a few minutes." When he saw the slightest raise of his mother's brow, he laughed. "It's business, Mom. I can't go into detail, but she's doing a job for my office."

"Oh."

"I brought her here to dinner because she was new in town. Doesn't really know anyone."

"Well, that was kind of you."

"Yeah," he said, "I'm a real kind guy."

He checked his watch and left shortly, still needing to stop at the store before picking B.G. up at the mall. He wasn't sure why he'd gone by his folks', and guessed it had been just to say hello. Or, maybe, he realized with a mild jolt, he'd wanted his mother to mention B.G. so he could talk about her. He could use an ear right now. But he'd chickened out. And talking to his mother about it . . . He really was in a state over this girl.

Greg pulled up to the southeast entrance of the mall a couple of minutes early. He left the car idling and watched for B.G.'s bus, as always wishing he could meet her at her house and save her this extra hassle.

She was pregnant, after all. Really pregnant now, her belly starting to round out like a perfect globe. She still worked, though, and never complained.

He sat there and couldn't stop remembering the doctor's words: *It's perfectly all right to continue to have intercourse.* Dr. Resniak had assumed he was her husband, the father of her baby. Didn't the doctor read his patients' records, for God's sake?

Of course, in many ways, Greg was much more a father to B.G.'s baby than this Jay was. Greg was *there*. He was the one arranging for her support. He was the one holding her hand at the doctor's office. He was the one she called first if a problem arose. He was the one who saw her belly grow, saw her suffer from the heat, and he was the one who had to worry about her health, her safety, her welfare.

He tried to push away the notion the doctor had etched indelibly in his mind. Sex. But it refused to go away, and sweat broke out on the back of his neck despite all his efforts to forget it. Sex with B.G.... He couldn't allow himself to imagine such a thing. First, she was pregnant. But more importantly, she was working for him, had contracted to do this job. What kind of an ass would he be if he took advantage of her?

On the other hand he most certainly could imagine making love to B.G. Something told him it would be beautiful, touching her, feeling the tender swollen flesh beneath him—

A tap on the passenger-door window startled him, and he sucked in a ragged breath.

"Hi," B.G. mouthed through the glass. "Want to let me in?"

And then she was sitting next to him, the car's air-conditioner fanning their faces. "Feels good," she said, giving him a smile. "The one on the bus was broken, and everyone was griping up a storm."

For a moment Greg stared at her almost in wonder. He took in the flush of her skin and the shine of her rich brown hair, the way a few strands had escaped the braid and lay on her neck. The curve of her bare shoulders and the way her long white cotton blouse fell over the fullness of her stomach. She was wearing a very short skirt, and her pale legs glowed in the dry heat, as if she'd just put lotion on them. Everything about her seemed slight and delicate and unutterably feminine: her slender fingers and forearms, her neck, the hollows beneath her high cheekbones. He couldn't help remembering the first moment he'd seen her, in the interrogation room, the manner in which she'd held her chin up, her full lower lip trembling. He'd wanted to protect her then. He still did.

His eyes lifted to hers. "What?" she said, a bewildered half smile on her lips. "Do I have spinach caught in my teeth or something?"

Greg shook himself mentally. He laughed and put the car in gear. "No," he said, "it's nothing like that."

"You were looking at me funny."

"Was I?"

"Yes."

"Sorry" was his only comment.

He cooked dinner—vegetables and pasta with a cream sauce that came in a container—while B.G. sat on a stool at the counter, recounting—almost word for word—her conversation with Grace Jacobs at her house that morning.

"...then she talked about her girls living a healthy life-style, how she liked to keep a close eye on them. She kept smiling and looking around the living room, as if she was filing stuff away in her head."

"She's a cool customer," Greg said.

B.G. nodded. "I wouldn't put anything past her." She paused. "The people who want my baby are from California. La Jolla. Their names are Sarah and Mel Levy."

Greg strained the pasta in the sink and listened intently. When B.G. was done, he said, "I can't believe you remember all that in such detail. You'd be an excellent witness."

She chewed on a piece of celery. "I have a good memory." She shrugged. "Maybe it's from all those years of remembering orders in the restaurant, I don't know."

"Whatever, it's quite a talent."

She shrugged and then a frown crossed her features. "I don't know about meeting these people, Greg, the ones who want my baby. It's... well, it's going to be hard to look them in the eye and lie, let them believe their dream's going to come true."

Greg stopped what he was doing and faced her. "They know it's illegal, B.G."

"Maybe they don't."

"Bullshit," he said. "They have to know that paying an exorbitant fee for a child is tantamount to slavery. Plus, they aren't even seeking a child in California. Ask yourself why."

"I suppose."

"Don't feel bad for them," he said. "At least not for going to Jacobs to buy a baby. There are other ways. Legal ways. And there are orphanages packed with kids desperate for love and a good home."

"It's not the same," she said quietly. "My baby will be... well, just born. Minutes old, you know."

He watched her closely, and he knew she was ready
to cry, but God, how she could control her tears. He'd
never known a woman who could do that. Vulnerable
and kindhearted and yet so strong.

They sat in the alcove off the kitchen and ate, Greg
having a beer with his food, B.G. an iced tea. She
didn't say anything more about the prospective parents, but he could tell how upset she was. It was
something no one had counted on. And truth was, he
felt a lot more sympathy for the Levys than he'd let on
to B.G. In this baby-for-sale business, too many got
hurt. For now, though, he needed to bolster B.G.'s resolve. And not just where the Levys were concerned.
It was becoming more and more apparent that B.G.
was having a lot of second thoughts about giving her
child up for a legal adoption. It tore at Greg's heart,
too. But hell, how on earth would she manage? What
sort of life would she and a child have? The only answer was welfare. And with B.G., that was not even an
option.

Not his problem, Greg had to tell himself. B.G. had
gotten herself in this fix, and the deal the county attorney had offered her was still as fair as she could
have hoped for. *You bet,* Greg thought. *B.G. took up
with that pretty-faced boy and now she's paying the
price. It could've turned out a whole lot worse. She
could've married him.*

While they ate, they talked about the mundane,
about Tucson and the weather, the freak late-spring
storm that had just struck the Colorado mountains.

"In June, no less," B.G. said, her fork poised in midair. "My grandma up in Colorado must be hating it."

"Your... Oh, right," he said, "your grandmother in Colorado."

"See? I have it down pat at all times."

"You certainly do," he agreed, and she smiled at him and then quickly dropped her gaze. She looked so pretty to him at his table that he couldn't help thinking how right it was for her to be there. He'd never tried to imagine the woman he'd someday marry, the woman he'd live with the rest of his life. The concept of a wife had never been one he'd even considered. But if he let himself, he could imagine B.G. in his life, in his home. He could see her fitting right in, cooking in his kitchen, sitting on his couch, driving his car.

Sleeping in his bed.

He drew in a breath and looked at her again, at her bowed head and the shining dark hair, and he realized with surprise that her pregnancy didn't matter to him; the baby was hers, and he'd seen her grow with it. He'd even seen the baby move and suck her thumb, for God's sake, and he felt a peculiar possessiveness toward the child. Irrational, nonsensical, but undeniable.

It was also ludicrous, the idea of him and B.G.

Later she helped with the dinner dishes, and then they walked out to the pool area at the complex with cups of coffee. They sat in recliners and quietly watched the sunset.

"This is a beautiful spot," B.G. said wistfully. "But I suppose you'll move when you get a law practice going."

"I'd like a house, sure. Why not?"

"No reason. If you can afford it, go for it."

"I intend to."

She sighed and then gave a short laugh. "And here I am happy as a lark in the bungalow. I think it's the greatest place."

"That's because it's the first time you've ever had a place of your own," he said, staring at the lavender sky. "But you'll do fine, B.G., once this is all over."

"I don't know," she said, and she took a long sip of her coffee, holding the mug with both hands. "I know I want to finish school and all that, but sometimes I think that... well... Oh, never mind..." Her voice trailed away.

"No, go on," he said.

"It's stupid."

"Tell me what you were going to say."

She was very quiet for a moment, and then it just seemed to spill out of her. "I think I should keep my baby. I try to work out in my head how I could make ends meet. I keep thinking there's got to be a way... Oh, heck," she said, sitting up, "I know it's impossible. We'd be poor as church mice." Then she rose to her feet, awkwardly, tears shining in her eyes.

"B.G.," he said softly, also rising, but she was crossing the flagstones, heading back to his condo, shaking her head. *Damn,* he thought, following, tossing the rest of his coffee into the sandy garden.

By the time he caught up to her, she'd grabbed her purse and was heading out his front door. Gently he took hold of her arm, trying to stop her. "Hey," he said, "come on, B.G. What you're feeling is perfectly understandable."

"Please let me go," she said. There was a catch in her voice.

But he closed the door and made her face him. "Come on, B.G., you can't just go off like this."

She ducked her head. "I just want to catch the bus and go home."

"I'll drive you," he said. "But I don't want you to go off alone as upset as you are."

Suddenly she raised her eyes to his. "You don't know anything about how I'm feeling or what I'm thinking."

"Maybe I do," he said carefully.

But she shook her head. "I just want to be alone." And then she disengaged her arm from his grasp and opened the door again.

Greg could see her shoulders shaking and the awful time she was having trying to stop a flood of tears. A dam inside him broke.

"Ah, hell," he said gruffly, and he took her shoulders and spun her around, kicking his door shut. "Let it out, B.G. For God's sake just let it out."

For a terrible moment she merely stood there as rigid as a statue, her eyes shining, a tremble coursing through her.

"Let it out," Greg said again, a whisper, and he pulled her against his chest, his arms going around her back, imprisoning her. At last he felt the huge sob well up inside her and burst forth. He held her tighter, his lips against her hair, and she wept. He felt more helpless than he'd ever felt in his life.

After a minute, one arm still cradling B.G., he got her to the couch and they sat. He stroked her hair, her slender back, and repeated, "It's okay, it's okay."

Between hiccuping sobs, she got out a torrent of suppressed emotions. "If only I could keep her...I'm so embarrassed... It's all so useless..."

He never knew whether it was B.G. who finally tipped her face up to his, or whether it was he who cupped her face in his hands, but somehow they were looking into each other's eyes. And then he kissed her.

At first it was the barest brush of their lips, his hesitant, hers trembling. But then something shifted. Before either of them could stop it or even think about the consequences, their kiss became passionate, their hands quickening on each other, searching, grasping, Greg for the first time touching her heavy breasts, fumbling with the buttons on her blouse, B.G. helping him, their mouths locked, their breathing fast.

He lowered his head to her neck, found the rapid pulse above her collarbone, the warm sweet swell of her breasts. He reached around her and quickly unsnapped her bra, and she fell back against the cushions, moaned while his mouth found a dark full nipple.

Greg drank her in. The incredible heavy soft warmth of her breasts. His mouth moved over her, one hand cupping that heaviness, the other venturing gently to her belly. He knew a beauty then that he'd only imagined before. She was everything he'd dared to dream. More. A tenderness toward her rushed through him, a forbidden craving to know all of her.

After a time he raised his head and they kissed again and again, whispering against each other's lips, his hands still on her breasts, her soft moaning a tune ringing in his head, driving him to a pitch of desire only one thing could satisfy...

HE PICKED HER UP, one arm beneath her knees, the other beneath her neck, and carried her, unprotesting, to his bedroom, where he lay her carefully on his bed. The only light came from the living-room lamp, which spilled softly through the half-open door and fell tenderly on her naked body.

Standing over the bed, his eyes on her, he took off his own clothes. Shirt, trousers, underwear. And then, while she watched, he lay down next to her and put a hand on the hard globe of her belly. "I won't hurt you?" he asked, and his hand moved upward, across the hollow to her breasts. He leaned into her, cupping a breast, drawing the nipple into his mouth.

"No," she whispered, "you won't hurt me, Greg. I want you, too."

He kissed every inch of her, from her lips to her neck, his mouth lingering on her breasts, her belly. He lowered himself onto the bed and kissed the warm flesh of her inner thighs until she arched her back and cried out.

He kissed her knees and moved upward again, his hand on her hot moistness, and then he eased himself over her, his belly just touching hers, her hands on his hips, guiding him.

They were very, very careful. His movements slow and deliberate, Greg entered her. Sweat broke out of every pore on his body as he held himself in check, afraid he'd hurt her, wanting her more desperately than he'd wanted anyone or anything in his life.

They moved together, Greg kissing her, feeling their sweat mingle, the hard bulge of her belly against his, an indescribable sensation that was wildly erotic to him, making him want to move inside her more quickly.

But he didn't. And the act of holding back took him to a height he'd never known. And then she was moaning and sobbing out his name and clutching him to her, her back arching, her breath labored. He pushed more deeply into her one last time, and his senses seemed to explode . . .

GREG JERKED bolt upright in bed and gasped as if he'd been punched in the gut. He was soaked in sweat. His head, his body, the sheets. There was light seeping in the windows, a pale light. Dawn.

"Dear God," he whispered, running his hands through his damp hair. It was a dream! He'd dreamed the whole thing!

Shaken, disoriented, it was long minutes before he could stumble into the bathroom and splash cold water on his face and neck. His knees were so weak he thought he might collapse right there.

A goddamn dream.

He showered shortly thereafter, still trying to free himself from the erotic hold of the dream, both hands against the back wall of the tiled stall, the cool water beating on his back.

Later, towel around his torso, he padded into the kitchen and made coffee. His glance strayed to the couch then, the pillows still disarranged. It hadn't all been a dream, he knew and remembering, he felt his stomach seize up.

Last night...he and B.G. on the couch. They'd kissed. Somehow they'd let it go a lot farther. He'd taken off her bra, touched her...

But he'd stopped there, catching himself, getting control. He'd been angry, too, but not at B.G. He could never be angry at her. But he'd been a real jerk, taking cruel advantage of her when her defenses were down.

He'd cursed and gotten up from the couch, pulling her with him, hastily helping her rearrange her clothes. But B.G. hadn't understood his anger, even when he'd given her that fumbling explanation.

"I'm an idiot," he'd said, trying to apologize. But she'd thought it was all her fault somehow, and she simply hadn't understood that he had a job to do, that he'd compromised her.

He'd driven her to the bus stop at the mall then and watched her get on safely, still beating himself up mentally. Some evening that had been.

Now Greg drove to work trying to put everything into perspective. It was no easy task. The trouble was, he could pull *himself* back together and stay clear on what it was he had to accomplish, but what about B.G.? As fragile as she was right now, Greg had to wonder if he'd blown the whole operation.

"Swell," he muttered, trying to sort everything out in his head, trying to feel in control again—when all he could really think about was that dream.

CHAPTER FOURTEEN

B.G. FELT DREADFUL the next morning. She hadn't slept all night, and her eyes were swollen from crying. She couldn't eat, couldn't think, couldn't hardly summon up the energy to get out of bed. The baby kicked and squirmed more than usual, and she felt gross and bloated.

She'd replayed the previous evening in her mind a hundred times, wondering, agonizing, searching for a way out of the impossible situation. How could she ever face Greg again? He must be so disgusted with her—a pregnant woman throwing herself at him. He must think that was what she'd done before, that was how she'd gotten pregnant in the first place.

She sat in the morning coolness of her backyard, still in her bathrobe, staring unfocused into the distance. Even Whiskers avoided her, as if feeling her mood. He sat in a beam of sunshine, licking a black velvet paw, his tail twitching.

It had been so good for a moment last night, so sweet. Greg had held her, and she'd thought he cared. She'd cried in his arms, sobbed helplessly, a thing she'd sworn never to do. She'd thought he really cared; he'd sounded as if he did. But in the end he'd only been using her, and he'd finally pushed her away and cursed.

I'm an idiot, he'd said, gallantly blaming himself. Well, she knew he didn't really believe that. And she'd never ever give Greg even a glimpse of her feelings again. Provided, of course, he could even bear to see her again, provided the operation was still on. Oh, God.

Whiskers turned his head toward the back door, and his ears twitched forward. And then B.G. heard something. Someone was knocking at her front door.

Greg. Her heart leapt in sudden hope, then faltered. No, he wouldn't take the chance of coming here, no matter what. So who...?

Slowly, ponderously, she pushed herself up and went into the bungalow. The knocking on her front door increased.

"Okay, okay," she said, "I'm coming."

She pulled the door open and felt herself go hot, then cold and trembly.

It was Jay.

"For God's sake, what took you so long?" were the first words out of his mouth.

"Jay," she whispered.

"Well, B.G., you gonna ask me in? Man, have you gotten fat!"

She looked down at the bulge her stomach made under her robe and flushed. Jay hadn't seen her for three months.

He strode past her into the living room and looked around. "Hey, not bad, baby. You're doin' okay."

"Jay—"

"C'mere," he said, turning to her and holding out his arms, so handsome, so damn sexy with that irreverent grin and long blond hair, the cowboy hat with its brim curled just so and the tight, tight jeans.

And then she was in his arms, her big belly pressed against him, and he felt so good, smelled so good, so familiar.

"Oh, Jay, what are you doing here?" she asked, her voice muffled against his chest.

"Well, now, I couldn't call, could I? You don't have a phone, you said. And I finally got enough bread together to get another car."

She pushed away from him. "You could've called me at work."

Shame-faced, he said, "I lost the number. You know how I am, B.G. I lose stuff like that." Then he held her at arm's length and studied her. "You look good, B.G. Fat, but good."

"I'm almost seven months pregnant, Jay. I'm not fat."

He was in one of his better moods, playful, charming, adorable. He patted her stomach. "That's my kid in there. Wow, it's really getting big, isn't it?" He pulled her close and gave her a hug. "God, I'm starved. Got anything to eat?"

Jay. He hadn't changed. But B.G. had. She'd been in another man's arms last night, and she was giving up Jay's baby for adoption, and she was involved in the Grace Jacobs sting—and Jay didn't know about any of it. The guilt she felt was almost overwhelming, as if she'd betrayed both Jay and Greg at the same time.

Jay dropped onto the couch and swung his scuffed cowboy boots up onto the coffee table, tilted his hat back with a thumb. "What're you still doing in your bathrobe at this hour, baby?"

"I . . . I didn't sleep well last night. I didn't feel so great this morning."

"Well, you better take care of yourself and that kid of mine. You know, B.G., it never seemed real before, but now with you so huge, I'm beginning to believe it. I'm gonna be a daddy."

No, you're not! she wanted to cry.

He patted the cushion next to him. "Sit down. Food can wait."

She sat. He put his hand on her knee possessively. "So, how'd you get this place? And the job? Boy, I sure was glad to hear you were doing okay. I was a real ass back there, wasn't I?"

"You sure were."

"Yeah, I know. So, tell me, how'd you score this place?"

She sat there and looked at his hand on her knee, her eyes burning with tears. "You really want to know, Jay?"

"Yeah, 'course I do." Then he gave her a swift look, and his eyebrows drew together. "There's no guy, is there? You're not living with some goddamn sugar daddy?"

B.G. put her face in her hands, not sure whether to laugh or cry. "Oh, Lord, Jay."

"Well, are you?"

"No, there's no sugar daddy."

"Good thing, baby."

"Jay, you're so...so damn irresponsible!" She took her hands away from her face and felt her cheeks grow hot with anger and near-hysteria. "Jay, you left me to get arrested. I spent the day in jail! What was I supposed to do? I was alone, broke, pregnant, accessory to armed robbery."

"Yeah, well, you got out of it."

"You know how? Do you really want to know how I got out of it?" She turned toward him, her fists clenched. "They put me in this room and gave me the third degree. I was scared, Jay. I was so scared. I didn't give them your name. I wouldn't tell them, and they threatened me. And then—" she sniffed and held a finger under her nose "—they sent a guy in with a deal."

"What do you mean, a deal?"

She looked down at her hands in her lap. "They needed a pregnant girl for this job. A sting, really. There's this lady lawyer who adopts out babies illegally, and they needed someone to go to her with a wire and get evidence against her."

Jay stared at B.G., his mouth open. "You?"

"Yes, me. I get this house, my doctor bills are paid, everything."

"They got you to do this, like some kind of undercover agent?"

She gave a short laugh. "That's me, Bettie Gay the undercover agent."

"Man, B.G., I can't believe it. You." He ran his hand over his face. "Who do you work for?"

"The Pima County Attorney."

Jay was silent a moment. "This, this lawyer, what does she do that's illegal?"

"She charges the adoptive parents a whole lot of money, pays the mothers, which is illegal. Falsifies legal papers. Makes the adoptive parents lie in court. All kinds of stuff."

"What's her name?"

"Grace Jacobs."

"Some smart cookie, huh?" Jay remarked.

B.G. shivered. "She's scary."

Then Jay shook his head. "B.G., you know, the cops didn't have a thing on you. They couldn't have held you. I mean, all you did in that store was go to the bathroom. You really are dumb sometimes. I can't believe it."

"I am not dumb, Jay. And even if they hadn't arrested me, where was I supposed to go? I didn't have a cent to my name. You even took off with my clothes. Jay, you left me totally stranded!"

"Yeah, yeah, I know. I told you—"

"I did what I thought was right. I'm supporting myself."

"Don't hand me the old guilt trip, baby. I'm doing okay now."

"So am I," she said.

"Well, B.G., I came down here to see if you wanted to go back to Phoenix with me, and here you are being a brat." His tone was injured, his blue eyes shining with indignation.

Her heart gave a treacherous thump, then sanity returned. "I can't, Jay. I have this deal, this job. I can't leave till it's over."

"And I sure as hell can't stick around Tucson. Even if I got a gig. Hell, B.G., you're working for the cops!"

"The county attorney. It's not the police."

He waved his hand dismissively. "Same thing." He stared at his boots for a minute, thinking, then he looked up. "You've been to this lady lawyer, this Jacobs woman?"

"Yes."

"So—" Jay put his feet on the floor and leaned his elbows on his knees "—how much is she going to pay you for the kid?"

He might as well have punched her in the face. "You'd sell our baby, wouldn't you? Anything for money, right?" B.G. stood up and looked down at him angrily. "Well, I have to tell you something, Jay. This baby's mine, and you don't have a thing to say about her. I've already got it all arranged. I'm adopting her out. I'm not keeping her, and that's that."

"How do you know it's a girl?" he asked mildly.

"What do you care?"

"Give me some credit, B.G. It's my kid, too."

"It isn't your kid, Jay, unless you pay for the doctor and take care of her and support her and worry about her. You're no father, not one bit."

"You sign any papers yet? About adopting the kid out, I mean."

"Jay!"

"Just answer me."

"No, I didn't. But I will."

"Sure, B.G., but don't I have to sign the papers too?"

"No," she said. And maybe she wasn't really lying. Hadn't Grace Jacobs said something about the court declaring the father's rights terminated if he abandoned the mother and child? "You better not cause me any trouble, Jay, not after what you did."

"I'm not going to cause you any trouble, baby. I'm just thinking."

"Don't."

"Look, maybe this deal can work two ways. What if you fool the cops and fool this lawyer lady, see, and deal directly with the family? Then we could get away clean with some real money."

The Levys. B.G. recalled every word on their application, their letter. They'd pay anything for a baby. "No," she said. "You make me sick, Jay."

"Hey, it's not my fault there's people out there who'll pay through the nose for a kid. Supply and demand. You gotta take advantage of it."

Wearily she went to the window and looked out at the dusty palm tree. "No, Jay," she said without turning around.

"I was just thinking. But, hey, I have to get back to Phoenix now, anyway. You aren't coming, I figure, are you?"

"No."

"Well, it's been good seeing you, baby. Give me that phone number at work again, okay?"

B.G. went into the kitchen and wrote the Casa del Sol's number on a pad for Jay. She handed it to him. "I do have a phone here, but I told you I didn't because you can't call me on it. It's bugged," she explained. All she wanted now was Jay to be gone. He was so slippery, always looking for some way to benefit himself. Not caring about anyone else. Why had it taken her so long to figure that out?

"Bugged," he said. "Wow, this is some sting you got going."

"It's real well thought out, yes," she said, thinking of Greg's meticulous planning. Greg. Jay. She hugged herself as if she was cold. It was probably already ninety in the sun.

"Say, baby, you got twenty bucks to spare? I'm about out of gas, and I gotta get back to Phoenix."

"Oh, for goodness' sake, Jay."

"Well, it won't kill you, will it? You got a real nice setup here, B.G."

She went into her bedroom and dug into her purse, which was sitting on the dresser. When she turned around, a twenty-dollar bill in her hand, Jay was there, standing right behind her. He put his hand on her cheek gently, gestured toward her unmade bed with his head. "We had some good times, though, baby, didn't we?"

She held out the money to him without saying a word. He took it, tipped his hat with a finger and grinned. "Yeah, we did," he answered himself, then he turned, and she could hear his bootheels thumping down the hall, across the living room and out the door. She stood in her bedroom, listening to his car start and drive away down Navaho Street, then she slumped onto the mattress and let the tears come.

THAT EVENING, the ring of the phone gave B.G. a start. She'd been napping on the couch while an old sitcom flickered on the small TV screen. She pushed herself up and hurried into her bedroom.

It was Greg. "Look," he said, "I didn't want you to think I was mad at you. It wasn't that."

She clutched the receiver so hard her knuckles turned white. "Then what were you so mad at?"

"I told you. Me. It was my fault."

"What was your fault, Greg?" She wasn't going to make it easy for him. She hurt too much.

"The, uh, well, you know... what happened last night."

"Uh-huh."

"B.G.? You okay?"

"Sure, I'm fine."

"Okay, good."

She wanted to scream at him, to cry out in pain, to tell him that Jay had been there. Jay, the father of her baby, who cared no more about her than he cared about a stray dog in the street. But she only clutched the receiver harder.

"It was my fault and I'm sorry. Very sorry," Greg was saying.

"Are you sorry you kissed me, Greg, or are you sorry you stopped?" she dared.

Silence. "Maybe this isn't a good time to talk."

"Why not?"

"What I meant was, we have to keep our relationship strictly business. We're doing a very important job."

"Sure."

"You understand? Good. I promise it won't happen again. We have to be professional."

"Right." But she wasn't listening. She was thinking about her baby and Jay and kissing Greg and hurting so much she thought she'd die. If she dared, if she had some guts and some money, she'd run away from both these men....

"Okay, so we'll be in touch," Greg said.

"Sure," B.G. said tonelessly.

She was still pretty upset the next day when Grace Jacobs phoned to tell her the Levys were going to be in Tucson that afternoon and wanted to take her out to dinner.

"They're here?" B.G. asked, her mind whirling.

"Yes, and they're very anxious to meet you," Grace said. "I hope you can make it."

B.G. thought quickly. She had to work the lunch shift that day, and she'd have to call Greg... "I can make it."

"Good. Now, you do realize that these people are going to be very curious about you. If you make a good impression, if they think you're attractive and intelligent, well, let's just say they'll be strongly motivated to consummate the contract."

"I get it. They'll pay more for my baby," B.G. said, hoping to get Grace to say something more.

"You're a very smart young lady" was all Grace said. "This evening, six-thirty at my office, B.G. And, my dear, wear something decent. If you need money to buy an outfit, let me know right now."

"No, I've got something that'll be just right," B.G. said.

"I trust you implicitly. See you this evening."

She had to call Greg. She could hardly face talking to him again; she'd thought she'd have at least a few days to gather herself before she had to see or talk to him again. She toyed with the idea of just not telling him. But this was too important. He'd want her wired for this meeting, she knew it. She closed her eyes and took a deep breath, then reached for the phone and dialed the now familiar number.

"Tyrrell," he answered.

"It's me."

"B.G." He voice was wary, noncommittal. "What is it?"

"Grace just called. I'm going to meet the Levys tonight at her office at six-thirty. Then they're taking me to dinner."

"Okay, good, that's great. I'll have the van pick you up at the mall as usual. I'll be there to wire you. Where's dinner?"

"I don't know. But I'll make sure to ask before we leave Jacobs's office so you'll know."

"Six-thirty at her office you said? So, be at the mall at five-thirty, okay?"

"I have to work this afternoon. It'll be tight."

"Get off early." There was a hint of exasperation in his voice.

"Don't worry, I'll manage."

"Listen, I've gotta go, got another call on the line. See you later," he said, and the phone clicked in her ear.

IT WAS EXCRUCIATING to stand there in the van while Greg wired her. The other men, the driver and the technician, waited outside while Greg ran the wire down her side, along the waist of her white maternity slacks. His hands felt cool and made her skin shiver. She had to fight to stand still and not flinch. She clipped the microphone to her bra and pulled her red-and-white top down quickly.

"Is that a new outfit?" Greg asked in the uncomfortable silence.

"No, but I haven't worn it much."

"It's nice."

"Grace wanted me to make a good impression," she said dryly.

"I'm sure you will." He averted his gaze. "You know what to say?"

"Yes, I know what to say."

"Don't be too pushy or they'll get turned off. We don't want that."

"I know, Greg."

"I'll see you afterward for debriefing. At your house. I'll park around the corner."

She walked into Grace's building right on time. Debbie, the receptionist, had gone home, but the door to Grace's office was open, and she could hear voices inside.

"Ah, here she is," Grace said as she went in. "Bettie Gay, this is Sarah and Mel Levy."

She shook hands and tried to smile; every place on her skin where the tape held the wire fast was crawling. Surely they could all see it.

Sarah held her hand for a long time, searching her face until B.G. was embarrassed. She was a short woman with curly red hair, a round figure and dainty feet and hands. Her diamond engagement ring was very large.

"You're very pretty," Sarah said finally.

"Thank you." B.G. ducked her head, horribly uncomfortable, knowing every word was being recorded, every word was being listened to by Greg and the technician.

"I took the liberty of making reservations for the three of you at Ovens. It's a friendly place, good food," Grace said. "Mel has the directions. I do hope you like it."

"We will, I'm sure," Mel said. He was tall and balding and wore glasses, a kind-looking man. "Shall we go?"

"Have a wonderful time." Grace beamed at them, a benevolent goddess of fertility.

It was awkward in their plush Volvo driving north to Ovens. B.G. sat in back, and Sarah kept turning around to talk to her.

"Grace sent us your application, you know," Sarah said, "so we almost feel as if we know you."

"I saw yours, too," B.G. said.

"I guess we have no secrets from each other then," Sarah said lightly.

No secrets. "I guess not."

"This is a bit strange, isn't it?" Sarah said. "Us meeting like this."

"I suppose so."

"You're feeling well?" Sarah asked. "Everything's going fine?"

"Sure."

"I had two miscarriages," Sarah said, "and that was the end of that."

"I'm sorry."

"Will you be uncomfortable if I ask some personal questions?"

B.G. gave a short laugh. "Maybe."

Sarah turned all the way around. "What I want to know is—what I'd *really* like to know—what does the father look like?"

"He's gorgeous," B.G. said. "Tall, lean, blue eyes, blond hair. And musically talented." *Take that, Greg,* she thought.

"Ohhh," Sarah sighed, "what a beautiful baby it'll be."

"Yes," B.G. said sadly, "a beautiful little girl."

Dinner was tense, and B.G. didn't eat much. They sat outside on a veranda, watching the desert sunset. The evening was warm, the air filled with delicious smells from the kitchen, conversation humming around them.

"Do you need money?" Mel asked once. "We can help you."

"Thanks, but Ms. Jacobs is taking care of that."

"Is there anything you need? Anything at all?" he continued.

"No, really. Ms. Jacobs told me everything should go through her."

"I know, but it doesn't hurt to ask, does it?" Mel said.

"Your due date is August nineteenth," Sarah said. "We'll be here as soon as Grace calls us. I've been shopping like crazy, getting everything ready. It's so close really, isn't it?''

B.G. almost choked on her food. This was sick. She wanted to tell them they weren't going to get her baby; she wanted to warn them, but she couldn't. She felt pity for them, but the fervent gleam in Sarah's eye frightened her. The woman was so desperate it was scary.

"And I've already enrolled her in the Valley Preschool. There's a waiting list, you know," Sarah was saying. "It's the best one in La Jolla."

"We're quite comfortably off," Mel said almost apologetically. "We can offer her the best of everything. We wanted you to know that. I don't know exactly what your arrangements are with Grace, but she assures us you'll be taken care of."

"Yes," B.G. said, then, as ugly as she knew it was, she asked, "Is she, like, charging you a fortune?"

Sarah patted her hand. "Now, don't you worry your head about that, Bettie Gay. We're taking care of all that, aren't we, Mel?"

"Yes, leave all that to us," he agreed, and that was all B.G. could get out of them.

The evening lasted forever. She would have pleaded exhaustion and gone home early, but she knew Greg was waiting for something juicy, some tidbit he could use against Grace. Finally they offered to drive her home, and she accepted gratefully, but on the way they saw an ice-cream shop and had to stop.

"You don't mind, do you? Mel does love his ice cream. It's his only weakness," Sarah said.

B.G. had a soda, but Sarah had nothing, saying she had to watch her weight. Then she wanted to know how much B.G. had gained so far and how much she'd weighed when she wasn't "preggy," as Sarah put it in her little-girl voice.

They dropped her in front of the bungalow at eleven and said their goodbyes. Mel told her to call them anytime, if she needed something or even if she didn't. He gave her one of his cards.

"It was so nice meeting you," Sarah cooed. "Maybe we can come again."

"Thank you for dinner," B.G. said.

"Take care of yourself," Sarah said, "and the darling baby."

B.G. let herself into her house and leaned her back against the door, drawing her first free breath in hours. Then she reached under her pretty new top and ripped the wires off, letting them dangle from her hand as she gulped in lungfuls of air.

Abruptly a light flicked on.

"Where in hell have you been?" Greg asked, standing in the kitchen, his face pale in the dim light.

"Weren't you listening?"

"Not after you left Ovens. I sent the van home and came right here."

She waved a hand negligently. "We stopped for ice cream." Then she walked to the couch and sank onto it, her head aching, her body heavy.

"Damn it, I was worried," Greg said, pacing in front of her.

"You should've kept listening then," she retorted, trying not to look at him, trying not to remember what that handsome face had felt like in her hands or the hard pressure of his lips against hers, against her breasts, the wild beautiful beat of his heart . . .

"Did they say anything we could use on the way here?"

"No, not a thing," she got out.

"I thought you had something there for a minute," he said, "but nothing happened."

"I did my best, Greg." She looked up at him. "I'm beat. You through with me?"

"What were they like?" Greg persisted.

"Rich," she said wearily.

"You think they'd testify against Grace?"

She shrugged. It was crazy, but she couldn't keep her mind on this conversation; all she could think was that Greg needed a haircut. She'd never seen his hair quite this long, touching the collar of his white shirt. And it looked a little messy, as if he'd lost a tiny edge of his control. A part of her exalted in the notion that he'd lost it because of her, but she was too exhausted to hold on to the thought.

"Okay," he finally said, "I'm through. Maybe you could make a date to see these people tomorrow. Lunch or something? We could try again."

The idea was staggering. "No."

"Can't handle it, B.G.?"

"No, Greg, I can't. This wasn't part of the deal."

"All right, forget it. Get some rest."

"I'll try."

"I'll be in touch," he said, and he went through the kitchen, down the hall and out the back door. She heard it close behind him and then there was silence.

The next morning, B.G. called Santino and told him she needed some time off. She packed a small bag and took all the cash she had, plus her credit card, which she'd finally paid off, and treated herself to a taxi down to the bus station. She bought a ticket to Phoenix. The trip was two hours and it went through some of the flattest, brownest, dullest countryside she'd ever seen.

She sat in the bus and felt a certain bitter relief. Let Greg worry, let him think she'd taken off for good. Maybe she had, too. Let Grace Jacobs and the Levys worry. She didn't care anymore. The only one she'd miss was Whiskers, and she'd left food and a window open for him.

Let them all stew. Bettie Gay Bryson was on strike.

She got off the bus and took a room at a decent-looking hotel near downtown Phoenix. There was an okay pool, and she sat in the shade all day, watching mothers with children, occasionally fathers. She ate in her room, ordering from the room-service menu, and she put her feelings on hold for the time being. She bought a paperback in the lobby drugstore and read and dozed under a big beach umbrella on the patio.

"Hot, isn't it?" a voice said, and B.G. looked up from her book to see a pregnant woman smiling at her.

"It really gets me," she replied, smiling back.

"Thank heavens I've only got a few weeks," the woman said.

"I've got two months."

And these were practically the only words she spoke all day. She slept well, the air-conditioning humming all night long, took a walk the next morning and headed back to the pool.

What did she owe them, any of them? They all wanted something from her—Grace, the Levys, Greg. Okay, she owed Greg, but he'd gotten some things on Grace already. He didn't care about her, not the way she cared about him. She had to learn to keep her defenses up.

She had the chef's salad for lunch and took a nap, but by late afternoon she was feeling bored and lonely and worrying if Whiskers was all right.

It occurred to her she could call Greg and tell him where she was, or at least tell him she was okay, but she couldn't bring herself to do it. He probably hadn't even noticed she was gone. *Give it a rest,* she told herself firmly.

And then, of course, there was Jay. Here in Phoenix, close by. Just out of curiosity, B.G. took the Phoenix phone book and looked up Maverick's to see where it was. She found the address on the map in the phone book—not too far away. Wouldn't Jay be surprised?

She sat there in her cool hotel room and considered what she should do. He'd asked her to go to Phoenix with him, hadn't he? And he was Kathryn's father. She could probably move right in with him, now, today. She could catch his first set at Maverick's. Maybe she should just turn up at the place, surprise him. Or maybe she should call and ask him to pick her up.

It was kind of lonely here, no one to talk to.

B.G. looked at the phone and reached her hand out toward it. One little phone call wouldn't hurt.

CHAPTER FIFTEEN

GREG KNEW he was breaking a cardinal rule again when he parked two blocks down Navaho and went on foot to B.G.'s house. As he walked, he studied the street, looking for anything out of the ordinary: someone loitering on a corner, someone sitting in a parked car. But there was nothing unusual that he could see. A woman was walking in her front door with a bag of groceries. A boy was mowing a tiny front yard that was scorched by the desert sun. He walked past an older couple; the man was leaning on a cane.

Using his key, he let himself into B.G.'s quickly and called out her name. Of course, he was pretty damned sure she wasn't there. After all, he'd called her at least two dozen times over the past two days. The question was, where in hell had she gone?

The first things he noted were the bowls of food and water left out for the cat, and the cracked window so the tattered feline could come and go at will. He checked B.G.'s closet next, heartened to see most of her clothes neatly hung up. The bathroom—no toothbrush or toothpaste or shampoo. No comb or brush.

He strode back into the kitchen, opened the fridge

door. There was a half-empty carton of milk, a few pieces of fruit, some yogurt.

It was then that he heard Whiskers coming in the window, the soft thump of the cat's paws on the linoleum as it hit the floor. It eyed Greg warily, apparently decided he was harmless and made its way to the food bowl.

If only the stupid cat could talk, Greg thought. "Hey, cat," he said, hands on his hips, "why don't you tell me where she is?"

He went back into the bedroom and picked up the notepad on the table by B.G.'s bed. There was nothing written on it. But just in case, he tore the top page off and held it up to the light. He could see the indentation of writing on it. He found a pencil in the kitchen and, holding it level to the paper, lightly brought up the writing. It seemed to be a telephone number. The prefix was local, and the other four numbers were legible. Also, a time was written on the paper. Or at least Greg thought it was a time. Too hard to read, though.

He went back into the bedroom, picked up the phone and dialed the number he'd found on the pad. It was a bus company, Trailways. He hung up and swore out loud. She'd split.

Even though he couldn't believe B.G. would have been stupid enough to use this phone knowing the line was tapped, Greg nonetheless called his office, speaking to the woman who monitored all the calls in and out of this location. He gave the number of the Trailways bus station to the woman on duty, asking, "Was a call made from this phone to that number?"

There hadn't been.

He hung up and realized that B.G. had looked up the number to Trailways at home, but been smart enough to call from another location. The little minx!

Greg drove over to the Casa del Sol next, hoping against hope that B.G. had only left town for a short time. If she'd quit her job, he'd know she'd gone for good. And he could guess where or, he thought, grimacing, to whom—good ol' pretty-boy Jay. With a stab he recalled B.G.'s description of Jay to the Levys: gorgeous, tall, lean, blue eyes, blond hair, musically talented. Oh, yeah, Greg remembered hearing all that over the wire. He'd never forget it, in fact.

At the restaurant he spoke to the Latino stud, Santino. At first he got nowhere. "Miss Bryson?" Santino scratched his dark mass of hair. "I cannot really say, señor. Maybe she's here, maybe she's not. In this business, who is to say? They come, they go." He shrugged eloquently.

"So let me get this straight," Greg said, keeping his temper in check. "You don't know if she quit or not."

Again Santino shrugged.

"Did she collect her final paycheck?" Greg asked, his tone a little less even.

"Who knows?" Santino replied. "The lady who writes the checks is not here."

Greg took a breath. He reached into an inside pocket of his suit jacket and pulled out his wallet, flipping it open. "Santino, my man," he said, "do you know what this is?"

Santino eyed the badge. Shrugged.

"This means I'm the law. Actually, a detective. I work for the county attorney. Now, you wouldn't want to upset the Big Man, would you?"

A shrug.

"Good. Then why don't you tell me if Miss Bryson is still working here."

Santino swallowed. Finally he nodded. "As far as I know."

"She didn't quit or give notice?"

"Not that I know, man. Hey, I gotta get back to the kitchen."

Greg stared at him coolly for a long moment, then nodded. "Go on," he said.

On the off chance that B.G. might have returned home, he used a pay phone down the street and dialed her number. Her machine answered and he hung up.

He spent the rest of the evening trying to figure it out, dialing her number at least a dozen more times, until he was so damn frustrated he threw the cordless telephone across the room, hitting the wall, breaking the phone. "Great," he grumbled.

He went to bed late, having gone for a jog, something he hadn't had a chance to do in a long time. But it hadn't relieved his tension. Nor had the shower. Studying was out; he was too distracted. And, naturally, sleep was not forthcoming, either. He kept remembering her clothes in the closet; the items were too precious for B.G. to have left them behind. So it stood to reason she'd only gone off for a couple of days. Or had she? Maybe she'd rushed out of there, remembering only to leave something for the cat, barely grabbing a few things. When he'd last spoken to her she'd been pretty upset. Trying to sound cool and distant, but he'd known. And whose fault was that?

His.

The worst torment was his memory of the other night. Memories, dreams, were supposed to fade with time. But while Greg lay in bed waiting for sleep to come, he could almost feel the soft texture of B.G.'s skin, the beautiful heaviness of her breasts, the sweet taste. He still couldn't separate reality from the dreams he'd had. It was sweet bitter torture.

And those other treacherous thoughts continued to creep into his mind. What if he had B.G. all the time for his very own? What if he could see her every day, talk to her about anything, anytime, touch her, listen to her laugh, see her putter around the kitchen, turn and give him that sweet shy smile?

And what if, he reminded himself, she was gone for good?

By ten the following morning the thermometer stood at ninety-seven. Greg drove to work with the air-conditioner blasting, still wondering about B.G. Was she hot wherever she was? She was always hot lately. Was she with Jay? Greg had never believed the guy was in Tucson, but he could very well be down in the valley, in Mesa, Tempe, Phoenix. B.G. could've run to him. In fact, odds were she had.

He lifted his hand in greeting to Rosemary when he passed her desk and entered Dick Mayer's office. This was not going to be pleasant.

"A Trailways bus?" Mayer said, frowning. "Then she's gone, damn it."

"Not necessarily," Greg said, still standing. "Most of her stuff is still at the house. And there's this cat..." Greg saw Mayer lift a brow. "She'd never leave the cat to fend for itself for very long."

"Right," Mayer scoffed.

"I'm serious. Plus, I don't think she quit her job, either."

"People walk off the job every day and never come back."

But Greg shook his head. "Out of character for this girl."

"So where is she? Tell me that."

"My best guess," Greg said, "is that she took off to visit her boyfriend. I've always suspected he was nearby."

"And what if this boyfriend persuades her to stay with him?"

"Then we've lost her."

"Uh-huh. That's just great."

Greg cleared his throat. "There's another possibility. One last thing I haven't checked. Grace Jacobs may know where she is. This could have something to do with her. Grant you, it's a remote possibility. But if B.G. isn't back by this afternoon, I'm going to check Jacobs out."

"Can you pull it off?"

Greg nodded slowly. "I don't see why not. Jacobs has never met any of the men in B.G.'s life."

"Hmm," Mayer said, thinking. Then he looked up. "Go for it. I want that girl back here. I want this job finished. We could charge Jacobs today on the illegal sale of infants, but we need more to make it stick in court."

"I realize that."

"So go find this girl of yours, Greg."

"I'll sure try."

Greg had not shaved that morning, knowing he might very well have to pay Jacobs this visit. He drove his Honda toward his sister Sandy's house and thought about how he was going to pull it off. Grace Jacobs was smart, smart and dangerous, and the last thing Greg could afford was a slipup. If—no, *when* B.G. returned, he wanted to be a hundred percent sure he hadn't blown her relationship with the lawyer. To put B.G. in jeopardy was unconscionable. He'd have to be very careful, and that meant he'd have to be convincing.

He caught Sandy at home. In a couple of weeks she was due to go back to work, her maternity leave over, but for now she was a stay-at-home mom.

"Good grief," his sister said at her door, "now *this* is a surprise."

Greg laughed and poked the baby in Sandy's arms with a playful finger, receiving a toothless smile before the infant hid his head in his mom's shoulder. "I need to borrow a couple of things from Art," he explained.

"Like Art has something you need?" Sandy asked doubtfully.

Greg nodded. "His pickup truck and that old blue-and-black checked shirt, the one with the tear in the shoulder. Art still have it?"

Sandy frowned. "Are you kidding? They're going to bury him in it." Then she cocked her head. "What's this all about, anyway? You doing undercover work or something?"

"Sort of," he said evasively.

"I'll bet this has something to do with your friend B.G."

"Sandy..." he said.

"Okay, okay," she said. "I'll get the shirt and the truck keys. But you're going to owe Art."

"Of course," Greg said, taking the baby from her arms as she headed for the bedroom upstairs.

The last stop Greg made before going to Jacobs's was his place, where he changed into Art's old shirt and a pair of his own jeans, which were old and half-shredded. He checked his appearance in the bathroom mirror. He rubbed the day's growth on his face and figured it was a good touch. The shirt, left hanging out, was perfect. The jeans might have been over-kill, but he didn't think so. His sneakers were appropriately grubby. But his hair...it did need a trim, but the razor cut showed. And that wasn't good. He could only hope Jacobs would figure his ego allowed for decent haircuts.

"Okay," he said into the mirror, pulling a baseball cap low on his brow, "let's do it."

He parked Art's old battered pickup truck in the lot next to Jacobs's building, figuring she'd watch him leave if she could. This was not a woman who left stones unturned. Then he took the stairs to the third-floor suite that housed her office. The secretary—

Debbie Hostlier the nameplate read—said she'd buzz
Ms. Jacobs and see if she had a free minute.

"You tell her it's a friend of Betty Gay's. A good
friend. She'll see me. Name's Jay. Just plain Jay."

"Mmm," the girl said, pushing an intercom button.

Jacobs kept him waiting a proper amount of time,
no doubt to show him who was in charge here. But he
knew the cold-blooded woman was dying to meet him,
the man B.G. had said was gone, disappeared. So he
waited, sitting in a comfortable chair, one ragged leg
crossed over his knee, baseball cap balanced on it. He
grinned a few times at Debbie, a little lewdly. The girl
let out a disgusted sigh.

After about ten minutes the door to Jacobs's private office opened and she appeared. She gave Greg a
pleasant nod, walked to Debbie's desk and handed the
girl a few manila files. "Would you type these up,
please?" Jacobs said. Then she turned to Greg. She
gave him a smile that didn't reach her cool blue eyes.
"Jay, is it? Won't you please come in?"

He shrugged and unfolded himself from the chair.

Grace Jacobs up close and personal was a stun-
ningly attractive woman, a real Nordic beauty in what
had to be a two-thousand-dollar suit. Everything
about her was flawless, right down to the barest hint
of blush on her high cheekbones. Greg was impressed—but not enough to erase his opinion of her
unethical and immoral approach to the law. In a few
months he'd be a full-fledged lawyer himself, and he
sure as hell hoped he'd never stoop as low as this mer-
cenary bitch. Seeing her like this made him marvel at

how well B.G. was handling her. And again he thought about how tough little Miss Bryson really was. B.G.— wherever she was.

"Just Jay," Grace was saying. "Why no last name?"

Greg sat down across from her and smiled. "No particular reason."

"You wouldn't be wanted by the law, would you, Jay?"

"Of course not, ma'am," he said evenly, pleased with that slight Western twang he affected. Of course, that was the way his entire family spoke. It wasn't all that hard to slip back into it.

Grace studied him for a moment and then smiled. "So I take it you're the father of B.G.'s baby."

"That's a fact, ma'am."

"I see. I must admit, Jay, I'm mildly surprised to see you here. Bettie Gay told me you'd disappeared."

He shrugged. "I did. I'm back for a day or two. Got some of her stuff in my truck."

"Hmm," she said. "And just how did you get my name? Did Bettie Gay ask you to come here?"

"No, ma'am," he said, and his face took on a serious expression. "Fact is, I ain't seen B.G. at all."

"Then . . . ?"

"Oh, I stopped by her grandma's place—she stays there house-sittin'—but she wasn't around. I found your name and number by her bed and looked you up in the book. Thought I'd drive over and see what B.G.'s doin' with a lawyer."

"I see," Grace said, thinking. Then, "Bettie Gay has decided to give her baby up for adoption, Jay. I'm helping her with the arrangements."

"Oh," Greg said, and he shifted uneasily in his chair. "Oh. Well, I guess if that's what B.G. wants..."

"It is."

"Well, I won't give her no trouble or nothin'. B.G.'s a real sweet girl. I want what she wants for the kid, you know?"

"Yes, I do," Grace said. "And maybe it's good you stopped by. You could sign some—"

"Now, ma'am," Greg interrupted, "I said I only stopped in Tucson to see B.G. I ain't signin' no papers. I'm outta here, lady. You won't get no trouble outta me, I promise."

"Hmm," Grace said again, her blue eyes boring into his. "Then why this visit, Jay?"

"Uh, when I couldn't find B.G. and I hung out for a time, well, I thought you might know where she is or somethin'."

"I see," Grace said. "But to tell you the truth, Jay, I don't have any idea where Bettie Gay is. Perhaps her grandmother up in Colorado became ill?"

"Maybe," Greg said, knitting his brows. "She's gettin' on in years. Maybe."

"Well," Grace said then, a polite dismissal. She began to rise.

Greg got up, too. He hated to push, but damn, if Grace had any idea at all where B.G. had gone, he wanted to know. "Pretty weird," he said at the door, shaking his head. "I'd've thought B.G. would've told her lawyer if she was leavin' town."

"Well, she didn't," Grace said, and by the troubled look she let slip, Greg believed her. So that left Jay. And now Greg was beginning to think B.G. really had gone to him.

He left the office building and shuffled across the pavement to his truck, got in and glanced casually up at the third-floor windows. Uh-huh, someone was peering through the blinds.

An hour later Greg was home. He'd stopped by Sandy and Art's, dropped off the shirt and truck, and he'd even stopped by the dry cleaner and the grocery store. He barely recalled any of that. Okay, he kept telling himself, he was worried sick about B.G. He was positive she'd run away because of him. But what really stuck like a knife and turned in his gut was the notion that he might never see her again.

THAT SAME EVENING B.G. opened the door to the house on Navaho, put down her bag and called out to Whiskers. "Here, kitty, kitty, kitty." And then the phone rang.

Her heart skipped a beat. She wouldn't answer it. No, she'd better. "Hello?" she said, breathless from rushing to the bedroom.

"B.G.?" Then he swore. "You stay right there. You hear me? Don't you move a goddamn muscle. I'll be right over." And then he hung up.

It wasn't ten minutes later that she saw car lights swing around the corner onto Navaho and then Greg's car pull up out front. Uh-oh, she thought, he wasn't even hiding his presence.

He slammed the door when he came in, too, and strode up to her, his expression furious.

"Now, look—" she began, but he grabbed her shoulders and gave her a chewing out the likes of which she hadn't heard since she broke her grandma's favorite serving platter.

"...go off like that without so much as a telephone call! What in hell were you thinking!"

But B.G. was only thinking one thing at that moment. No man, ever, had dared to lay a finger on her in anger. "You let go of me, Greg Tyrrell!"

He dropped his hold and stepped back, as if only then realizing he could have hurt her. "I'm sorry. I—"

"And you get this through your head, mister. I go where I want when I want."

"Look, B.G.—"

"Look nothing," she interrupted. "As long as I help bust that lawyer of yours, what I do on my own time is none of your business. Why should you care, anyway?"

She seemed to have gotten him on that one. He scrubbed a hand through his hair and said nothing, and B.G. couldn't help but wonder if, by some miracle, he really did care. But that was impossible. All her experience and all her logic told her there was no way. He only cared that she might have skipped out on him and the sting operation.

"I went to Jacobs," he said after a moment.

B.G. had to fit her mind around his words. He'd been to see Grace Jacobs. She stared at him, and that was when she noticed the full day's growth of beard on

...is face, the uncombed hair. Even his T-shirt looked worn, and those jeans were absolutely ratty. She shook her head, uncomprehending.

"That's right," he said. "I used the father cover story and went this afternoon." He was glaring so hard at her now she had to look away. "I told Jacobs my name was Jay," he said.

B.G.'s head snapped up. "Jay?"

"That's right," he said in a hard voice. "Clever of me, wasn't it?"

She swallowed. Of course. He'd known the name from that phone conversation with her grandma.

"I wouldn't give Jacobs a last name," Greg said. "But then, I don't know his last name, do I?"

B.G. swallowed again.

"Oh," Greg said, "by the way, how is good old Jay, anyhow? Was he surprised to see how pregnant you are? Or maybe he's been dropping by here from time to time. Maybe—"

"Stop it," she gasped.

"Struck a nerve, did I?"

"Stop it, Greg," she repeated, "I want you to leave. I'm tired. Very, very tired." She could have told him then that she had run to Phoenix, that her hand had been on the phone ready to dial Jay's number, but she hadn't done it. She could have told Greg all that. But she didn't.

He said nothing more. He only stood in the middle of her living room glaring down at her, big and menacing in that small space, looking completely different from his usual self, an edge to his voice she'd never heard before. And it occurred to B.G. that this was a side of Greg he'd never want anyone to see, especially not her. Something had pushed his buttons so badly he'd lost his usual iron control. It had been her leaving without telling him, she knew. *Good,* she thought spitefully.

Finally he spun on his heel and left. She heard his car start, saw the lights swing back onto the road, heard the tires squeal. Her brain was reeling. If she hadn't known better, she'd have said Greg Tyrrell, handsome, brilliant, unattainable Greg, was jealous. But then, as always, her thoughts came crashing back to earth. She was just a cracker from Florida, poor and uneducated and fat as a cow. What would a man like Greg ever see in the likes of her?

CHAPTER SIXTEEN

B.G. HAD AN APPOINTMENT with Dr. Resniak on July fifteenth. At thirty-two weeks she'd gained twenty pounds, and he was quite satisfied with her progress.

"Well, everything's going fine, Bettie Gay. No problems, no more bleeding. The baby hasn't dropped yet, and there's no sign it'll be a premature delivery. You never know, though." He smiled. "I always wish I could just tell my patients what season of the year they'll deliver, instead of the exact date. Rarely is a baby born right on time."

"I'm getting pretty impatient," she said, "and the heat bothers me a lot."

"Hellish climate for pregnant women, I know. Stay inside during the day."

"So, you can't tell if my baby will be born on time?"

He shook his head. "It's up to Mother Nature."

She left the office feeling down. Her pregnancy was going fine, but that was the only thing that was. Well, she'd had another meeting with Grace, and Greg had said there were a few things he could use. Jacobs was canny, though, and so far she hadn't mentioned numbers, despite B.G.'s pressing her.

But beyond that things were not very pleasant. Thank God she had her job and Santino to cheer her up.

Her problem was, she realized while she waited at the bus stop, she'd arranged her life around Greg. Typical of her, she thought, depending too much on a man again. And he'd enabled her to do it, even encouraged her to do it. Her only stab at independence was her job, and she'd stuck to her guns about that, thank goodness.

The bus came, snorting hot diesel smoke, but it was mercifully air-conditioned inside. She sat there, her purse resting on her knees because she had no lap left, escaping wisps of hair sticking to her neck with perspiration.

What would happen when she delivered her baby and her job for Greg was done? That'd be the end of her money, the cute little bungalow. The end of Greg. However unsatisfying, however pathetic, at least she still got to see him, to talk to him. She could pretend he cared a little. She had something to look forward to.

Then, of course, it would be the end of Kathryn, too. She'd go to some nice family, straight out of B.G.'s body to strangers, and then B.G. would be totally, utterly alone.

Oh, deal with it, she told herself, watching the now familiar streets of Tucson slide past the bus window. *Stop feeling sorry for yourself.* She might have been raised like common folk, but her grandma had never raised her to be a coward.

The next day Grace Jacobs phoned and wanted another meeting. B.G. called Greg to let him know, and they arranged a time to meet at the mall, the usual routine. The conversation was short and impersonal, strained. B.G. hadn't heard from him at all for a week, with the exception of a couple of messages he'd left on her machine. She'd returned his calls, but he hadn't been in the office, and someone named Rosemary had taken the messages for him. "He's in court this week. Grand jury," Rosemary said.

"Oh, well, just tell him I phoned," B.G. said.

"How are you doing, B.G.?" Rosemary asked.

B.G. was surprised. "Do you, I mean, do you know who I am?"

"Yup. I type up all the reports, transcribe all the tapes. I know everything there is to know about this operation."

"Oh."

"Listen, honey, you're doing a real good thing here. We're going to nail that Jacobs woman because of you. I don't know if Greg tells you that often enough, but he should."

"Really?"

"See? I knew it, he doesn't tell you a damn thing. Trust me—you're doing a terrific job."

"Thanks," B.G. said. "Gosh, I didn't realize other people knew what I was doing."

"The whole office knows, honey. And we're all rooting for you."

"Oh, wow, that's real nice of you."

"You be careful, though. That woman is dangerous. We think she...well, she might have...hurt a girl who wanted to talk about her operation."

B.G. felt shock grip her. "She did?"

"Well, we aren't sure. But don't you worry. You're never alone with her, anyway. And I'd swear she doesn't suspect a thing. You're good, honey. You take care now."

"Thanks...Rosemary."

That had been days ago, and B.G. hadn't said a word until the moment she was alone with Greg in the van.

"Why didn't you tell me Grace hurt some girl who was going to rat on her?" she asked angrily, feeling claustrophobic and sweaty in the back of the closed van.

Greg looked at her in surprise. "How did you...?"

"Rosemary told me."

He frowned. "Damn, she's a gossip."

"Oh, so that's only gossip. What happened? Did Grace have the girl beat up?"

"Something like that," he replied calmly.

B.G. studied his face. "I have a right to know, Greg."

His gaze slid away, and he got busy untangling the wires in his hands.

"Tell me."

"There was an accident. The girl was...killed. We have no idea if Jacobs had anything to do with it."

"Oh, God."

"Don't worry about it. You're always wired when you see Jacobs. We're right outside in the van."

"What if she comes to my house again? She did it that one time. What if she does? You won't be there."

"It won't happen. She has no reason to."

"But she could." B.G. felt her heart pounding. Sweat broke out on her neck, her forehead. "It's so hot in here."

"Take it easy, B.G. Just a second. I'll wire you, and then you can get out of here."

She wiped her forehead with the back of her head. "Okay, hurry up."

He lifted her tunic and placed the transmitter, the wires, ran them deftly along her skin. She clipped the mike to her bra. It should have been old hat by now, but this time was different. This time she was scared.

Greg must have sensed her anxiety, because he put his hands on her shoulders and made her meet his gaze. "It's okay, B.G. Nothing's going to happen."

"Easy for you to say." She felt his fingers on her shoulders and a familiar tremor coursed through her. She felt suddenly dizzy, the interior of the van beginning to spin.

Greg kept his hands on her shoulders. He was saying something, but all she could think was how desperately she wanted to collapse against his chest. Couldn't he tell she was crazy in love with him?

She heard him ask, "You want to call the meeting off this time? You could phone Jacobs and tell her you're sick or something."

She shook her head, drew a shaky breath. "No, I'll do it. I'll be okay. It's just so hot in here."

"You're sure."

"Yes, I'm sure. Just, open the door."

She was better sitting in Greg's car with the van following. The air-conditioning blasted her in the face, and her panic subsided. But the longing, the craving for Greg, maybe that was permanent. She tried hard to chalk it up to hormones. Lately she'd suffered the wildest emotions: sudden spurts of panic, intense moments of sadness, bursts of joy when she heard the deep timbre of his voice. It had to be hormones. One more month and it would be over. *Hang in there,* she told herself.

"Ready?" Greg was asking.

"Sure," she said, opening the car door, "no problem."

Grace Jacobs was her usual cool and blond and confident self. She got Debbie to fetch B.G. a lemonade with lots of ice. She was solicitous, the perfect concerned mother.

"You should've taken a cab. I'll pay. For goodness' sake, it's a furnace out there."

"I'll take one home," B.G. said.

"Absolutely. Debbie will call one for you. Remind me to tell her when we're through." Grace rose and walked around her desk. "The Levys called again. They're very anxious."

"So am I," B.G. said truthfully.

"You're to call me the second you feel a pain, before you even call your doctor. I check my messages constantly when I'm not in the office. I just want you to be clear on the process. You'll sign papers in the hospital that allow the baby to be placed directly with the adoptive parents. As soon as she's given a clean bill of health, the Levys will take her with them."

B.G. felt the weight of her decision like a suffocating blanket of hopelessness. Maybe it wouldn't be the Levys who took Kathryn, but someone would, and the result would be the same—her baby would be gone.

Grace cocked her head. "You're not having second thoughts, are you, B.G.?"

She raised her head quickly and hardened her voice. "No, I just feel lousy today."

Grace leaned back against the edge of her desk, her long slim legs crossed at the ankles. "I wanted to speak to you about something else. Your...the father of your baby stopped by to see me a while ago."

B.G. ducked her head. "I know." Greg's visit, she remembered in alarm.

"I thought he was gone for good."

"So did I."

"He won't cause any problems, will he?"

"No, I talked to him."

"It'd be easier all around if he signed the relinquishment papers, but he seemed a bit...hesitant," Grace said. "Now, we can have the court terminate his rights, but we'd have to prove abandonment, so if he showed up again and made any noise, things could get tricky. You know, B.G., I really hate these kinds of complications."

Damn Greg! "I'll get him to sign those papers. I know where he is now," B.G. said.

"Let me ask you a question. Will money take care of this little hitch in our plans?"

"You mean, pay him off?"

"Precisely."

"How much?"

Grace shrugged. "A few thousand. Say five grand."

"That's too much for him," B.G. blurted out. It was as if the whole scenario was really going to play out the way Grace Jacobs thought it would. Somewhere in the back of her mind she knew Greg was listening to every word, but it didn't matter. Right now she was living the lie they'd created.

"Fine. Say twenty-five hundred then."

"All right," B.G. mumbled. "I think he'll go for that."

"Can you contact him? I want those papers signed."

"It might take a while." B.G. frowned. "If you're so free with your money, the Levys' money, then how come you won't tell me how much I get? Here I am, ready to pop, and I don't even know how much I'll get. I need to make some plans, you know." *Don't push too hard,* Greg had reminded her in the car only minutes ago, *or her lawyer can yell entrapment and get her off.*

"You'll get at least five thousand."

"I want more," B.G. said. "I'm not going through this for peanuts."

"You're a very greedy girl," Grace said coolly.

"Me? What about you? How much will you make? Twenty, thirty grand?"

"I'm the one taking all the risks," Grace said with composure.

"Try having a baby sometime and then tell me that," B.G. said. Grace folded her arms and pinned B.G. with her ice blue gaze. In a very soft voice she said, "Bettie Gay, my dear, don't you go getting on your high horse with me. You've signed a contract, and nowhere in it does it say how much money you get. I do my best for all my girls, but I will not abide greediness.''

B.G. shivered inadvertently, even though she could feel sweat dampen her armpits. ''I want ten thousand,'' she mumbled.

''You'll get what I decide is fair,'' Grace said, her voice menacingly quiet, steel sheathed in velvet.

''It's my baby,'' B.G. said sullenly.

Grace smiled. ''No, it isn't, dear. It's mine, signed, sealed and shortly to be delivered.''

There, B.G. thought. *Greg, did you hear that?* She said nothing more to Grace, not a word.

''Now, that's better, B.G. I'm glad we had this little chat. It's always good to understand each other, isn't it? And I do want the father to sign the papers. Soon. His name is Jay, isn't it? Good-looking man. A little more mature than I expected. You did give his age as twenty-six, but then, I suppose he's lived a hard life. All that traveling and those late nights. Cigarette smoke and beer.'' She gave a delicate shudder. ''I certainly hope you don't indulge in those unhealthy things.''

Grace smiled again, and it was more frightening than any frown. Her eyes remained clear and blue and remote, utterly untouched by emotion. ''So, that's it, dear. I think we've covered all the bases. Call me when you get hold of Jay.''

B.G. pushed herself up. She was trembling, as if Grace's threats could really touch her. As if Greg and two other men weren't just outside in the van listening to every word. She believed now that Grace Jacobs really did kill that girl who crossed her. She was convinced of it.

"I'll have Debbie call that taxi for you," Grace said kindly, as if nothing unpleasant had gone on between them. She dug in her handbag and held out a twenty-dollar bill. "This should cover it."

"Thanks," B.G. muttered, properly chastised.

"And it's a good thing you'll be taking a cab. Look." She pointed out her window. "It's going to rain. It's the monsoon starting."

Outside the building, B.G. made sure to get into the waiting cab in case Grace was watching, then had it let her off around the corner where Greg was waiting. She got out slowly, handing the driver the twenty-dollar bill, not even bothering to get the change. She felt as if she were dissolving in the heat.

"You were great," he said, taking her arm. "Jacobs did herself in today."

B.G. was soaked in sweat. She was still shaking, feeling those ice blue eyes on her, the silken voice, the danger that emanated from the woman like a living thing.

"You look pale," Greg said. "Do you feel all right?"

"She scared me," B.G. said. "I believe she killed that girl. I really believe it."

Greg stopped for a moment and turned B.G. to face him. Heat radiated up from the sidewalk, and she felt weak. "She's really tough," he said. "You were..."

She swayed, putting a hand to her forehead, which was beaded with sweat.

"B.G.," he said urgently, "are you okay?"

"No," she whispered, and he took her arm and hustled her down the street and around a corner to where his car was parked.

"I'm taking you home," he said, and she didn't argue.

She leaned against the hood while he unlocked the doors, climbed in, started the engine and turned on the air-conditioning. Then he came around to her side and opened the door for her. "It'll be cool in a minute," he said. "Should I take you to the doctor?"

She shook her head.

"Okay." He spoke clearly, leaning close to her hidden microphone. "Earl, Mike, I'm taking her home. Get the stuff back to the office and tell Rosemary where I am." Then he took off his suit coat and threw it into the back seat. "You can take the wire off now," he said, then went around to the driver's seat.

"So this is off the record?" she asked, reaching under her top, leaning forward, pulling at the tape, unclipping the microphone, leaning back tiredly.

He said nothing for a time, and B.G. sat there quietly, trying to relax, feeling the cool air blowing out of the vents as Greg pulled out onto the busy street. She put her head back against the new-smelling upholstery of the car and closed her eyes.

"Better?" he asked after a minute.

"Uh-huh."

"You shouldn't have gone today. I told you—"

"But you're glad I did."

He didn't answer.

She felt the car stopping, starting, felt every pot-hole and bump, every turn. Sounds were curiously muted, the air whispering onto her hot face. Silence hung between them, and it was as if time were suspended.

She finally opened her eyes and looked out the side window. "Where are we?" she asked. "This isn't on the way home."

"I'm not taking you home. Not just yet."

"Where are we going?" she asked wearily.

"I don't want you to be alone in your house right now. You're upset."

"I'm all right."

"No, you're not."

"Greg, you don't have to baby me."

"I'm not babying you. It's been a tough day. You're done in. Let's just take a ride. You can relax. And besides, it's going to cool down and rain. I'll show you."

She looked out the window. The city slid by, battered, whitened by the violence of the sun, everything glaring, reflecting, crouching under the burden of heat. "I don't see any rain."

"You will."

He drove north, up past the road to his house, beyond that into the foothills of the Santa Catalina Mountains, stopping at a turnoff.

He helped her out of the car, and the heat smote her again. "Greg," she said, "what are we doing here?"

"Watching the rain," he said, "and relaxing." Then he pointed toward the southwest, and she saw the thunderheads boiling up on the horizon. Faint thunder rumbled, far-off, deep-throated, and he stood close to her, a hand on the small of her back. "The desert Indians celebrated their new year on the day the monsoon first arrived in July," he said. "It was life to them."

"It's really going to rain?"

"Buckets. You know those posts with measurements on them, the ones where streets dip? Up to eight, nine feet on them? They'll be filled with water. People drown."

"In the desert?"

"Yes, in the desert."

She looked out over the city; the whole Tucson valley lay before them, settled into its ring of mountains like a cupped palm crisscrossed with lines of dry streambeds and roads.

The storm was coming toward them, a blue-black gathering of massive thunderheads churning up into the afternoon sky. And the rain advanced slowly, an enormous gray curtain drawn along by a godlike hand. It fell from the clouds in long slanting plumes, and in places bright stripes of sun spilled through.

B.G. could barely see through the rain to the shadowy mountains across the wide valley. A cool breeze lifted strands of her hair, and she closed her eyes and raised her face to it.

"Look," Greg said.

She opened her eyes. Jagged white spears of lightning leapt from the black clouds to mountaintops, and the thunder growled louder.

Then the first drops of rain fell, bouncing in the pale dust, big drops like pebbles that dissolved into splotches on the ground after an impossibly long time.

It was magic, cool life-giving rain falling harder and harder, lightning cracking the sky open, the trees and bushes bending under the onslaught. A fresh pungent smell rose from the earth, and B.G. breathed it in.

"We better get in the car," Greg said.

"No," B.G. replied, "let's stay out in it for a little while."

So they stood there in the rain, faces upturned, hands out to catch the precious stuff, and got wetter and wetter.

"It's the first time I've felt truly cool all summer," B.G. said, water streaming down her face.

Finally they climbed back into the car, dripping all over Greg's immaculate upholstery.

"Never mind," he said. "It's only water." Then he turned to her, searching her face, and she could see his nipples and the hairs on his chest through his soaked shirt. Outside the car the rain slashed down, and lightning lit up the sky like a neon sign.

"I think we should go," she said, abruptly aware that her own clothes were plastered to her body, her swollen belly, her ponderous breasts. She plucked at her top, pulling it away from her skin, but she knew he'd seen already, seen her as if she was naked. She pushed back wet strands of hair and stared straight ahead through the blurred windshield.

"You're soaked," Greg said in an odd choked tone. "I don't have anything to dry you off with."

"So are you." She didn't look at him.

"I'll take you home in a minute," he said, "when the rain lets up a little."

"Okay."

She felt his hand on her arm; she flinched.

"You're cold," he said softly.

"No," she denied.

Silence filled the car, a heavy silence that the noise of the storm outside couldn't erase. B.G.'s skin crawled with tension, her heart pounded.

"You were very brave today," he finally said.

"I don't know if I can do it anymore, Greg," she breathed.

"It's almost over."

"Sure, sure it is."

He turned the key in the ignition and the engine hummed into life. "The rain's letting up," he said. "I'll take you home now."

She sat there, exhausted, as he drove through the rainstorm, the wipers swishing hypnotically, the tires hissing on the wet asphalt.

Despite her protests he drove her straight to her house.

"What if she's got someone watching me?" B.G. said. "I wouldn't put anything past her."

"You're in no shape to be out walking in the rain," he said. "No one's watching you. She figures you're scared of her after today."

"I *am* scared of her."

Getting out of the car was an effort. B.G. felt like a hippo, and her walk was no better than an ungainly waddle. Greg must have had trouble, she thought, keeping the distaste he felt off his face. She unlocked her door, and he followed her in. Whiskers was curled up on the couch. He raised his head and stared with emerald green eyes as B.G. sank down beside him.

"Is there something here for you to eat?" Greg asked.

"Sure, don't worry."

"I want you to take it easy. I wish you'd quit that damn job. It's too much for you."

"Leave me alone, Greg."

He stood over her, his hair mussed and still damp, his clothes wet. "How are you, B.G., really? You seem . . . nervous." His voice was soft, concerned, as if he cared.

She shook her head, speechless.

"You can tell me," he said.

Tears sprang to her eyes and her throat ached. She shook her head again, unable to speak.

"Is it Jacobs? I promise she won't get near you. I swear to you you'll be safe."

She could still only shake her head.

"Then what is it?"

B.G. took a deep quavering breath. "It's my baby. I only want to know if you found a family, someone to take my baby. I wish I could choose the Levys," she said wistfully. "They seem so perfect, but I guess that's not possible."

"No," he replied quietly, "it's not. They haven't even applied to the Tucson social services. It wouldn't be legal."

"But you have found someone?"

"Yes, there is a family," he said quickly. "It's all legal."

She gazed up at him. "A . . . a nice family?"

"The best."

"Do I . . . will I meet them?"

"Only if you want to."

She stayed silent.

"I have the preliminary relinquishment papers at the office," Greg went on. "You can sign them anytime. I, uh, I didn't want to press you about it. There's no real hurry."

She put her face in her hands, and then she felt Greg's touch on her head. "Aw, don't do that, B.G."

Tears squeezed between her fingers; she was aware of him kneeling beside her, pulling her toward him. She gave in, leaning against him, letting the tears come, and he stroked her hair, her wet tangled hair. Her breasts and her stomach were pressed against him, but she didn't care.

"It'll be okay," he said, and he was damp and cool, smelling of rain and the wet dust of the desert, and her heart broke into a thousand pieces because she knew she was going to lose it all—the man she loved and her own sweet baby girl.

CHAPTER SEVENTEEN

IT WAS HER LAST DAY at work, and the crew at the Casa del Sol threw B.G. a going-away party. They all had cake and ice cream in the kitchen before the dinner rush and wished her well. She was asked to come back after the baby was born—tactfully, no one asked anything more about the baby—but B.G. was evasive, saying she didn't even know if she'd be staying on in Tucson.

"At least stay through the autumn and winter," one of the waitresses said. "If you leave in the summer, you won't remember anything but the godawful heat."

"I'll see," B.G. said.

"Besides," Santino put in, "we really want you to come back here."

"Maybe," B.G. said, ducking her head.

And then they gave her a present, a tiny musical Earth Ball on a silver chain. Santino put it around her neck and said, "For luck, B.G., wherever you go."

"For luck," everyone chimed in.

She left shortly afterward, her purse in one hand, her other hand at her throat, gripping the beautiful silver ball. Her eyes were brimming with tears. Halfway down the block, waddling ponderously, she turned and waved, and the tears rolled down her cheeks.

It was a long four blocks home. Even though it was six-thirty and the sun was low in the summer sky, it was still hellishly hot, the heat coming up from the concrete sidewalk in shimmering waves, making distant buildings appear to wiggle. Palm trees drooped. Orange and lemon and grapefruit trees sagged. The land ached under the desert sun. B.G. walked along, breathing deeply and evenly, concentrating on her steps. It would be over soon. Any day now. And yet, even as uncomfortable and miserable as she felt, at least Kathryn was hers for now. But she had to stop thinking about that. She simply had to do what was best for the both of them.

A car moved alongside her slowly, nearing the stop sign at the next corner. B.G. only noticed it because the driver, a man, gave her a long look. But he moved on, and she shrugged it off. Ever since Rosemary had scared the pants off her several weeks ago with that story about the dead girl and Grace Jacobs, B.G. had been anxious, seeing things that weren't there, men in dark cars following her. She knew it was paranoia. Heck, she'd spoken to Jacobs on the phone a week ago, and everything had been hunky-dory. Grace had even told her she was working on that "extra" money. Everything was going as planned.

Greg was pleased, too, especially with Jacobs's money commitment on the telephone. One more nail in the woman's coffin, he'd said.

"We've got her, B.G.," Greg had said a week ago. "We'll pick her up and charge her formally at the hospital when she shows up with her legal documents. But you'll remember to call me first?" he'd said.

"Sure," she'd replied.

"I mean it, B.G. You're almost due. If you even feel a pang..."

"Yes, yes," she'd said, "I know. Call you. You've told me hundred times."

"That's right. And quit that damn job. I'm having nightmares about it."

"I gave notice," she'd told him.

"What? A two-week notice?"

"No, one week."

"Damn it, B.G...."

But she'd put him off by threatening to hang up. It had worked before.

At times, such as now when she was walking, trying to concentrate on not being too ungainly, pictures would fly unbidden into her mind. She'd see herself all skinny and happy standing with Greg and Kathryn on top of a mesa, watching the summer sky darken with thunderheads. Greg would explain the summer-monsoon phenomenon, and the baby would clutch B.G.'s neck with pudgy fingers, and Greg's arm would slip around her waist as the first raindrops spattered their faces.

Of course it was all a fantasy. And fantasies weren't bad. But the obsessive dreams she had about Greg and her baby were pure torment, so painful she couldn't bear them, and yet to stop thinking and dreaming about Greg was a punishment she couldn't endure.

And she remembered, too, alone in her bed at night, the feel of Greg's lips on hers, on her neck, her breasts—a sweet painful memory that made her ache for him. She told herself it was the pregnancy. It had to be. And yet she knew it was more. She'd been in love before, oh, yes, but never like this. Never with such . . . power. A power that consumed her.

At last she reached her bungalow and let herself in, dropping her purse on the coffee table. She arched her back, putting a hand at the small of it, holding the Earth Ball in the other hand, feeling its warmth.

And that was when she heard the refrigerator door slam shut.

Her heart leapt. Someone was . . .

Then he rounded the corner into the living room, a can of soda in his hand.

"Jay," she breathed, so dizzy with fear she thought she might faint.

"Hey, baby," he said, giving her his lady-killer smile, "did I scare you?"

"Good God, Jay," she said, dropping heavily onto the couch. "Why do you do this to me?"

"Hey, baby, come on."

Then she looked up sharply. "How did you get in here, anyway?"

"Same way as your cat." He shrugged. "Just like a big ol' tomcat, baby, I come prowling around from time to time."

She sighed. "That's not funny."

"Okay," he said, sitting next to her, tucking a damp lock of her hair behind her ear, "I'm sorry I scared you. Hey, you sure are about ready to pop. Man-oh-man, B.G., that's amazing. I never thought you could get so big."

"I'm due any time now." Lord, she felt tired; she didn't even have the strength to tell him what a jerk he was. Kathryn was his child. Weren't men supposed to cherish their pregnant women? Carry the groceries, all that? *Greg* seemed to worry, though....

"I've been thinking things over," Jay said, and he leaned back, swung his booted feet onto the scarred table and looked at the ceiling. "Yeah, the gig's still going at Maverick's, but the money sucks. Really, three of us sharin' this pad down in Tempe and—"

"I don't care, Jay," she said. "I just don't care anymore. I want you to stop popping in and out of my life. I mean it."

Jay took a long drink of the soda, his throat muscles working. "Well, then," he said, belching, then giving her a boyish smile, "guess I better get down to brass tacks, then."

"Please do," she said, looking straight ahead, so tired. "And then I want you out of here, Jay."

"Oh, I'll get out of your hair. But first I got this little plan." Jay smiled and ran a hand through his long blond hair. "I told you before, but I've been thinking about it a lot since then. Got it all clear in my head now."

"What, Jay?"

"Well, about this lady lawyer and all. Let's face it, she's the one who'll make the bucks. And what do these dudes from California care so long as they get the kid?"

B.G. sat up. "Not this again, Jay."

"Listen," he said, flicking an imaginary piece of lint off his knee, "we eliminate the middleman, B.G., and sell these folks the kid ourselves. I figure they'd pay twenty, thirty thousand. And what's more, this lady lawyer can't do nothin' about it. I've been doing a little research, and I hear I gotta sign off on the kid. Now, if I refuse to sign off..."

"Oh, Jay," she said in dismay, "I should've known you were planning something. Well, it won't work, you creep. You abandoned me! I don't need you to sign anything."

"Well," he said, grinning, "I'm what you might call unabandoning you now, baby. I'm gonna go see that lawyer and tell her I'm not signing anything. I want my kid. Then we drive to California and deal with those dudes direct. What do you say, baby?"

"I say go to hell." She got up and took a deep breath. "Just get out of here. Leave me alone."

"You're forgetting," he said, coming to his feet, "I'm the daddy, B.G. I got rights, too."

"And you're forgetting," she said, turning to him, hands on her hips, "I made a deal with the cops. If you try anything stupid, they'll nab you, Jay. I won't let you ruin this. Kath— The baby deserves a home. A real home. I can't provide that. You sure as hell can't provide it. But the county attorney can. I won't let you ruin this, Jay. I've come too far. I won't let you do this."

He looked at her soberly for a long minute and then shrugged. "Tell you what," he said. "I gotta play tomorrow and the next night in Phoenix. I'll call you. You think it over."

"I have thought it over, Jay. Now please just go. I'm very tired. Please."

"Okay, okay," he said, and he did go, this time by the front door.

B.G. fed the cat and took a cool shower. No more baths; she could barely get up out of the deep tub. She had a little bowl of cereal for dinner, but it gave her instant indigestion. Everything did lately.

Absently fingering the Earth Ball, she thought about calling Greg, telling him about Jay's threat. But she cringed at the idea. Not only would she be giving Jay up to the cops, but worse, Greg would learn all about what kind of person he was, and she couldn't stand the idea of that. Jay knew she could turn him in if he tried anything; he'd never dare take the chance of that happening. If he really was planning on holding up the adoption, all she had to do was threaten to turn him in to the county attorney. At heart, Jay Pearson was a coward.

No, Jay wasn't going to screw things up. He was just mouthing off.

B.G. went to bed feeling a little dizzy and more exhausted than ever. She knew her time was very close. She turned out the light, failing to notice that the little address book by the phone was turned to Jacobs, and tried to get comfortable. God, how she wished it was all over, Kathryn with her new parents, a wonderful future ahead of her. And as for herself... well, somehow she'd get over the loss. Somehow she'd get over Greg. But in her heart of hearts she knew there were going to be scars....

IT TOOK A LOT to rattle Grace Jacobs, and you could count on the fingers of one hand the number of times in her life she'd been rattled. This was one of those times.

It began when Debbie buzzed her. "Miss Jacobs, there's, uh, well...Jay Pearson here to see you. I think you better—"

"Jay? Oh, no, not that man again. What does he think he's doing?" She sighed, annoyed.

"Uh," Debbie said in a low murmur, "it's not the same man."

Grace raised a brow. Bewildered, curious, she got up and opened her office door. Indeed it was not the man who'd come to her office a while back saying he was the father of Bettie Gay's baby. So who on earth was this?

She walked directly to him and said, "Mr. Pearson, is it? I don't believe I've had the pleasure. I'm Grace Jacobs." She stuck out her hand and shook his. In her high heels their eyes were level. She instantly assessed this man, five-ten, 160 pounds, the sexiest smile she'd ever seen, and those insolent blue eyes. He was so far from her type—a cowboy in grubby clothes and dirt under his nails—that she was amazed her initial thought was of how absolutely darling he was.

Without missing a beat she said, "And what can I do for you, Mr. Pearson?"

He nodded toward Debbie, then said, "This is kinda private, ma'am. I'm here about Bettie Gay Bryson."

"Bettie...?" What was going on here? Jay. There couldn't be two Jays. "Why don't we step into my office, Mr. Pearson,'' she said smoothly, smiling, an alarm beginning to sound in her head.

He sat across from her, slumping in the chair, his cowboy hat off now, casually dangling from an index finger. His devilish blue eyes met hers. ''Bettie Gay, B.G., that is,'' he began, ''must've have told you about me.''

Grace leaned forward. The alarm was getting louder. ''Go on,'' she said.

''Well, it's like this, ma'am. I left for a time, that's true, but I'm back now, and I ain't signing no papers to adopt out my kid. I'm real sorry if B.G. led you on.''

He was still talking, something about leaving town with Bettie Gay, but Grace was too shocked to really listen. All she could see was the other Jay sitting in that same chair, the tall lean fit body, the smooth handsome face, the intelligence in his eyes, the haircut that had seemed too perfect. *My God,* she thought, *if this is the father, then who...?*

''...we don't want no trouble, ma'am, and that's why I came by. Now, B.G.'s kinda mixed up right now, but the fact is, I ain't signin' nothin'. I know I got rights, I checked.''

''Yes,'' Grace whispered, ''you do.''

''So I'm heading back to Phoenix,'' he said, ''but only to get my stuff, see? Then I'll be taking care of B.G. and the kid from there on out.''

''Uh-huh,'' Grace said, thinking furiously. Who did this punk think he was, anyway? She saw nothing ''darling'' about him now.

Jay Pearson got up from his chair and settled his hat on his head, tugging at the curled brim. "It's been a real pleasure, ma'am," he said, that impish gleam in his eyes.

"Yes," Grace said coldly, "hasn't it."

When he was gone she sat back down, buzzed Debbie and told her to hold all calls, then she steepled her fingers beneath her chin, her brow furrowed in thought. This punk, this Jay Pearson, she could handle in a New York minute. A little extra money was all that was needed. But the question remained: who in hell was this other man? Someone else trying to cash in on Bettie Gay's pregnancy?

Maybe. But Grace kept seeing that very handsome face, the confidence in his deportment, that haircut. This Jay who'd just left her office fit the role of Bettie Gay's lover. But the other one... She should have seen it before. Damn, she should have realized that, take away the shabby clothes, he and Miss Bettie Gay Bryson would mix about as well as oil and water.

B.G. HAD JUST WALKED out back to water her sad wilted geraniums when she heard a car pull up out front, and instantly her heart gave a glad leap. Greg. Who else could it be? But then she realized that it was most likely Jay again; Jay who, like a pit bull, got hold of something and just wouldn't let go. Like his career. His great career.

She put down the plastic watering can and went inside, wondering if he'd at least knock this time, when she saw through the window Grace Jacobs coming up the walk.

B.G. answered the door, her heart in her throat. Everything was all set with Grace. And if this was a confirmation about more money, well, wouldn't she have telephoned?

"Hello, Bettie Gay," Grace said, and she came right in, her eyes moving around the living room quickly, darting.

"Hi," B.G. got out, standing there, still holding the doorknob.

Grace swung around to her. Her glance slid from B.G.'s face to her stomach and up again. "Well," she said, "I'd say you're due any day." Her tone was uncharacteristically cold.

"Uh, yes, I guess I am."

"Mmm." Grace headed, without asking, into the bedroom, looking around. She even opened the closet door and then closed it and went to the bathroom, poking her head in. "I suppose Jay is just waiting with bated breath. He came to see me this morning, you know."

All the blood drained from B.G.'s face. Jay had... And then she was hit with another blow—Greg had also gone to Grace's office, said his name was Jay! Oh, dear God! But which Jay was Grace talking about? *Think,* B.G. commanded herself. *Think fast.* It must have been Jay, the real Jay, who'd gone to Grace as he'd threatened. That meant Grace had been visited by two different men, and now she was suspicious. Suspicious? She was furious! *Think.*

"Jay?" B.G. said in a little voice as Grace strode into the kitchen.

"No more games," Grace bit out. "Two men have come to my office now, two of them, both claiming to be Jay, the father of your baby. I want to know what you're up to, Bettie Gay. I demand to know what you're trying to pull here." She opened the back door and looked into the yard. Whiskers went flying out.

B.G. stood behind her and swallowed hard. "Omigosh," she sputtered, thinking, thinking. "Two men . . . Oh, I bet I know what happened."

"I'd like to hear it."

"My brother . . . I'll just bet that creep told you his name was Jay. Yes," B.G. said, her mouth cotton dry, "that greedy son of a gun. I just bet he showed up and tried to pull something on you."

"Your brother," Grace said tightly.

"Uh, yeah, Bill. Billy. He, uh, came by here last night. Just showed up out of the blue."

"You don't have a brother, Bettie Gay."

"Oh . . . the papers I filled out for you. Well, I do have a brother, a half brother, Billy, like I said. He's such a creep. I don't ever tell anyone about him. He's been to jail. He's a terrible person. I just never tell people . . . And now I bet he's told you some silly story. Oh that Billy!"

"I see," Grace said. "So you're telling me that the man who came by my office when you took your little jaunt to Phoenix is really the father of your baby. Is that correct?"

"Yes. That's Jay. Yes." *Oh, God,* she thought, and she could feel her baby stirring, kicking, awakened by the sudden tension thrumming inside her.

"You're lying."

B.G. turned the color of ash. "Why would I do that?"

"I don't know. But you're going to tell me. There's no way in hell that man fathered your child. I know that now. I was a fool not to have seen it before." She turned away and pulled open a cupboard door, then another. Next she started on the drawers. "Who are you, Bettie Gay?"

But B.G. couldn't answer. She was too shocked, held immobile as she watched in fear as Grace methodically opened every cupboard and drawer, searching, and B.G. knew in another second she'd find it. . . .

"Well, well," Grace said, standing over the drawer where B.G. kept the wire paraphernalia, staring at it. "What have we here?"

B.G. was silent.

"And just who are you working for? The police?" Grace came toward her slowly, her blue eyes chips of ice.

B.G. took a step back.

"Oh, you're clever," Grace said, smiling grimly. "You really had me fooled. But that was a bad slip-up, the two men both coming to me."

B.G. stared at her for a long moment. It was useless. The jig was up. With all the courage she could muster, she squared her shoulders and met those cruel eyes. "To answer your question," she said, "it's the county attorney I'm working for. He's going to nail you. He's already got all he needs."

Grace seemed to weigh that. After a terrible minute she said, "Not quite, my dear, not quite. You see, they'll also need *you* to testify."

B.G. should have seen it coming. Grace was still talking, but at the same time she was reaching into her handbag and pulling something out. Then, when it was too late to react, B.G. saw the gun lifting toward her. A small lethal-looking handgun.

"Yes, Bettie Gay," Grace said, "they'll definitely need you to testify. But I don't think you'll be available."

"You . . . you wouldn't."

"Oh, not here I wouldn't. But we're going to go for a nice ride together."

"I won't," B.G. breathed.

"Then I'll have to shoot you right here and now." She cocked the gun.

"But you won't get my baby. I'm too valuable to kill. Think of all that money you'll lose," B.G. bluffed.

"Neither you nor your baby is valuable enough to jeopardize me or my operation," Grace said coolly. "There's always another pregnant girl out there. There're millions of you girls. And to tell the truth, scarcity just makes the merchandise more valuable. As the song says, you have to know when to fold them." She gestured with the pistol. "Now get moving."

"All right," B.G. whispered. "All right."

"Good girl. Now, I want you to go out the door ahead of me and walk slowly to my car. No tricks, Bettie Gay. I'm very good with this little thing. A lady has to protect herself, after all. Now let's go. If you try anything, anything at all, I won't hesitate. Think of your baby, Bettie Gay. Now move. We're going for a drive.''

B.G.'s feet felt like lead, but she managed to put one ahead of the other. Out the kitchen, through the living room, out the front door. The baby gave a great kick as she stepped onto the walk, but Grace was right behind her, gun hidden from sight, but ready.

''Keep moving,'' Grace said harshly.

B.G. did as she was told.

ACROSS THE STREET and down half a block a man sat in his car, sweating, watching. When the two women got into the BMW, he reached for a radio handset attached to his dashboard.

''Hannah,'' he said into the mike, ''this is Norman. I want you to patch me through to Tyrrell. Pronto.''

''Roger'' came Hannah's voice. ''Hold on.''

The man fingered the mike, waiting. And when the BMW pulled away from the curb, so did he, tires squealing.

CHAPTER EIGHTEEN

WHEN GREG'S cellular phone sounded, he was just pulling on his pants after showering at the gym. It was Norm, and he was racing south on Mission Road, following a silver gray BMW registered to Grace Jacobs.

B.G. was in the passenger seat.

"What?" Greg yelled.

"It looked like your girl just went with her. I couldn't tell whether she was forced. But I'm on her tail, passing Speedway now."

"Don't lose them. Call the sheriff. I want backup. You got that, Norm? Jacobs is dangerous. I'll be there in five minutes. If she turns off anywhere, call me immediately. And don't try to stop them yourself."

"Got you, Greg."

He zipped his fly, not bothering to tuck in his shirt. He grabbed his suit coat and gym bag and ran out to his car, cursing the locked door, the recalcitrant key, the heat, the blistering hot steering wheel. He tore out of the parking lot, squealing around the corner, possibilities racing through his head. It was nothing, a false alarm. Grace Jacobs was just checking B.G. out again. Why, then, was she speeding down Mission Road? It wasn't on the way to her office. She could have gotten suspicious. How? Why? There'd been no sign of anything like that on the tape, not a word. And why had B.G. gone with her? She knew better. She'd been scared stiff when Rosemary had let slip the business about that girl being killed, and she wouldn't have gone with Jacobs voluntarily, not without telling Greg.

So, she'd gone involuntarily, and that scared the hell out of him.

He'd promised her, reassured her, sworn she couldn't be harmed. He clenched the steering wheel more tightly, his hands slippery with sweat.

Norm was a good man; he could handle the situation. What if he couldn't, though? What if he lost Jacobs's car?

B.G. must be terrified. She was so brave, never complaining. He could have pulled her off this case weeks ago—they'd had enough on Jacobs—but he'd wanted to hammer that last nail in her coffin so there wouldn't be any chance she could get off, no matter how many smart lawyers she hired. And now B.G. was paying the price.

He swung left onto Mission, cutting off a delivery van, barely noticing. Norm hadn't called back. That was good, he hoped.

B.G. shouldn't have to go through this. No one should, but B.G. in particular. Eight and a half months pregnant. Goddamn it, he should have taken her off this!

He pulled past a huge truck as if it was standing still, heading south, beyond the city, out into the flat dry wastelands surrounding Tucson. Where was Norm? Where was that silver BMW? He strained his eyes ahead into the hot glare, and it occurred to him with utter clarity that if anything happened to B.G. and her baby, he didn't know how he'd be able to go on.

GRACE JACOBS hadn't spoken a word for half an hour. She drove fast, with fierce concentration, and the small chrome pistol lay in her lap within easy reach. B.G. was sick with fear. Her heart pounded and she felt weak. Cold sweat dotted her skin.

She had no idea where Grace was heading. She'd never been here before. They were out of the city now, in an empty flat blistering-hot section of desert. A sign a few miles back had said San Xavier Reservation, wherever that was.

How on earth was she going to get out of this? She couldn't run, she couldn't put up much of a fight, she could barely move. And Greg had no idea where she was. No one did. She'd just be another dead body someone found in the desert.

No! She couldn't give up. If she died, so did Kathryn, and that was unthinkable. There had to be something she could do. Jump out of the car if Grace slowed down, hit her, fight back, snatch the gun. Something.

Grace must have seen her sidelong glance at the gun. "Don't even think about it," she said in a hard voice.

"Is this what you did to the other girl?" B.G. asked, and she had the satisfaction of seeing Grace's head whip around. "Won't it look pretty suspicious if another one of your girls disappears? They'll know you did it. You can't get away with it this time. You better just turn around and—"

"Shut up," Grace said.

"Drop me off then, right here, and run for it. Mexico's not far."

"Mexico," Grace said scornfully. "I think not."

"You're as good as behind bars. Don't be stupid," B.G. pressed.

"I may be a lot of things, Bettie Gay, but stupid is not one of them."

B.G. subsided, looking out the window as the brown featureless desert raced by. It was so hot that not even rattlesnakes stirred. God, she was scared. *Greg,* she thought, *you promised me.*

But it was her fault; when Jay had threatened to go to Jacobs she should have alerted Greg. She should have figured this could happen. But then she'd have had to tell Greg all about Jay, and she hadn't wanted to.

And now look where it had gotten her.

Well, it was no use looking for someone to blame. Right now she was in deadly danger without a soul to help her, so she'd have to figure out how to get away all by herself.

Grace drove on. Traffic thinned out, the sun beat down, bleaching the land, making everything white and desicated. Even the stalwart saguaro cacti wavered like ghosts in the waves of heat rising from the parched ground. B.G.'s mouth was equally parched, and her heart was leaping with panic.

The BMW turned off onto a rutted dirt road and headed deeper into the untracked desert. Soon there was no one for miles around, not a car, not a house or a gas station, nothing. Finally Grace pulled the BMW to a stop, parking it at the base of a rise. A dry sandy gully ran alongside the road, the pebbles in its bottom glaring white under the sun.

Grace got out, taking the gun with her. B.G. opened her own door, ready to run if she could, but Grace was already there, holding the gun on her.

"Out," she said, gesturing with the barrel.

"No," B.G. said with false bravado. "Shoot me here, right in here, and get blood all over your pretty leather upholstery."

"I should have seen that you were trouble right from the start," Grace said.

"You were too greedy," B.G. dared.

"Unfortunately you're right, but the problem can be remedied. Get out."

"No." B.G. folded her arms. If Grace shot her in the car, Greg would make sure she was caught and he'd prove it was B.G.'s blood. He'd see Grace go to the electric chair.

But Grace just leaned forward, grabbed B.G.'s arm and yanked her off balance, so that she half fell out of the car. She fought back, but her bulk prevented her from moving quickly, and the lawyer was surprisingly strong.

B.G. lost. She was pulled onto her knees in the burning dirt, dragged, jerked upright. She finally stood, breathing in huge gasps, shaking.

"Move!" Grace said, gesturing with the pistol to a spot behind the car.

B.G.'s mind whirled uselessly. It was over. She was out here in the middle of the desert alone with a gun pointed at her. *Greg,* she thought, *I love you. I really do. I wish Kathryn was yours and now I'll never be able to tell you.*

What happened next surprised her almost as much as it surprised Grace. She lunged, with all her considerable weight, right at the woman, and Grace stumbled backward, the gun flying out of her hand to land with a puff of dust just out of B.G.'s reach.

Awkwardly, she tried to get to it, but Grace was slim and much faster. Her hand was closing around it when there was an explosive blast of a gun, stunning both women into immobility.

"FREEZE!" GREG YELLED, holding Deputy Norm Clasen's gun on Grace Jacobs. He plunged down the hillside, digging his heels in, sliding between the clumps of cactus. Beside him, Norm covered the lawyer with his shotgun.

All Greg could think on his precipitous descent was that B.G. was there, alive, and that he'd pull the trigger if Jacobs made a move. He'd never shot anyone, didn't even own a gun, but to save B.G. he wouldn't hesitate.

Jacobs swiveled her head to him, back to B.G., then to Norm. Her face was hard and white, her pistol still trained on B.G.

"Drop it, Jacobs," Greg said, "or the next shot's for you."

He heard B.G. cry his name, and from the corner of his eye he saw her slump to the ground, but his eyes were on Jacobs.

For a moment the tableau was motionless: the woman with the ugly little gun, B.G. on the ground, Greg with Norm's big .38 police special in his outstretched arms, the deputy with the shotgun, all under a scorching midday sun that made everything appear faded and unreal.

Then Grace Jacobs lowered her arm and dropped her pistol, and Greg breathed again, dizzy with the receding adrenaline, his nerves leaping under his skin. He didn't move until Norm had kicked Grace's gun aside and cuffed her. As the deputy read her her rights, he rushed to B.G., gently helped her to her feet and enclosed her in his arms.

"Greg," she whispered in a ragged voice. "Oh, Greg."

"Are you all right?"

"Yes. She didn't do anything." She had her arms around his waist, clutching at him convulsively. "I was so scared, Greg. How did you know? How did you...?"

He stroked her sweat-soaked hair back from her face. "I had a man on you, B.G., for the last two weeks."

"You did?"

"I didn't tell you. I didn't want you to worry."

She buried her face in his chest, and he heard her sob, once, a tearing sound. She was trembling, her body shaking, and he held her close, drinking in the feel of her, the scent, the warm living texture of her skin and hair, the bulge of her belly, pressed hard against him. They were safe, both of them. He closed his eyes and thanked God.

"Okay, Tyrrell, I'll take this one in," Norm said, his shotgun dangling from one hand, his other on Grace's elbow. "Can I have my gun back now?"

Greg handed it to him, butt first, glad to be rid of it. "Thanks, Norm," he said.

"I'll see you later. You'll need to fill out a report."

"Later, yeah, okay."

"You can take care of this lady now?" Norm asked, gesturing at B.G.

"I can handle it, Norm."

When they were gone, Greg relaxed his hold on B.G., but she still leaned against him, looking up into his face. "I thought I was dead," she breathed.

"I wouldn't have let that happen," he said. Then, "You were very brave, B.G. You're the bravest person I've ever known."

She shook her head silently, tears brimming in her eyes. They stood there like that for a little while, drinking each other in, looking, just looking at each other, and then Greg saw a strange expression flicker across her face.

"What?" he asked, fear shooting through him.

Her eyes widened, and he felt her stiffen in his arms.

"What, B.G.? What is it?" he asked frantically.

"Oh, my Lord," she said, "the baby."

He'd never driven so fast in his life. This trip back along Mission Road seemed to take forever. There was B.G. in the seat next to him, one hand on her stomach, and every few minutes she'd start breathing very hard, and he could see her turn inward, totally concentrated on what was going on in her body.

"Are you all right?" he kept asking.

She even managed to smile. "I'm fine. I'm okay. The pains are still pretty far apart. You can slow down, Greg."

"The hell I can," he muttered. He used his cellular phone to call her doctor and the hospital. He called Rosemary, too, steering with one hand.

"She's in labor," he told Dick Mayer's secretary. "We're on our way to the hospital. Norm Clasen is bringing Jacobs in. Tell Dick.'' And he hung up before Rosemary could reply.

He pulled up in front of the hospital emergency entrance and raced inside, urgently explaining to the nurse that he had a woman about to give birth. By the time he'd turned around, B.G. had come inside, walking slowly and carefully, stopping to lean against a wall with one hand.

''My God, what are you doing?'' he asked.

''It's okay, Greg. It was just too hot in the car.''

Then the nurse came up with a wheelchair, and B.G. sank into it. The nurse asked a lot of questions Greg didn't understand and started to wheel her away.

''Wait,'' B.G. said to the nurse. ''Greg? Will you...could you stay with me?''

He took her hand in his. ''You want me there?''

''Yes,'' she whispered, ''please.''

By the time Greg had put on the hospital gown and cap and entered the labor room, B.G. was on a bed, a nurse hovering close, taking her blood pressure, checking her pulse. B.G. smiled and held out her hand. ''They think it'll be pretty soon,'' she said, then she gasped and started breathing hard again, and Greg felt useless, unable to do anything, watching her pain.

''She's doing great,'' the nurse said. ''Did you two go to Lamaze classes?''

What were Lamaze classes? Greg wondered. And then he remembered Dr. Resniak's telling him about them, and how B.G. was supposed to go to them, and he felt a spurt of guilt. But there wasn't time for that, not now.

''No, I saw...it...on TV,'' B.G. gasped.

''Where's the doctor?'' Greg asked the nurse.

"Oh, I won't call him again until she's ready for the delivery room. There's plenty of time."

"It's okay, Greg," B.G. said.

"She's going to be fine," the nurse said reassuringly. "It's a perfectly normal labor."

B.G.'s baby was born three hours later. Greg was there, watching, marveling, forgetting everything in the miracle of birth.

"A perfect little girl," Dr. Resniak said. "Congratulations."

Greg leaned over B.G. and smiled. "You did it."

The baby cried, that husky newborn infant's wail of chagrin, and B.G. grinned back at him. "Yeah, I did, didn't I?"

THE MINUTE B.G. HELD her baby in her arms she knew she'd never be able to give her up for adoption. The revelation was so clear and so positive she never questioned it. She sat in her hospital room, propped up in the bed, and held the tiny girl to her breast, studying every detail: the miniature fingers and toes, the perfect paper-thin fingernails, the fine dark hair on her head, the unfocused eyes of undetermined color, the button nose, the rosebud mouth, the waving arms with their circlets of flesh at the wrists.

"I'll be the best mother ever," she told her baby. "I'll never leave you."

She knew, unquestionably, that she'd be able to raise her child with love and care. She didn't need to be rich. It didn't matter. She'd take care of her baby; it was what she was meant to do all along.

She told Greg that before he left the hospital. She explained to him that she was very sorry if someone was expecting to adopt her baby, but she couldn't give her up. He didn't seem particularly surprised.

"I know you'll be able to do whatever you want, B.G.," he said.

"Thanks for being with me," she said.

"It was pretty exciting," he said. "How do you feel?"

"Great. Tired. Happy." She paused. "Scared to death."

"You'll do fine, B.G. You can do whatever it takes."

She ducked her head. "I'll never forget what you did for me."

He put his hand on her cheek and gazed at her tenderly, and her heart was so full it almost burst. "You did it all," he said.

She looked up at him and searched his face. "I'm going to name her Kathryn."

"After your grandmother?" he asked.

"And after your mother."

"My mother?"

"Uh-huh," B.G. said. "Kathryn. For the most beautiful little baby on earth."

CHAPTER NINETEEN

GREG LEFT B.G. to rest and headed over to the county attorney's office. He drove the familiar streets oblivious to his surroundings, still high as a kite from the experience of seeing the baby's birth. It struck him that all the success, all the money in the world, couldn't buy anything nearly so wondrous.

In the parking lot at the office he sat for a time thinking about that. For as long as he could remember he'd had his goals, that driving need to overcome his blue-collar background. He'd discounted marriage and a family, positive the burden would hold him back. And he'd almost achieved his ends, the bar exam right around the corner. But suddenly he had to ask himself what it all meant if there was no one to share it with. There was B.G. with her new baby, willing to tackle the world so that she could know the joy of motherhood. It seemed B.G. was a whole lot braver than he was.

Greg found Dick Mayer in an expansive mood, having just finished an interview with a local TV station concerning the arrest of Grace Jacobs.

"We're charging her on no less than twelve counts," he told Greg in his office. "We've got her on kidnapping, possession of a deadly weapon with intent to kill, grand larceny, perjury, making false statements and the unlawful placing of children for adoption, just to name a few. She'll go to trial and be behind bars for a long, long time."

"That's great," Greg said.

"How is Miss Bryson, by the way? She and the baby doing all right?"

"They're both fine," Greg said, and then he told Mayer about her decision to keep the baby. Kathryn.

"She's sure?" Mayer asked.

Greg nodded. "One hundred percent. And you know what? She'll do fine."

"She's a scrapper," Mayer agreed. "And we owe her a lot."

"What about the couple you lined up for the adoption?" Greg asked.

Mayer shook his head. "It was very tentative. I made no promises. They'll understand."

"And the Levys?" Greg had to ask. "The people Jacobs was going to sell her baby to?"

"I spoke to them on the telephone. They're disappointed, but Mel Levy, the husband, said he wasn't surprised. He even said he'd testify in court against Jacobs."

"B.G.'s going to feel pretty bad about them. I guess they were nice folks."

"They'll find a child," Mayer said. "It just takes time. But this one will be a legal adoption, I bet."

"For their sakes I hope so," Greg said.

After talking to Mayer, Greg stopped by Rosemary's desk to tell her about B.G.'s decision.

"I knew she'd keep her," Rosemary said.

"What, are you into mind reading now?" Greg said.

"Could be," Rosemary said. "Would you like to know what I see in your future?"

"Uh, no thanks."

"Chicken," she said.

He wrote up his report and filed it, then left the office for B.G.'s to pick up some things she was going to need for the next couple of days.

He was still feeling high as he drove, and he couldn't stop thinking about B.G., the tiny pink infant in her arms. All these months with her, watching her belly grow with the baby, knowing it was a little girl... Hell, he felt like the father, for God's sake.

Greg let himself into the house and immediately saw the open cupboard doors and kitchen drawers—Jacobs, he knew, looking for something out of the ordinary, finding that wire and transmitter. B.G. must have been terrified, knowing the game was going to be up at any moment. He should have been with her. And again he thought about how extraordinarily brave she was. He had a flash of memory then, an image of Grace Jacobs aiming that gun at B.G. out in the desert. His heart kicked in his chest. A few seconds, if he and Norm had gotten there only a few seconds later, B.G. and her baby would have been dead. He took a deep breath and let it out slowly.

He found her overnight bag in the closet in the bedroom and tried to figure out what to pack for her. The bathroom stuff was easy. But her clothes... Half of what she owned was going to be way too big. Okay, he thought, holding up a shirt and some shorts, he'd take a few pieces he remembered from when she'd first gotten to Tucson. Funny, but he recognized everything. But then he recalled that he'd been the one who'd taken her shopping. It seemed like years ago.

He was ready to zip up the bag when he thought he heard a noise out front. And then he heard the front door open. What the . . . ?

He strode into the living room, not at all sure what to expect. And that was when he saw him, Jay, recognizing him instantly from the convenience-store video.

Jay was just closing the door when he saw Greg. He jumped a little. "Hey," he said, "who in hell are you, man?"

Oh, yeah, Greg thought, it was definitely the guy who'd left B.G. stranded. Long blond hair, the cowboy hat pulled low on his brow. Jay.

Greg leaned against the doorjamb and folded his arms, glaring at him. "The name's Tyrrell," he said after a long moment. "And I'm real glad to meet you at last, Jay."

Jay looked bewildered. "Where's B.G.?" he asked.

Greg stared at him for another moment and then said, "Why don't you sit down and we'll have a little chat."

"Yeah? Like, why should I? And where's B.G.?"

"Tell you what," Greg said evenly. "We can do this the easy way or the hard way—your choice." And then he explained how it was, all about the nice jail cell just waiting for him. Jay Pearson sat down. A half hour later they were headed over to Greg's office.

"I don't see why I gotta sign papers, man, giving up my kid," Jay said on the ride.

"Like I told you," Greg said. "I'm not going to have B.G. worried that someday you'll turn up and try to pull something."

"I never really meant that stuff about selling the baby," Jay said.

"Now, how did I guess?" Greg asked dryly.

"No, really, man, I—"

"Just shut up and get this through your head," Greg shot back. "You're done screwing up B.G.'s life. You're going to sign papers relinquishing all rights to Kathryn. You're going to pay that money back to the store and then, if you want, you can visit B.G. and tell her you're out of her life. If you don't sign the papers, you can talk to the sheriff about that robbery."

"All I got is eighty bucks, man," Jay protested.

"Yeah, well," Greg said, "sixty-five of it was stolen."

Jay swore under his breath.

"And you know what?" Greg said. "If I were you, Pearson, I'd get a life."

B.G. WAS TOTALLY UNUSED to so much fuss. Apparently word had spread around the hospital about how she'd been working for the county attorney and then almost been killed that morning. Some of the nurses knew Grace Jacobs, too, from the many times she'd waited just outside the delivery room with adoption papers in hand.

"She's a vulture," one of the nurses said to B.G. "We're all so glad she's been caught."

Flowers arrived from the county attorney, and B.G. was sure that Rosemary had sent them. Someday, B.G. thought, she was going to make it a point to meet the lady. All the while that people came and went, little Kathryn slept through everything in a bassinet beside B.G.'s bed, her tiny fists like pale flowers. She was the most beautiful child B.G. had ever seen. How could she ever, in a million years, have thought she could have given her up?

She must have finally dozed off, because when she opened her eyes again, it was dark outside her window. She looked down at the baby and felt that incredible warmth spread through her, and wondered how her own mother had been able to leave her. Maybe the sins of the fathers weren't always visited upon the offspring. She remembered then that her grandmother didn't even know about her pregnancy, and now Kathryn Bryson had a perfect little grandchild. First thing tomorrow, B.G. decided, she'd call Grandma and tell her everything. Maybe in a month or two she could visit.

But how? She didn't even have a place to live! Oh, the county attorney would probably let her stay in the bungalow for a little while, but what then? And if she went back to work at the Casa del Sol, who would care for Kathryn? How was she going to make this work?

B.G. took a deep breath, felt the soreness in her body and told herself not to panic. She'd take it one day at a time. Lots of people had gone through the same thing. You survived. The key was love. So long as she and her baby had each other, nothing else mattered.

A dinner tray was brought in and she ate every bite, knowing she needed her strength. Then two more nurses coming on shift stopped in to see her and the baby and tell her how glad they were that Jacobs was finally arrested. A "pink lady" brought more flowers, beautiful summer blooms—they were from the crew at the Casa del Sol.

"How on earth did they know?" B.G. wondered aloud.

"You were on the evening news," the girl said. "You're a celebrity."

"Me?"

"Oh, yes. Several reporters have tried to get in to see you, and the switchboard's been lighting up with all your calls."

"Wow," B.G. said.

She wondered where Greg was. He'd left hours ago, saying he was going to stop by her place and get a few things she might need. He'd left so quickly after the baby was born that she was starting to wonder if something was wrong. The job for the county attorney was over; maybe Greg was done with her entirely.

Despite the euphoria that had buoyed her all afternoon, she felt a sudden stab of sadness. Never to see Greg again, never to hear that wonderful deep voice or see that smile... And even if she stayed in Tucson with the baby, she'd probably only see him at Grace Jacobs's trial. Maybe not even then. She simply could not fit her mind around that possibility—never to see Greg again.

Without realizing it, she began to cry softly. She reached over and tried to pick Kathryn up out of her bassinet, but the position was awkward. So she sat up and swung her legs carefully over the side of the bed, and then she was able to pick up her baby.

She sniffed back her tears and said in a whisper, "Do you know I'm your mommy? Do you know how much I love you?'' It felt right, too, so natural and perfect to cradle her sleeping child against her breast. How on earth could she be sad about anything?

"Are you supposed to be sitting up?'' came a voice from behind her, and B.G.'s heart gave a glad leap. "Shouldn't you be lying down?''

She turned and couldn't keep from breaking into a big smile. "I'm fine. We're both fine.''

She could see that his arms were full. He was carrying her bag and a big bouquet of flowers, a box of candy with a pretty red ribbon and a stuffed panda bear. "Oh, Greg,'' she said.

He put everything on the chair by the window and then shrugged shyly. "Everything's closed,'' he said. "I'm afraid the flowers and other things are from the grocery store. I hope they're all right.''

"They're beautiful, Greg,'' she said, and then looked down at Kathryn. "Her first toy, too. I can't believe it. So many firsts.''

Greg walked over and crouched down next to them. "Can I?'' he asked, reaching out tentatively to touch the baby's tiny hand.

"I don't think she'll break, Greg.''

"You never know,'' he said, and Kathryn wrapped her fingers around one of his.

"I took the liberty of calling Sandy,'' he said then, his eyes lifting to B.G.'s. "You remember my sister? The one with the baby?''

"Sure,'' B.G. said.

"Well, anyway, she and Art have a garage full of baby things. You know, an old crib, high chairs, baby tubs, all that stuff. She wants you to have whatever you need.''

"Oh, Greg," she said again.

"And as soon as you and Kathryn are ready, well, we'll drive over and pick out what you need to get started."

"I don't know what to say," B.G. began, and then the tears came again. She couldn't stop them.

Greg seemed a little embarrassed, too, so tactfully he changed the subject and told her about Jay, everything, right down to his signing of the relinquishment papers. "Maybe I should have asked what you wanted, B.G.," he said then, "but, well, I figured you'd agree. He's no father. Hell, he's barely figured out he's an adult."

"Some taste in men I have," she said, and her gaze lowered to the baby. But then she raised it again. "That's history, though. And you did the right thing, Greg. I hadn't even thought all that out yet. As it is, I only just decided to keep the baby. Although," she admitted, "I think I knew in my heart all along that I could never give her up." She paused. "And today, your being with me for the birth, Greg—that was so special. I'll never ever forget it. And now calling Sandy, the crib and all . . ."

"Well," he said, and he stood, walking to the window, turning back to her, leaning against the frame, "I think I'd better explain. No," he said then, "I'm not saying this right."

"What?"

"Hell." He raked a hand through his hair. "Here I'm about to be a lawyer and I can't find the right words."

"I don't . . ." she began, but he shook his head at her.

"Let me just get this off my chest from the beginning, okay?"

"Sure," she said, bewildered.

"It's like this," he said. "Ever since I can remember, I've set goals for myself. Lofty ones. Some I reach, some I don't. But mostly I've been on a pretty straight line. One of my goals, you might say, has been to stay single. I saw a lot of my friends in both high school and college get involved and then married, and, well, somehow it seemed as if they were always scraping by, you know?"

B.G. nodded. What on earth was he driving at? Did he really think she didn't know all this about him?

"Anyway," he went on, "I always told myself that yeah, sure, I'd get married and start a family someday, when I was older, had my law practice firmly established and all that. But, well, recently..."

"Go on," she prompted, daringly, carefully, a seed of hope and disbelief ready to sprout.

"Well, damn, B.G.," he said, "then I met you." He took a deep breath. "Ever since I saw you in that interrogation room, there was something, a strength, a beauty... You had nothing. Zilch. And yet, and damned if I know how, you made me feel as if you had everything in the world that I didn't. I guess I... I must have forgotten how to really live, the important things, that is. And then today, when I almost lost you..."

"I can't believe this," she whispered.

He laughed suddenly, and his eyes met hers. "I guess I better get to the point then. I want you to marry me, B.G. I want you and the baby to be a part of my life."

She was speechless.

"I know this must seem pretty sudden," he said, "or maybe not. Maybe you've seen this coming for a long time." Abruptly he sobered. "My God," he said, "maybe you don't love me..."

But she was shaking her head and crying again, and between her tears she told him she loved him.

"You do?"

"Oh, yes," she said. "I think I've loved you from the start, Greg."

"Then it's okay?" he said. "I mean, you and me and the baby?"

She bit her lip and nodded.

"Then tomorrow I can arrange for us to get married and move all your things into my place?"

Again she could only nod.

"Will you please say something?" he said. "Anything?"

And finally she did. "Sure," she said, and a moment later they both laughed.